GHOSTS AND GOLD DUST

THE GHOST VEIN MINE COZY PARANORMAL MYSTERIES 1

KELLY ETHAN

This was a labor of love for me. I am a neurodivergent mom of three neurodivergent boys. Emotions, social interactions and romantic entanglements and their nuances can escape me.

So writing Ghosts and Gold Dust with it's romantic subplot was hard and I think I've done it justice. I hope you all love this book as much as I do.

GHOSTS AND GOLD DUST
THE GHOST VEIN MINE COZY PARANORMAL MYSTERIES 1

Welcome to Ghost Vein, Nevada. Where the mine runs deep and so do the lies. The gold's cursed, the ghosts are chatty, and murder never stays buried for long.

Down on her luck, Rue Maddox inherits a haunted saloon turned bookshop café in a cursed Wild West reenactment mining town. The last thing she expects is to find a dead body behind her building or to be accused of murder. Now Rue is suspect number one in a crime she didn't commit.

But Ghost Vein isn't your average tourist trap. The mine is haunted, the locals are obsessed with cowboy costumes, and Rue's late Great Aunt Ruth turned out to be the town's last curse-breaking witch.

With a dead tour guide, a too attractive grumpy sheriff, a town full of ghosts and secrets, Rue must solve the mystery before another body drops or she ends up six feet under with only ghosts and gold dust for company.

Small town life just got weirder. And Rue? She might be the only thing standing between Ghost Vein and something far worse than bad tourist reviews.

Perfect for fans of paranormal cozy mysteries, haunted Western towns, and amateur sleuths.

Unlock the lighthearted magic and mayhem in Ghosts and Gold Dust. Book one in The Ghost Vein Mine Cozy Paranormal Mysteries by Kelly Ethan.

ONE

Rue was not having a good day.

"It's just one little interview. This could be the career for you." Evelyn Maddox smiled at her daughter. "Then, you could move into the condo next door. We'd be besties in matching pink condos."

Fighting the convulsive shudder that threatened to topple her, Rue forced a smile. "As great as that sounds, I'm not psychic, Mom. Human or animal. So, working at the local pet salon doesn't cut it for me. I'm a library assistant, not a pet psychic."

"You shelved books for four hours a day. That doesn't make you a library assistant. Besides, that was in Denver. This is Florida." Evelyn fluffed her lavender colored, tightly permed curls. "Betsy says her bichon is depressed, and her vet suggested a pet psychic. Apparently, it's well-paid." Evelyn flapped the newspaper. "And look, an ad for a pet psychic, just down the road. It's fate."

"Fate I can do without," Rue mumbled under her breath and grimaced as a trickle of sweat rolled down her cleavage. Florida was a tad more humid than Denver. She'd moved when she lost her job and her lease on the same day. Her mother had suggested moving into her condo in the retirement village while she hunted for a job. But grown-up daughters in their late twenties should never share homes with their mother. That way lay a perm-filled, saccharine-sweet, weight gain comment minefield.

"Enough of that attitude, missy. You aren't so big I can't send you to your room without dinner." Evelyn eyed her daughter's abundant cleavage. "Although fewer carbs might not be a bad thing. You don't want to spill out of your bikini and give an old man a heart attack."

Crossing her arms over her chest, Rue glared at her mother. "Since when do I wear bikinis? And when do I swim at all? I'm a redhead. I burn just thinking about the sun. And you said I looked healthy when I arrived."

"That was three months ago. I thought you'd find a job a little bit quicker." Evelyn snapped the newspaper in Rue's face. "A pet psychic is an important job here in Florida. Pets need help too."

"Psychic help? Somehow, I don't think it's as important as, say...vaccinations, registration, and other things." Rue rolled her eyes and snatched the newspaper from her mother's hand.

"Don't sass me, child. I'm providing a roof over your head." Evelyn sniffed and wiped her counter with a rag, rubbing Rue's fingerprints away. "And we need to talk about you picking up after yourself a little more. You aren't a child now."

"And I'm not a clean freak either." Rue let her head thump onto the counter her mother had just wiped. Evelyn had always been a clean freak, but it got worse after her husband's death a few years ago. Six months after her father died, Rue's mother declared her old bones weren't taking another Colorado winter, and she'd moved lock, stock, and aching joints to Florida, where she had her sister nearby.

Rue had elected to stay in Denver and keep working in a library job. She loved her mother, but she didn't want to live with her full-time. And after Dad died, she'd just wanted to stick around the same place he'd lived and loved. Her mother, on the other hand, couldn't wait to escape the cold and his memory. Rue guessed she could understand it. She'd always been a chip off her dad's block, instead of the precious little princess clone of her mother. And didn't that still burn in Evelyn's craw? Mom always got a wrinkled nose when Rue's dad rumpled her auburn hair and declared a bookshop hunting day. He loved books and told her they were his family. His real family. The Maddox family was spread all over the states. Mom, on the other hand, only had a younger sister, Alexandra, in Florida. She now had a condo in the same retirement compound.

"I am not obsessed with cleaning. I just prefer a tidy living environment." Evelyn glared at her daughter.

Sighing, Rue lifted her head. "All right, you're not a clean-obsessed Floridian at all."

"I suppose that's somewhat better. Now let's get back to your job interview."

She gritted her teeth. "I am not a pet psychic. Besides, I thought you disliked anything to do with magic?" Her mother hated magic, refused to recognize anything supernatural. Shifters, ghosts, witches, vampires, garden gnomes, anything slightly left of center was out according to her mother's rules. Dad on the other hand loved magic and had even snuck books on it into the house before her mother had thrown them out. From then on, if her father wanted to stay married, there was no magic mentioned. Rue would never have demanded anything like that from a partner, but her mom was a rule unto herself. Whenever Dad talked about his family, her mom shut him down...*hard*. Magic and the Maddox family were taboo subjects.

"I don't hate magic. I just find it useless. But that job." She tapped the newspaper. "Getting paid to pretend you can read a pet's mind. It's a gold mine. Just take the paycheck and lie. It isn't hard, Rue."

The idea of her rule-abiding, magic-phobic mother telling her to lie and fake psychic powers was all sorts of wrong. Rue preferred her dad's way of thinking. He'd been all about monster rights and had no problems working alongside shifters, witches, or vampires. As long as one asked politely before taking a bite, her dad was fine. *Not. Her. Mother.* In fact, this whole new behavior felt off. "You all right, Mom? You seem a little on edge."

"I'm fine. Just annoyed at my lazy daughter. We're living together, so we need to pull equal weight around here. Especially as you're not paying rent." Evelyn narrowed her eyes. "You know rent? That thing that you pay people to stay in their homes for three months."

Yeah. Three months. *Three long months.*

"I am fully aware of what rent is. I am twenty-eight years old, not ten. Dad would have never..." Rue trailed off. Mentioning Dad in a heated argument was not the way to appease her mom.

Evelyn cleared her throat and drew out a pile of envelopes, dropping them onto the counter. "Yes, well, your father isn't here. But your bills are and I'm sure the rest is just junk mail." Her face screwed up and she moved to snatch the envelopes away, but Rue got to them before she did. "Ah, there might be one or two of mine among them."

"It's okay. I can sort them out and even if it's all bills, it's nice to get mail."

Rue flipped through the pile and frowned. "These date back a month."

Evelyn avoided Rue's gaze. "I forgot to give them to you. As I said, nothing important you need to deal with now."

Her mother was acting weird, and Rue wanted to know why and how it was connected to her junk mail. "You're probably right. But it isn't like I have a job interview to go to. I'll open them now." Rue huffed a laugh as she sorted the mail. "You never know, I might have won something."

Evelyn grabbed the mail and tried to yank it out of Rue's hand. "No. No. It's all rubbish. I'll just throw it out."

"Are you high on Florida sun, woman?" Rue moved her mail away from her mother. A partially open envelope caught her attention. She picked it up and noted it was from a lawyer in Reno, Nevada, and someone had opened and resealed it. *Someone called Evelyn Maddox.* "You opened my mail? Isn't that a crime?"

"It isn't when one's daughter is freeloading from you," Evelyn snapped back.

"Uh huh. Nice to finally know what you think. But it doesn't explain opening my letter."

"It accidently opened as I was collecting the mail. That's all. You don't need to read it. The lawyer doesn't have anything to say that will interest you."

Rue raised her eyes from the envelope. "Unsealed long enough to read it? Well, I guess it's my turn then." Watching her mother, she drew out the letter. Mom paled, and a muscle twitched in her jaw. Evelyn Maddox was upset, and Rue wondered why a letter from a strange lawyer would cause the normally unflappable woman to lose it. She scanned the contents, and a furrowed line appeared on her forehead as she processed the letter's content. A short, to the point letter from a lawyer in Reno, stating that her Great Aunt Ruth Maddox had passed away and willed her heritage saloon-turned-bookshop and café in Silver Vein, Nevada, along with a sizeable bank account, to Rue.

Ruth Maddox had passed away six months ago, but it had taken some time to track Rue down. Plus, there'd been an issue with unanswered phone messages at her current residence in Florida. Rue read that line again. *Does that mean...* She looked up at her mother's guilty expression. "Have you been erasing my phone messages? Messages from a lawyer about my inheritance?" She'd gotten rid of her mobile phone a couple months ago since she didn't have enough funds to pay the bill and had been relying on her mother's phone to keep in contact.

Evelyn shook her head. "No. I haven't received any messages from a lawyer."

"According to this, none of the lawyer's messages were passed on." Rue pointed at the letter and then at her mother. "Seriously, you can't even look me in the face. What's going on with you?"

Letting out a shaky breath, Evelyn finally made eye contact with her daughter. "You don't understand. Silver Vein is like a whole different world. You do not want to go there. Just sell the place and pocket the money. No good ever came out of that town, no matter what your father used to say."

Dad? Rue narrowed her gaze at her mother. "What does this have to do with my father?"

Evelyn threw her hands up in the air and began to pace. "The Maddox side of the family. Magic this. Magic that." She spat out the words. "It's not normal. Not ladylike. I made a deal with your father when you were born. No more magic. No more Ruth Maddox. He kept his promise except for a few times when he snuck you out to meet your Maddox cousins. You didn't think I knew about it, but I did."

"What's that got to do with not passing on my phone messages? Don't you understand how this inheritance will change my life? This could set me up. And it's a bookstore." Rue flapped the letter, imitating her mother's previous actions. "I've always wanted to own a bookshop. So did dad."

"Problem is your great aunt and that town."

"You knew her."

"I met her once and once only." Evelyn clenched her lips. "We met when your father and I got married. She went on and on about witches and curses and how the next generation could inherit the Maddox family gifts. It made me violently ill. I made your father promise he would never let that side of his family near us. *If* he wanted to stay married. He had no choice."

"He's not here anymore and I'm an adult. I can't believe you kept this from me." Rue stood, flabbergasted at her mother's manipulating. Her mom could be rigid, but this was going too far.

"I'm protecting you. You don't want to get caught up in magic. In something you don't understand." Evelyn stiffened, her hands two white fists at her sides.

"I'm not your clone, Mom. I'm not prejudiced against the supernatural. This is my life, and I want to see Silver Vein."

"You were always a copy of your father. He would've dived headfirst into the magic too. Is that what you want to do? Throw away your life? Then go ahead. But don't call me when it's time to pay the price because magic always has one. Silver Vein is where Ruth lived and died. And I'm pretty sure magic killed her. Think about that when you're playing with your bookshop." Evelyn slapped her hand on the counter before storming out of the condo.

Rue gripped the bridge of her nose. Her mother's histrionics drove her crazy. She couldn't believe she'd kept all this from her. Rue looked down at the letter, taking note of the lawyer's contact details. No matter what her mother said, this could be the beginning of a new life for her. Away from her mother's condo. Away from pet psychic job interviews. Away from the soul-sucking heat and humidity of Florida.

A new life. A new start. Just what the fake pet psychic ordered.

TWO

"Come on, sweet girl. You survived driving in Reno traffic, a fox, and that raccoon incident. You can do this." Rue squinted through the dusty windshield as her rust-bucket of a car wheezed. Her friendly lawyer, who'd refused to step inside Silver Vein's boundaries, had bought her an old car so she could drive to Silver Vein after her flight from Florida. Rue blanched at the memory of being wedged between two older women rabbiting on about slot machines in Reno. They'd argued for hours, but it beat the silent treatment her mother had given her in the weeks leading up to her trip. Evelyn Maddox held grudges. It'd be a cold day in Florida before she forgave Rue for visiting Silver Vein.

Rue gripped the steering wheel so hard her knuckles turned the same shade as her sunscreen-slathered face. "Everything's fine. Just get me to Silver Vein, sweet girl, and I'll treat you to a nice oil change." The engine gurgled and Rue winced. Maybe she should have let the lawyer splurge a little on a better car. She had her Great-Aunt Ruth's money now, but she didn't want to spend too much until she assessed the financial state of Ruth's store. "It's all good.

We'll get to Silver Vein and settle in. Who needs guardrails anyway?"

The road coiled around the mountain, each curve daring her to find out just how bald her tires really were. The incline was steep enough to make her rust-bucket sound like it was dying. Somewhere under the hood, sweet girl let out a death rattle.

"No. No. Not now," Rue crooned to her car. "You can do this."

Sweet girl let her death rattle build in response.

Rue rolled down the window an inch or so to let in a little air. Instead, a gust of wind buffeted her, sending her auburn hair into a frenzy. One strand stuck to her strawberry lip balm and sun-screened face. Another whipped across her eye, causing it to water. The rest of her hair formed a fiery halo of frizz that would make Medusa proud and her mother cringe.

"Cool, okay. I always wanted to die in a tangle of hair on the side of a mountainous road that will probably eat me and my sweet girl car alive. But it's all good." Rue closed her window and spat a mouthful of hair out, blinking wildly as she focused on the road.

To her left was a sheer rock wall. To her right, nothing but sky and a drop that went on forever. Florida had spoiled her with flat roads and gentle curves. She didn't know much about Nevada but had kind of expected a desert. Instead, it was more like trying to drive up a vertical cliff face, blindfolded and being judged. Just like the coyote currently standing in the middle of the road ahead, staring at her.

Rue slammed the brakes. Her poor sweet girl coughed then shuddered to a stop. "No, no, no, no, no." She sat in the still car, blinking frantically before dropping her head on the steering wheel. A silence settled so thick, she heard her own heart pounding. Or maybe her car was getting ready to explode? Lifting her head, Rue sighed and rubbed her reddened forehead. This was not a great start. Her mother would have called it an omen to flee back to Florida and her plan of matching condos. She peered out the window. The obnoxious coyote turned its head and focused on the car as if judging her driving ability. "I'm a safe driver. Present situation aside." The coyote blinked once, twice, then prowled out of sight.

"I gave up central air and mimosas for this?"

In response, sweet girl gave a final death rattle and added a long, drawn out moan. From somewhere far above, Rue swore someone cackled...or it could be her fevered imagination. It was an even toss, right now. Madness or magic. Gathering herself together now that the coyote had disappeared, Rue slipped out of the car and opened the hood. An ominous creak greeted her as she peered inside. Honestly, she had no clue what she was looking for. Rue bargained with the engine. "I will literally sacrifice my first paycheck to give you a spa retreat and an overhaul if you just turn over."

A rumbling tow-truck pulled up behind her, kicking up dust and stones.

A tall, lanky figure climbed out, wiping his hands on a rag before shoving it into the pocket of his stained blue coveralls. He had some scruffy stubble and straight blonde hair tied back in a ponytail. He also sported the world-weary expression of a man who'd been in this situation before.

"You broken-down, overheated, or distressed?" He squinted at Rue's rust-bucket almost as if the old car offended him.

Rue straightened, brushing road grit off her pale blue

tank top and faded denim shorts. "Little from column A, little from column B, and I think my car's experiencing A, B, and C."

The man walked around sweet girl and peered under the hood with a hiss. "There's your problem. This thing is held together with spit."

"Yeah." Rue sighed and tried to smooth her wind-frizzed auburn hair into something vaguely bun-shaped.

He looked up and grinned. "Name's Jesse. Lucky for you, I'm the local mechanic. You new to the area, Sunshine?"

"Rue Maddox." She curled her lip. "Sunshine is for someone not broken down on the side of a murderous mountain. I just inherited a...building. In Silver Vein."

Jesse's eyebrows shot up. "Oh. You're our new bookstore saloon owner."

She blinked. "That sounds like an extremely specific profession."

"Well," he said, slamming the hood of Rue's car down with the finality of a man declaring time of death, "it started out as a haunted watering hole, but now it's Silver Vein's reading nook. I guess it depends on how the ghosts are feeling that day."

"Great. Right. Can't wait." Rue gulped at the mechanic's casual reference to ghosts and her new inheritance in the same sentence. She definitely wasn't in her mother's Florida condo anymore.

Jesse dusted off his hands. "Since it's nice to be neighborly, how about I hook up your car and give you a tow into town? I can take your car back to my workshop and have a look if you want?"

Beaming, Rue scrambled for her bags. "That would be

great, as long as you aren't a serial killer." At least something was going right.

"Pretty sure I'm a run of the mill mechanic." Jesse winked.

Ten minutes later, Rue rode shotgun in Jesse's old Ford, her suitcase and large bag wedged in the back with a box of jumper cables, a large toolbox, and what looked suspiciously like a mannequin leg. "Do I want to know why you have a plastic leg in your truck?"

"You never know when you might need a helping leg."

"Shouldn't the phrase be helping hand?" Had she stepped onto a comedy movie set without looking? Because it felt like a punchline was missing or maybe he was a serial killer with a mannequin fetish?

He took pity on her confused, glassy stare. "I was helping deliver some mannequins to a store in town. I didn't realize a leg got left behind."

"Sounds plausible. As long as you aren't a serial killer, I'm good." Rue ignored Jesse's rich chuckles and peered out the dusty window as the landscape sped past. The road ahead levelled out, twisting into habitable landmarks, revealing Silver Vein in all its dusty glory. She gawked at the sight before her. Talk about something out of the ordinary. It looked like someone had built a movie set and forgotten to tear it down.

Wooden and brick buildings with false fronts stood shoulder to shoulder. Signs proclaiming their business were painted in a kaleidoscope of different colors but all united by the same looping, gold script. *Silver Queen Hotel. Bucket of Blood Saloon. Miss Kitty's Crinolines and Curios. Boone's General Store.*

People in corsets and cowboy hats roamed the boardwalks. A man in full miner gear, with a rubber pickaxe over his shoulder, was arguing with a woman dressed like Annie Oakley. And all the while, the woman continued to sip what Rue presumed was coffee from a takeaway cup. A small dog crossed in front of the couple.

Rue whispered, goggled eyed, "Am I hallucinating, or did I just see a poodle in a bonnet?"

Jesse didn't even bother to glance up. "That's Priscilla. She runs one of the tour's now, since her owner's hips gave out."

Huh? A poodle running a historical tour. Maybe her mother was right about the town being different. Rue rolled her window down, almost hanging out as she took in the wild west glory that was the re-enactment town of Silver Vein, Nevada.

A bell above an old saloon clanged in the wind as they pulled up. The building was tall and narrow, all sun-bleached wood and creaky charm. The outside was painted a faded sage-green and an antique copper color had been used for the window frames, door trim, and the decorative molding along the false front. It gave the aged building elegance without being shiny and over-the-top. Near the front door, an old whiskey barrel had been turned into a colorful flower planter. The building's top floor windows were framed by lacy, mismatched curtains. A black, wrought-iron-ringed patio jutted out from the top level. Probably providing its owner with an amazing Main Street view.

A faded sign, with gold script proclaiming Silver Tongue Saloon Bookshop and Cafe, hung lopsided off the building. Charming, yes. Structurally sound? Rue had her doubts.

Beneath the sign, an old wooden hitching post still stood. And someone had tied their fire-engine red bicycle to it.

"There you go. Door to door service." Jesse tipped an imaginary hat and clambered out, avoiding the tourist crowd as it surged around him. He hauled Rue's bags out and dumped them on the boardwalk in front of the saloon.

Rue stepped out slowly, letting the noise of the babbling crowd wash over her. Her eyes trailed over the plank porch, the lopsided saloon sign, and the little chalkboard by the entrance that read "Today's Special: Ghost stories and strong coffee. No whiskey 'til noon. No feeding the ghosts or the goat."

She exhaled, long and low. "Okay. This is a hallucination or the weirdest Hallmark movie set ever."

Jesse leaned over and gently pinched Rue's arm, causing her to squeak in surprise. "Nope. You ain't dreaming. Welcome to Silver Vein, or as the tourists call it, Ghost Vein, Nevada. Home of cursed gold and the Ghost Vein Mine. We put the 'fun' in dysfunctional."

Blinking a few times in case the image in front of her was a mirage, she stepped up onto the boardwalk.

Jesse pushed Rue's bags over next to her, offering a lopsided smile. "Welcome home, Maddox. You'll get used to our weirdness or...you won't, and you'll leave." He shrugged. "Who knows which way you'll go?"

As she was about to comment on the unique marketing of not feeding ghosts or goats, a cold, distinct *pinch* on her backside had her yelping and spinning but coming face-to-face with absolutely nothing and no one.

Except Jesse, who wasn't within pinching distance. He waggled his eyebrows and smirked.

"Did something just…"

"You'll get used to it," he said, deadpan. "Some of the miner ghosts are…handsy."

Rue reached down with one hand and snagged her duffle bag, clutching it to her chest like a shield. "I guess that was a welcome pinch?"

A low, ghostly chuckle drifted over Rue before dissipating. She swung her head around wildly, trying to catch a glimpse of her jokester pincher.

"You can only see them if they want you to." Jesse jerked a thumb over his shoulder. "That one likes to pinch and run."

Rue backed up, nodding mechanically. "Okay. Invisible ghost pincher. Guard my butt. Got it." She retreated until she hit a wall. "Thanks for the lift."

He winked and clambered back into his truck. "Consider it a freebie. I'll look at your car and get it back to you when I can." He waved and pulled onto Main Street with Rue's rust-bucket in tow.

Holding her duffle bag with one hand, Rue reached out and snagged her suitcase. She gave into her fight or flight surge of adrenaline and burst through the swinging doors.

Inside, conversation screeched to a halt. The expectant silence felt as if she'd walked into a high-noon showdown but with lattes, gluten-free muffins, and middle-aged cosplayers.

Behind the long counter stood a short woman with dark curls piled into a hairnet, wearing jeans and a flannel shirt. Beside her, a teenage girl, all eyeliner, sarcasm, and a saloon girl outfit paired with thick, black boots, stood open-mouthed and mid-pour, staring at Rue.

A handful of locals and tourists, in a dizzying array of cowboy hats and dusty costumes, turned to stare, forks halfway to their mouths and cups paused midair. Rue did what any totally normal, not-flustered person would do. She dropped her bags to the ground and raised one hand in a limp wave. "Hi. Sorry. I was just booty assaulted by a dead miner."

A titter rose through the bookshop café. At least one tight-corseted young woman filmed Rue on her phone.

Clearing her throat, Rue tried again. "I'm Rue Maddox. I inherited the saloon. And, uh...the apartment upstairs. From my great-aunt Ruth?"

The tension snapped, with the combined inhale of the locals present. The name Maddox meant something in Silver Vein, at least to the town's residents.

The curly-haired woman set down the drink she'd prepared and wiped her hands with slow, deliberate movements. She walked around the counter and stuck out a hand. "Tamsin Moreno. Folks call me Taz. I worked with your aunt Ruth for years. And I was her friend."

The teenager gave a half-shrug and continued with her order. "I'm Cassie, and I come with the building."

Rue blinked. "Like...furniture?"

"She's more like our temperamental espresso machine. Hard to get rid of and prone to sudden hissing and cursing." Taz crossed her arms. "You need to understand something, Rue. This place? The Silver Tongue? It's part café, part bookstore, and part town landmark. And it's not just walls and timber. It's *ours*. Mine. Cassie's. The regulars'. It's Ruth's memory."

Rue opened her mouth. She had no clue what to say, but there was no need as Taz held up a hand and kept on talking.

"So, before we roll out the welcome wagon, what exactly are your intentions for the saloon?"

The room went deathly still. Even the espresso machine seemed to hold its steam.

Peering around the café, Rue spotted a cowboy reenactor picking his teeth with a small stick, an older woman in a bedazzled sun visor who sipped tea from a mason jar, the young woman still filming on her phone, and others, all staring at her. A mannequin missing a leg, dressed as a saloon girl, posed on the window seat with a book.

Her brain fritzed, completely blanked, so naturally Rue defaulted to bad humor. "I mean. Intention wise...I don't intend to *marry* the saloon, if that's what you're asking?"

No one laughed.

Not even the snarky teenager.

She cleared her throat. "I just...want to see what the place is about. Get a feel for the town. The business. Figure out what I'm doing before I make any decisions."

Taz studied her for a long moment, then nodded once. "Fair enough. For now."

Sagging, Rue exhaled. "Thanks for understanding."

Nodding, Taz gestured to the back of the building. "Apartment's up the stairs to the right. Bathrooms are labelled Outlaws and Queens. You work out which group you are. Don't open any locked doors. And if you hear someone whispering, ignore it until after your second cup of coffee."

Rue stared. "Is that a rule or a threat? And does that mean I need to start drinking coffee?"

Cassie smirked. "Yes."

"Yes to which one? Because I'm kind of a tea drinker and..." Rue stopped babbling and tried to regain a shred of dignity. And immediately stumbled over something warm, fuzzy, and surprisingly solid. "Whaaa." Rue flailed her arms, struggling to regain her balance as a brown and white miniature goat darted out from between her legs.

The goat made a beeline for a half-eaten cupcake perched on the edge of a nearby table. With all the stealth of a sugar-obsessed toddler, it chomped the cupcake in one bite and licked the wrapper with gusto.

"Uh. Is that a health code violation?" She'd only just inherited the place and didn't want to get shut down any time soon.

Loud, raucous, honest-to-goodness belly laughter bounced off the timber walls and filled the air with warmth. Even the lights overhead flickered and glowed brightly. The tourists cracked up. The locals cackled. Even stone-faced Cassie snorted with laughter.

Taz wiped a tear from her eye. "That's Nacho. He comes with the building too, although he's more of a free-loading visitor than a fixture."

Nacho bleated proudly, lips still dusted with pink frosting.

And for the first time since Rue had driven her rust-bucket car up the side of a mountain and got pinched by a handsy ghost, she felt...not like an outsider. Not exactly an insider either but someone in between. Someone who *might* one day belong, if she was given a chance.

THREE

"Well, well," a voice purred, deep and oily. "What do we have here?" A skinny man of middling height with a purple and black pinstriped waistcoat and a black, dusty top hat shoved through the crowd of café onlookers. He was followed by a small group of costumed tourists. He paused in front of Rue and gave her a slow, sweeping once-over. "Planning to stay a while? I'm sure I could show you around town. Hit the highlights of ole Ghost Vein?" He winked.

Yuck. It looked like even supernatural towns had lechers. Rue gave him a look that could curdle milk.

"Back off, Tobias," Taz said without missing a beat. "She's not part of your creepy little world."

Tobias gave her a mocking bow, then turned to address his group of tourists, all corsets, cowboy hats, and selfie sticks. "Ladies and gentlemen." His voice boomed through the renovated saloon.

Ignoring his antics, Rue took more note of her surroundings now that her anxiety of first introduction had faded. The original building had been a saloon and still had that element in its decoration. The café counter was a long wooden bar with cast iron bar stools. The wood had a scratched and dented look that showed decades of wear and tear. Behind it, an espresso machine hissed and burped, alongside gleaming display cases of sugary baked goods. A swinging door obviously led to the café's kitchen. To one side hung shelves filled with mismatched antique teacups, mugs, old glass bottles, and chipped China plates. The main floor of the café housed scarred wooden tables and high-backed chairs, all in a kaleidoscope of different painted colors. The bookshop was accessed through a cased opening.

Rue poked her head in and nearly drooled at the floor to ceiling wooden shelves that held every size book she could dream of. Thick, patterned rugs covered the floor, and plush armchairs clustered near a large window looking out onto Main Street. Cozy nooks with the odd armchair had been carved out between the tall bookshelves and display cases featuring mining antiques. She loved the whole welcoming, cozy feel of the bookshop side of the old saloon. The tour guide's booming voice drew Rue back into the café.

"Welcome to the historic Silver Tongue Saloon. Once the very heart of Ghost Vein's dirty deeds, now it limps along as a café and bookshop. Unless it reverts to its nefarious activities which, frankly, would be an improvement."

"Hey." Cassie snapped.

He ignored her and continued to rattle on. "This building dates back to the late eighteen hundreds. Built when the town was still known as Silver Vein, before it earned its more infamous nickname, Ghost Vein." He let his last words hang for dramatic effect for a few seconds before continuing. "The town's new moniker was named for eight miners who disappeared and were never seen again. There were whispers of a cursed gold cache, hidden deep in the mine by the owner, Elias Grimshaw. Who then disappeared himself. Those rumors still echo through this town. And some say the ghosts of those miners cursed the mine and the town to this very day."

She might find the tour guide creepy, but he spun a good tale. Rue found herself wanting to know more. She subtly shifted away from the table Nacho the goat was nosing around looking for more snacks to steal.

The tour guide gestured toward the back of the saloon, where small antique mining tools were on display in glass cabinets next to shelves of new and secondhand thrillers and romance novels. "The Ghost Vein Mine was plagued with accidents and cave-ins, all under mysterious circumstances. Wailing and ghostly voices filled the mine's tunnels. And rumor has it whoever finds the cursed gold... won't live long enough to spend it."

One of the tourists gasped. Another pointed her phone at the ceiling, following a wispy trail of smoke or steam.

Maybe it was a ghost? One was certainly solid enough to pinch her booty. Rue subtly rubbed her offended body part. She looked at Taz. "Gold?"

Taz rolled her eyes. "You'll hear about it ten times a day. The mine was mainly silver, but the rumor is the owner, Elias Grimshaw, found gold and didn't want to share it so he hid it in the mine somewhere. This town is all about stories and gossip. So, take it with a grain of salt."

Rue looked down as Nacho tried to eat the rest of the cupcake paper.

"Or possibly a goat-sized antacid," she muttered. Rue focused back on the tour guide; his story had definitely caught her attention. "A cursed gold cache?" she asked, keeping one wary eye on him. "Miners disappearing? Do you have any proof of that? Or is it all a rumor like Taz said?"

Tobias folded his arms, leaning against the counter. "There is historical evidence of eight miners disappearing when the town was called Silver Vein. The gold's real enough, although no one's ever found it. As for the *curse...*" He shrugged. "The previous owner, Ruth Maddox, believed it."

"Wait. Ruth believed in the curse?" So much for the savvy business owner image. Believing in a curse sounded kind of flaky.

Taz gritted her teeth at Tobias' words and gave Rue a long look. "Ruth was a witch. She had certain...ideas."

Nearly choking on her own breath, Rue spluttered. "I'm sorry. Ruth Maddox was *what?*"

"A witch," Cassie piped in casually, tossing a towel over her shoulder. "You'll get used to it. Plenty of witches and other creatures in town. That's half the appeal of Ghost Vein. Cursed gold. Ghostly miners, witches, vampires, shifters. You name it, we've probably had someone pass through."

Taz grinned. "Cassie's right. There are plenty of witches in Ghost Vein. We don't exactly advertise it with bumper stickers, but it's not a secret. Some shops in town offer witchy services and supplies. Something about the town appeals to those of us who are supernatural. Ruth was special, though. She was a curse-breaker. That's why she settled here. She'd heard about the town and its residents and the cursed gold."

Rue's mouth opened. Then closed. Then opened again like a confused fish.

"Witches are common," Taz told her gently. "Curse-breakers aren't. There's usually only one or two per generation, and it normally runs through family lines. Ruth was it...until she died."

The floor tilted under Rue's feet. Not physically, but like her inner balance had shifted. "And people didn't like their curses being ruined?"

Taz gave a tight smile. "This town makes its money off ghost stories, cursed gold, and wild west shenanigans. Ruth had a habit of disrupting certain plans. Took the wind right out of some of our residents' sails."

"Oh, I get it," Rue muttered. "Yikes. I can see the clash."

Right on cue, Tobias clapped his hands, making himself the center of attention again. "Tell her how Ruth *really* died."

Eyes narrowing, Taz glared at the guide. "Tobias..."

"She was scared to death," he declared, brown eyes glittering. "By the Ghost Vein curse itself. She meddled and the curse killed her."

The tourists gasped at his dramatic words, their eyes wide as they followed the discussion.

Stomping out from behind the counter, Taz growled at the guide. "She had a heart attack at boot scooting, you jackass. Not everything's about the curse."

"She meddled, so she probably *thought* it was a curse." Tobias puffed up. "You don't understand these things. You're just a dabbler in magic. You don't have a natural born gift."

"That's it. Get. Out," Taz snapped. "You're banned. Go sell your lies and snake oil somewhere else."

"You can't ban me. You're not the owner." He smiled, smarm oozing from every pore.

Taz turned to Rue and pointed. "She is."

Rue swallowed around a suddenly dry mouth. She *was* the owner, ghost pinching and all. She stepped up next to

Taz, stiffened her spine, and nodded. "I'm the owner. And I don't tolerate bullying in my own building, especially not about my great aunt. You're not welcome here, Tobias."

The guide's smug smirk vanished. "You'll regret this. You just blacklisted the most popular tour guide in Ghost Vein."

"Guess we'll have to rely on cupcakes and cute goats then." Rue smiled sweetly. How was that for stepping up and taking charge? Maybe this wouldn't be such a disaster after all.

As Tobias stalked toward the main doors, he lashed out with one boot, kicking the cast iron spittoon that had been holding the saloon door open. It clanged across the floor with a metallic shriek before thunking against a table leg. The saloon fell quiet.

Taz didn't blink at the dramatic exit. "That..." she said with a slow smile at Rue, "was your first step toward owning the place. Kicking out the trash." Taz patted her shoulder. "You'll do fine, Maddox. You've got Ruth's spine, even if you don't realize it yet."

Rue wasn't so sure as she watched Tobias prance along Main Street. Her chest tightened with the weight of the remaining customers' eyes. One thought rose above the rest...

What the heck did I get myself into?

Rue trailed Taz as she showed her around the bookstore and café. "I'm just saying, I've shelved books, but I don't know how to run a bookshop. Or a café. Trust me, you don't want to eat my baking. You could use my biscuits as rocks."

Taz waved a hand as they passed through the swinging

half-doors that separated the kitchen from the café. "It's not rocket science. It's coffee, books, and reheated pastries. You'll be fine. We buy our pastries ready made from the diner every morning. So, it's easy peasy. Plus, Cassie has a friend who works in the bookshop part time. He's happy to go full time if you need him."

"I need him." Rue nibbled her lip. Customer service wasn't her thing. She liked the non-contact of shelving books. Silver Tongue Bookstore and Café was charming, quaint, and totally overwhelming. Rue rubbed the back of her neck. "Don't suppose you have a manual? How not to screw up your inherited business? A pamphlet?"

Taz giggled. "Sure. Right next to Ruth's ghost repellent."

"Really?"

"No. Not really." Taz thumped Rue on her shoulder as they returned to the café side of the saloon. The front saloon doors creaked open, and heavy boots hit the wooden floorboards with deliberate steps. Taz's eyes widened and she huffed. "Prepare yourself."

"What?" Rue swung to meet the newcomer. And her first thought was inappropriate activities with handcuffs and a willing partner. Tall, broad shouldered, with a square jaw with just enough stubble to add to his rugged look. His sheriff uniform fit like it'd been tailored by someone who knew exactly how to show off tight biceps. And his blond, buzzcut, military-style haircut had grown just enough to make it windswept. All this made Rue immediately suspicious. Good-looking men were her kryptonite, and it never ended well.

"Sheriff." Taz nodded at the new guy.

He returned the nod then his gaze turned to Rue. "You the new owner?"

Rue shifted her weight from foot to foot as his deep tones washed over her. "Depends. Are you here to welcome me or slap me with a fine for some nefarious wrongdoing?" Her *blurt-everything-out* whenever she felt awkward would probably get her arrested soon enough.

He didn't smile. "Tour guide has filed a complaint. Said he was verbally assaulted and wants to press charges for harassment."

"Oh, for..." Taz stepped between Rue and the sheriff. "Tobias was disrespectful about Ruth, so Rue kicked him out. Which she had every right to do. We can refuse service, especially to rude customers."

The sheriff's gaze flickered back to Rue. He scanned her from her blue tank top to her faded, dusty, denim shorts to her purple flip flops. It wasn't flirty but more *assessing*. Like he was mentally cataloging her faults and potential risk to the town.

"So," he grunted. "You're Ruth's great-niece. The *absent* one."

Oh, there is a wagon load of attitude in those words. "Excuse me?"

"You weren't here when she passed. You didn't visit. No one knew Ruth had any family."

Her hands went to her hips in a smooth, almost choreographed movement. "Okay, well, *I* didn't know I had a ghost-hugging, curse-busting great aunt living in Ghost Vein, so maybe we're both surprised."

The sheriff didn't flinch at Rue's take-no-prisoners attitude. "Name's Silver Vein. Not Ghost Vein."

"Right." Rue crossed her arms. "Ghost Vein's just for the tourists. The curses, the missing miners, the handsy ghosts, it's all just good old-fashioned marketing."

"You don't fit in here." He looked pointedly at her colorful footwear.

"I just got here," she shot back. "But thank you for the warm, judgmental welcome."

He let out a slow breath and gave Rue a look that suggested he wasn't used to people talking back.

Rue met his look head on. She didn't care how square his jaw was. She wasn't going to be scolded in her own building by a stranger.

After a long pause, he nodded once, almost with grudging respect. "Just doing my job and protecting the town."

"Then maybe you should check on the tour guide spreading lies about a woman who can't defend herself."

He studied her for another beat. Tension crackled between them. Sharp, simmering, and completely unwanted. Uninvited. Rue stiffened. He wasn't just suspicious, he was *mad*. About what, she had no clue...unless he didn't like redheads? Or maybe he'd been close to her great aunt and hated the idea of someone else taking over? She refused to soften. Even if a tiny part of her understood his reaction.

"I knew Ruth." He kept his voice low and clipped. "She was sharp. Private. She didn't trust just anyone." His jaw worked for a second before he added, "I don't know why she left this place to a stranger."

The words hit harder than Rue expected. *Stranger*. He was right even if she didn't want to admit it. Rue lifted her chin. "I didn't even know she *existed* until the will showed up. So, maybe you could ease off the judgment?"

"I take it you grew up in a city?"

"What's that supposed to mean?"

The sheriff shrugged. "Just wondering if you've ever

lived in a small town before. We do things a little differently here."

Behind the counter, Taz and Cassie had paused in their drink making and were eating up the tension.

Rue folded her arms. "Do you have something against big cities?"

"Nope. Just think come season change, you might want to swap the flip-flops and shorts for something that won't get you hypothermia. Otherwise, I'll have to file an incident report about your poor fashion choices.'"

Rue refused to acknowledge the goosebumps already prickling her arms. "I'll be sure to pencil in a trip to the flannel aisle."

Silence stretched between them as he stood in front of her, not saying a word.

Thankfully, Nacho, the miniature goat, reappeared and launched himself onto a nearby chair, triumphantly claiming another cupcake in a single frosting-smeared bite.

"Taz, if you don't keep that goat from stealing food off plates, I *will* write you up for a health code violation."

Not even flinching, Taz winked. "You'd have to catch him first. And you know he bites."

The sheriff pointed a warning finger at Nacho and stomped out of the saloon without another word.

The moment he disappeared, Rue let out a breath.

Taz glanced at her sideways. "And that, Rue Maddox, is Ghost Vein's one and only single sheriff. Cole Dawson."

"I can see why he's single," Rue sneered.

Cassie smirked, licking cupcake frosting off her finger. "You say that now. I give it a week before we're working out a cute, combined nickname for the two of you."

Rue rolled her eyes, but her cheeks burned. And, okay,

maybe she was a *little* cold. But she'd freeze solid before she admitted it to Captain Judgy Jawline.

"Come on. Let's show you the apartment." Taz grabbed Rue's suitcase, leaving her the duffle bag. She led them up a creaking staircase. Taz paused at the top of the landing next to a pale blue door to catch her breath. She flung it open without any fanfare. "Ruth had the place renovated a few months ago. Brand new kitchen, fresh paint, new bathroom. Got someone in to charm the plumbing too. No more cold showers even in winter."

Rue gave a distracted nod, her mind still back in the saloon, arguing with the sheriff.

Taz hesitated. "If you're wondering about Ruth, don't worry. She didn't die here."

"She didn't?"

"Nope. It was at the *Boot Scootin' Boogie Night* at the Dusty Mule, another saloon. And it was definitely a heart attack. No curse attached. Collapsed mid-two-step." Her voice cracked slightly. "She went out dancing. Just how she wanted."

Her heart squeezed. Rue hadn't even met the woman and still...grief caught her off guard. "I'm sorry for your loss," she said quietly.

Dumping the suitcase on the floor, Taz handed her a keyring. "Settle in. You've got a couple days before the town drives you mad."

Rue managed a smile. "You're giving me a few days before you show me the ropes?"

Taz snorted. "Try tomorrow. Eight a.m. sharp. We've got work to do."

And with that, she turned and headed back down the stairs, leaving Rue to settle in.

Stepping inside, Rue dumped her duffle bag next to the

suitcase. The space was...beautiful and not what she'd expected. The apartment opened into a cozy living room with warm, honey-colored floors and soft sage-green walls. The couch and armchairs looked brand new, plush and overstuffed. Someone had picked comfort over style, and it worked. A few bright colored throw blankets lay tidily folded over the arm of the couch. The kitchen, tucked along the back wall, was all shiny, white tiles, flashy silver appliances and glossy, gray stone counter tops. Rue opened the fridge and grimaced at the empty shelves. "Looks like take-away for dinner tonight." She'd get Taz to show her where the local store was and get a load of groceries in.

Rue wandered into the main bedroom, and it even had a cute little bathroom, tiled in a charming blue tile. Wide windows and lacy curtains framed the room. She popped back into the living room and spotted a black, wrought iron patio off the combined living and dining area. "Perfect." Rue breathed out the word and kept exploring. She opened the door to the second, smaller bedroom and froze as she spotted three medium-sized boxes stacked neatly against the wall, all labeled Ruth's Stuff.

She swallowed, a knot forming in her throat. Rue wasn't ready to look through her great aunt's belongings. She didn't know the woman, but it felt invasive. Without warning, the room pressed in on her, thick with someone else's memories. A cool draft coiled around her ankles, feathering up her legs and spine. Rue spun around.

No windows ajar.

No doors open except for the front door.

The air was still. *Too still.*

She rubbed her arms, very aware she still wore her Florida shorts, tank top, and flip flops. Rue glanced back at the boxes. The unopened answers waiting for her, the remnants of someone else's life. "Later," she said out loud, stepping back. The apartment didn't respond. But for a moment, the draft swirled again as if someone or something had heard her.

Clearing her throat, Rue dragged her suitcase into the bedroom and was halfway through unpacking when a loud crash, sharp and sudden, echoed through the silent apartment. She froze. The sound hadn't come from inside but nearby. *Below maybe?* Grabbing her keyring, Rue exchanged her flip flops for a pair of plain, black, slip-on shoes and cracked the open apartment door wider. The hallway was lit only by a small open window at the top of the stairwell, just above the landing.

Rue squinted through it. The window looked out over a narrow alley behind the saloon, where shadows stretched long and crooked. She frowned. Something felt...off. "This better not be Nacho raiding dumpsters," she muttered to herself and crept downstairs. At the bottom of the stairwell, she passed through the rear corridor, where old storage closets and cleaning supplies lived, and found a steel-reinforced door at the end of the hallway. "Definitely not part of the charming Old West aesthetic."

She pushed the unlocked door open and stepped outside.

The air smelled like old beer and rotting food. She shivered. A large green, rusted dumpster squatted at the side of the old building. This was the business end of Ghost Vein, hidden from the scenic boardwalk and photo opportunities. Stepping toward the dumpster, gravel crunched under her feet. That's when Rue spotted a black boot-clad foot. "What?" Had someone passed out? "This isn't a saloon, you know." Moving closer, Rue peered at the figure. *No,* she corrected herself mentally. A body. Facedown, half-shadowed by the dumpster. Wearing a pinstriped waistcoat with a discarded, dusty top hat, laying on its side,

"Oh, snapping duck poo." Rue's stomach flipped. The figure, the body, was Tobias, the mouthy tour guide she'd kicked out earlier. She shuffled closer. Blood streaked one side of his face, seeping into the gravel next to him. His fingers clutched a crumpled piece of paper and a small, yellow stone with sharp edges and a honeycomb texture to it. *Gold?*

Focusing on Tobias, Rue dropped to her knees and felt for a pulse. She knew in her bones it was pointless, but she still needed to check.

Nothing.

No pulse.

Rue pulled her hand away and stared at the slick red covering it. She recoiled, breath shallow, fingers shaking.

The back door slammed open, and Taz's voice rang out. "Rue?"

Rue stood and turned slowly, bloody hands outstretched.

"What...?" Taz backed up, eyes wide.

Rue raised her hands, palms up. "I didn't...I just...he was *already* dead."

Taz's face was white as flour. "Is that blood?"

Rue looked down at her hands. So much for a fresh start. She looked back at Taz. "This wasn't in the brochure."

Welcome to Ghost Vein...

FOUR

"Come on through, Doc. The sheriff's expecting you."

A man in a deputy's uniform lifted the yellow crime scene tape and waved through a woman of average height with blonde-streaked brown hair, wearing athletic wear and holding a bag tight to her chest. The deputy remained near the edge of the tape, waving off onlookers and gently steering camera-happy tourists back toward Main Street.

It took Rue a second to process who the deputy was. "Is that Jesse? Why is my mechanic wearing a deputy's uniform?" She whispered to Taz.

Taz, who hadn't stopped rubbing soothing circles on Rue's back since she'd called the sheriff, leaned in with a low voice. "Yep. That's our friendly mechanic. He's also the sheriff's best friend. They served together in the military, years ago."

"Of course they did." Rue blinked a few times, trying to bring the mechanic-slash-deputy into focus. Everything felt vague like a dream...or a nightmare. Except for her sticky hands. That felt real. Too real.

The woman Deputy Jesse had let through the crime

scene tape walked straight to Rue with a nod at the sheriff. She dropped her plain black bag at her feet and knelt in front of Rue. She calmly reached into her bag and drew out gloves, swabs, and evidence bags. Tugging on the gloves, she shot a sympathetic glance at Rue. "How ya holding up, sweetie? I'm Doc Halliday. I'd say welcome to Ghost Vein, but you're probably over our town now."

Rue didn't answer, couldn't seem to find her voice. Instead, she nodded awkwardly. Social scenes, let alone crime scenes, weren't really her thing. Who knew what to say, especially when you'd just found a body?

Doc Halliday didn't seem fazed and instead used her sterile swab to give Rue's bloodstained hands a quick professional once over to collect the evidence of the tour guide's blood.

"This is Rue Maddox. She's Ruth's great niece. And the new owner of the Silver Tongue." Taz introduced Rue and patted her shoulder. "Doc here is the best. She's a tea drinker too."

Doc glanced up and winked. "Fellow tea drinkers unite. I just wish we'd met under better circumstances." She discarded the swab in the evidence bag and grabbed another. She turned back to Rue. "Just hold still a little longer, sweetie. I'll be done soon enough."

Rue finally managed to speak. "I didn't...I didn't do it. Hurt him, I mean. I just found him."

Doc's expression didn't shift. She was all calm and professional. "That's for the sheriff to sort out, honey. Not my job. I'm just the evidence girl right now." Once she finished with the swabs, she peeled off her gloves and packed them and the evidence away. She patted Rue's shoulder with a firm hand and stood. "Taz, sweet hot tea is the best for shock. It'll help settle her once the sheriff releases her. I'll handle the stiff." Doc winked and grabbed a fresh pair of gloves and her bag, then headed toward the body, where the sheriff now stood, glaring down at the victim.

"Doc's one of the good ones, Rue. I promise she'll help sort all this out." Taz crouched beside Rue again and searched her expression. "Did you get a good look at him? The body, I mean?"

Rue swallowed a few times before answering, her tone flat. "It was the tour guide. The man I asked to leave Silver Tongue."

"Tobias?" Taz's eyes flared wide and her lips tightened.

Holding out her hands, Rue stared at the rusty discoloration that still stained her pale skin. She fought the roll of her stomach, focusing on Taz's words. "He was wearing that striped waistcoat. His top hat was next to him on the ground. And he was holding a rock with some yellowish paper.

Taz tilted her head. "Rock?"

"It was yellowish, not like the fake gold stuff you buy at the store. It looked old."

"A nugget." Taz breathed out the word.

"I don't know. I don't have much experience with real or fake gold. He had a piece of paper, crumpled around the rock. It looked stained and old, and I didn't want to touch it...the blood and stuff." She ground to a halt and stared at her hands again.

"You did the right thing."

Sheriff Cole Dawson approached from the other end of the alley. His expression was grim and unreadable. He stopped a few paces away, arms crossed.

Taz stood and moved in front of Rue. A momma bear protecting her cub.

"Taz." He nodded, his voice like gravel. "You can both go inside for now. I'll speak to you separately when I'm done out here."

Straightening, Taz glared. "Rue didn't do this. She *couldn't* have. She's been in town for *less than a day*. So, where's her motive?"

Rue placed a hand on Taz's arm, her voice soft. "It's okay. If I were him, I'd suspect me too." Her response must have surprised Sheriff Cole, as a flicker of some strong emotion passed over his face for a few seconds. Surprise at her honesty? Approval? Whatever it was, he hadn't expected it from Silver Vein's newest resident.

He gave Taz a pointed look and nodded toward the saloon. "Get her inside. We'll speak soon."

Shifting, Taz grabbed Rue's hand and carefully led her back inside the saloon and into the kitchen. "Sit," Taz ordered, already bustling around, a woman on a mission. She pulled down a black mug with the words "Witches steep it better" stenciled in white on the side. "This was Ruth's favorite tea mug. She hated those tiny pretty teacups. She always said they were great for looking at but if you needed a caffeine hit, size mattered."

Her words surprised a rusty chuckle out of Rue. "I agree. Sometimes the more tea the better."

Taz bustled around the kitchen. "Go on. Sit."

Following her instructions, Rue sat and hid her trembling hands in her lap. The kitchen smelled of cinnamon and caffeine. The warm vibe of the room seeped into her bones, and she relaxed on the stool.

Taz dumped three heaping teaspoons of sugar into Rue's tea, shrugging at Rue's look of shock. "Doc said sweet tea. So, sweet it is."

"He looked so smug earlier today. Annoying, but alive.

And now he's...he's just..." Rue trailed off, staring into space.

"Gone," Taz finished gently, setting the mug in front of her. "The tea should settle your nerves." She leaned against the counter and crossed her arms as she waited for Rue to drink.

Holding the mug, Rue gingerly took a sip, grimacing at the saccharine sweet taste. "I've been here hardly any time. And already I've found a body, the sheriff thinks I'm his number one suspect, and a miner's ghost pinched my butt."

"Ghost Vein works fast. The town grows on you."

"That's *not* reassuring." Rue gave Taz a tired look.

Lips quirking, Taz shrugged. "Didn't say it was."

A loud throat clearing caught Rue's notice, and she stiffened as Sheriff Cole stood at the entrance of the kitchen.

"Taz, could you give us the room?"

Her spine snapped straight, and Taz stood to attention. "She's been through enough, Cole. You should..."

"It's okay," Rue interrupted softly, still looking down at her too sweet tea. "Really, Taz. I'll be fine."

Not budging at first, Taz looked from Cole to Rue. Then, sighing, she shot the sheriff a glare that could've curdled milk. She pointed a finger at him. "Mind your manners, Sheriff." She turned on her heels and stomped past him.

Sheriff Cole then moved into the room with slow, measured steps. He didn't sit, just stood, pulling out a little notepad he flipped open, pen poised to take down Rue's every word. "Tell me your movements before you found the victim."

Rue closed her eyes for a moment, gathering the threads of her thoughts. "I was upstairs unpacking. I heard a noise. I'm not sure what it was. It wasn't loud, just not what I was expecting, I guess. I thought I'd better check it out."

He nodded and waited for Rue to continue.

"I grabbed the keys Taz had given me and stepped out onto the landing. I looked out the tiny window. I couldn't see anything, but something felt off. Actually, I thought Nacho had knocked something over. Or maybe got caught somewhere. I found the alley door and stepped outside...and there he was. Face down."

"You recognized him?"

She shook her head. "Not at first. I checked for a pulse and spotted the top hat and saw the costume." She paused and took a wobbly breath. "I realized it was the guy I'd asked to leave the saloon earlier. The tour guide."

"Tobias." Cole scribbled in his notebook.

"Right." Rue nodded absently. "In my head, I just call him the guide."

"Had you met him before?"

"No. Only earlier, in the café."

"When you threw him out."

Rue stiffened, eyes narrowing. All the fight and energy that had drained from her earlier flooded back with his words. "*Asked.* I asked him to leave because he was being disrespectful about Ruth. I wasn't violent. I didn't even touch him. I didn't *throw* him anywhere. He left voluntarily."

Cole glanced up briefly at her strong words but said nothing.

She kept going. "And why would I kill him? I didn't even *know* him. What motive would I have? For that matter, what motive would anyone else have?" She hesitated. "I mean...he was holding something. It looked like gold. Maybe someone killed him for that?"

Cole frowned. "What gold? There was nothing found on him."

"What?"

"No gold," he repeated. "Nothing like that was found on the body."

"That's..." She shook her head. "No. I saw it. He was holding a weird, yellow rock and a crumpled piece of paper. It looked old, parchment or something."

The sheriff wrote her words down, slower this time.

"It didn't sparkle," Rue added. "It didn't look like the stuff you buy from a tourist shop. You know how some of the stores sell souvenir gold that looks like the color was spraypainted on? This looked older."

Cole stopped writing. His gaze lingered on her for a long, unreadable second. "Did you or Taz leave the alleyway for any reason after discovering the body?"

"Taz found me checking for a pulse, then called the police." Rue paused for a few seconds before continuing. "She had a blanket, and we both went inside while she found it and wrapped it around me. Then we went back out and waited for you to come."

"You didn't see anyone else around at any stage?"

She shook her head. "No one until you turned up."

Nodding, Cole stuffed his notebook and pen into his pocket, turned, and disappeared for a moment. When he returned, he had a small pack of cleaning wipes. "Hold still," he muttered.

Rue flinched when he gently reached out and wiped her hands then her cheek, the cool sting of the wipes at odds with her heated cheeks. He still glared, but he was gentle. She caught a glimpse of dried blood on the wipe and looked away. Rue swallowed, praying the contents of her stomach stayed put.

After a long pause, Cole crumpled the wipe and stowed it in his pocket. "You can't leave town."

"I wasn't planning to," Rue responded, her cheeks heating up.

"I'll speak to Taz now. You stay in here until she comes and gets you." He turned on his heel and left without waiting for a response.

Rue blew out a breath. Sheriff Cole Dawson was a force unto himself. Having him wiping her hands and cheek had discombobulated her. Before the hand wiping incident, she would have said he was a burr in her behind but now...she wasn't quite sure how she felt. Rue wrapped her hands around the tea mug and let its warmth battle with a deep chill in her bones that wouldn't go away. She took a sip of the too sweet tea, then another. Her body felt limp, exhausted, but her mind wouldn't stop spinning. She'd touched a dead body, the creepy tour guide was gone, and she was right in the middle of it all.

Rue snorted. Heck, she probably *was* suspect number one. Her mother would blame the town and the I-told-you-so would be epic. She could hear her mom now... *"Magic always ruins things, Rue. I told you Silver Vein was danger-ous."* Her fingers tightened around the mug. "Maybe she's right. But I'm not crawling back to Florida yet."

The door creaked and Taz popped her head in. "Still alive?"

Rue offered a tired smile. "Barely."

"You'll be fine. We've got your back." Taz clapped her hands. "Now get that Florida booty up. You'll feel better if you're up and doing rather than brooding."

Taking Taz's words to heart, Rue pushed her tea mug aside, took a deep breath, and followed her out into the café.

Stopping and whispering to Cassie as she cleaned the

counter, Taz whipped around and beamed a wide smile at Rue as she entered the café.

The way Taz had spun around and the guilty look on Cassie's face made them look like toddlers with their hands caught in the cookie jar.

"Hey." Cassie squeaked the greeting out with over-the-top perkiness. "Glad to see you haven't collapsed in a sobbing heap. Way to go." The teenager held two thumbs up, then glanced at Taz, who rolled her eyes at the girl's too obvious encouragement.

"Subtlety is not your forte, kid." Taz shook her head.

A smile broke out on Rue's face without warning, surprising even herself. "You don't need to cheer me up. I'm okay." She peered out the large front windows at the front of the café. Tourists peeked in, noses pressed to the glass, ignoring the closed sign on the door. Or maybe they were hoping to see another murderous scandal to gossip about. Rue planted her feet apart, hands at her side. "FYI, the sheriff closed us down for a couple of days while he investigates." She gave them both a look. "And I didn't kill the tour guide."

Cassie snorted. "Yeah, well, plenty of people in town wouldn't care if you did."

"Cassie," Taz warned.

"What?" Cassie crossed her arms. "It's true. I'm not saying *she* did it, I'm just saying...heaps of people wanted him gone."

Rue raised a brow. "Why?"

Taz sighed and leaned against the counter. "Tobias was a popular guide. He started out with historic mine tours, then switched to theatrical ghost tours. Light on facts, heavy on acting. The ghost tours were more popular and lucrative. He liked to call himself a part-time historian, but he was just a bad actor with a flair for spooky drama. And a gift for rubbing people the wrong way."

"Or just rubbing them." Cassie fake gagged. "He thought he was a player, but he was just a creep. I saw him arguing with the mayor yesterday. Even *she* couldn't stand him, and she's a politician."

"She isn't wrong." Taz turned back to Rue. "There are rumors about him getting too cozy with female tourists of a certain age. And he always snuck around the museum and the mine. He thought he could get away with anything because he was popular with the tourists."

Rue stared out the window at the growing crowd. Some of the tourists had even taken to banging on the doors and window. She sighed. "Doesn't matter whether I did it or not. People will think I killed him. And it's going to tank the business before I've even had a chance to *start*."

"Honestly?" Taz coughed. "It'll probably be the opposite." She gestured toward the gawkers at the window. "They're all gonna want a look at the potentially murderous new owner. The morbid curiosity alone will probably bring in half the county."

"Awesome. I've become murderous clickbait. And the sheriff will lock me up and throw away the key."

"Cole's a grouch, but he's no fool. He'll see you didn't have time to murder anyone."

A scratching sounded from the bookshop side of the saloon. Rue froze, eyebrows arched high. "Please tell me you have rats or mice?"

"Nope." Taz and Cassie shook their heads in an almost choreographed movement.

"Maybe it was the goat? He's around, isn't he?" Rue asked hopefully.

Cassie shook her head. "Nacho's in the storeroom licking the wall again."

Ick. That didn't sound hygienic or healthy for the goat. Rue grimaced. She really wanted the noise to be the goat.

A loud thunk sounded from the bookshop, followed by a flutter of paper.

Taz groaned. "That better not have ruined any stock. You hear me?" She marched out of view, swiftly returning with a thick book. She held it up. *Nevada's Lost Veins: A Mining History of Silver Vein and Surrounding Ghost Towns.* Taz handed it to Rue. "Apparently, the ghost, whoever it is, thinks you need reading homework."

"I...I'm sorry? What?"

"Ghost," Cassie said casually. "Books fall a lot when they want someone's attention."

Taking a step back, Rue shook her head. "No. Nope. I'm a ghost free zone. Magic and ghosts were no-go when I was growing up."

"Let me guess...your mom?" Taz cocked her head to the side, taking in Rue's words.

"She *banned* any mention of the paranormal, including any witchy family members. I didn't see my first shifter until I moved out." Rue stared down at the book in her hand. "I had no clue I even had a great aunt. And now I find out that not only did Ruth exist, but she was also a *curse-breaker witch?*"

Taz gave a sympathetic smile. "Ruth had the gift, and it mostly runs in the family line. If she passed the saloon to you...there's a good chance *you've* inherited her witchy gifts as well."

A cold chill settled over Rue, and her face suddenly felt frozen.

"Also, ghosts tend to hang around here in town. So, Ruth might be lurking," Cassie added, not helping.

Sending Cassie a frown, Taz shook her head.

"Hey, I'm just saying." Cassie held up her hands. "Maybe it's not Ruth. It's Tobias?"

As one, all the women shuddered.

Rue backed up, holding up a hand. The other clutched the book. "You know what? I might go upstairs."

Taz reached out. "Rue…"

"Nope. I might have a shower, maybe lie down. Sleep this day away." Rue turned and fled up the stairs to the relatively safe haven of her new apartment. She really needed to rewrite her life plan to include no murders or ghosts. Maybe her mother was right. Sell the saloon and purchase a matching condo in Florida next to her. Watch her soul drown in the humidity of Florida.

At least the condo wouldn't harbor the ghost of a recently murdered, creepy tour guide.

FIVE

It was the humming that drove Rue out of bed. A girl could put up with handsy ghosts and books falling by themselves, but when an invisible someone starts crooning lullabies over your bed, a woman has to draw a line.

She remembered Taz bringing her soup the night before. Then she collapsed into bed, exhausted. Her sleep hadn't been *bad* exactly. Just...weird. She'd dreamed of places she didn't recognize, voices that sounded almost familiar, and a soft, female humming threaded through it all. Then a loud bang outside the building jolted her awake in the middle of the night. She hadn't slept much after that.

Now, just after sunrise, Rue stomped downstairs, tugging at the hem of her plain green T-shirt. Her well-loved jeans were faded but comfortable. She'd given up on her frizzy auburn hair and shoved it into a messy ponytail.

The Silver Tongue Café and Bookshop was still closed, at least until tomorrow, by sheriff's order. Which Rue hoped meant she could sneak into the kitchen and have a quiet, ghost-free moment with her tea. Anything or anyone bothering her, whether corporal or non-corporal, would get a verbal spray. No ghosts before caffeine. Slipping into the kitchen, Rue found Taz bustling around, already fully caffeinated and in the middle of a muffin-baking operation. Nacho, the miniature goat menace, sat at her feet.

Rue slid onto a stool with a sigh. "I thought Silver Tongue didn't make its own food. That you ordered stock in?"

Taz swung around with a hand to her heart. "Wow. You're quieter than your great aunt when she was on a sneak."

"Comes from years of avoiding my mother."

Snickering, Taz placed Rue's witch mug with steaming hot tea in front of her. "We normally do order the food in, but I thought you might like some home-baked goodies today. I'm not a professional baker, but I make a mean blueberry muffin." She snatched a cooling blueberry muffin off a rack and placed it on a plate in front of Rue. "Get some food into you. It might help you feel better."

"How did you know I'm feeling tired?"

Taz raised an eyebrow. "Because you look like poop and have bags under your eyes. I'm guessing you didn't sleep great?"

"That's generous. I feel like something Nacho dragged in."

"Don't insult Nacho." Taz fed the goat a piece of muffin. "He has standards."

Rue smiled and took a grateful sip of tea. "Thanks for this. All of it."

"Baking is my love language." She winked and pointed at a pot bubbling on the stove. "I made some vegetable soup for you as well. Once it's cooled, I'll leave it in the fridge for you."

"I'm never going to be able to pay you back for all your

help." Rue stared into her tea. "I had some weird dreams last night. There was humming. Lullabies. A woman's voice...I think. It was kind of comforting until I heard a bang outside. Then I just panicked. I draw the line at a ghostly nursemaid. A single girl has standards." She nibbled her muffin. "Mmm. This is delicious."

"Fruit and sugar. Nothing better." Taz smiled gently. "The humming was probably Ruth."

Rue swallowed her mouthful before speaking. "Say *what?*"

"Your great aunt. She had a thing for old lullabies. Used to hum them when she was baking." Taz shrugged. "She's probably checking in. Making sure you're settled and safe."

"I'm not sure if that's comforting or horrifying," Rue muttered. "But I guess it's nice she's keeping an eye on me."

"Good. As long as it's Ruth and not Tobias." Taz smirked at Rue's wide-eyed expression.

"Ugh." Rue grabbed her tea and took a healthy swig. "Please don't say that. I only met him for a few minutes when he was alive. I didn't like him then, and I doubt death improved his personality much."

"Not everyone who dies, murdered or not, becomes a ghost. And even when they do, it's not immediate. Sometimes it takes a while. But you don't need to think about it. You need to keep busy."

"Hard to forget I found a murder victim and I'm probably suspect number one."

Slapping a colorful brochure in front of Rue, Taz pointed at the map on the back. "Go do the tourist thing. Head to the museum. Learn about the town and its history. And breathe. Relax, even if it's only for a few hours."

"Is this your way of saying *get out of my kitchen?*"

"Yep. With love and respect."

Rue eyed the glossy brochure. She wasn't sure she wanted to leave the building and brave public opinion. But the idea of wandering through a museum without a humming ghost had its appeal. She snatched up the brochure and swallowed the last of her muffin. She mumbled a goodbye and headed out.

The air outside was crisp and cool for a spring morning and freezing for a former temporary Floridian. Rue shivered in her short-sleeved T-shirt. A slight breeze drifted over her with just enough chill to raise goosebumps. She glanced down at Nacho who trotted beside her. "If Sheriff Cole saw me now, what are the odds he'd lecture me for my attire?"

Nacho bleated and nudged Rue's leg with his head.

She reached down and scratched the back of his head. "Yeah, I think so too. So, let's hurry up before he spots us." Rue glanced at the map on the back of the brochure as they walked. She tried to ignore the way people looked at her. Some seemed curious, some suspicious. Rue guessed she couldn't blame people. Being discovered kneeling next to a dead body, with your hands covered in blood, wasn't the best impression. If Silver Vein had a newspaper, she'd lay bets the title would be "Saloon heiress or stone-cold killer?"

She lowered her head and avoided the stares. "I feel like everyone's waiting for me to confess or run through town on a murderous rampage."

Nacho bleated, then raced ahead of her.

"Thanks. Great pep talk, goat." Thankfully, the museum wasn't far. It sat perched on the edge of Main Street, nestled between the old post office and a witchy gift shop that sold curse-repelling crystals and cactus keychains.

Climbing the wide stone steps, Rue pushed the heavy oak door open and stepped inside. Nacho led the way.

Her love of history kicked in despite her worry. She

drifted past a display case full of old pickaxes and battered canteens. Her fingers itched to touch aged maps and faded letters pinned behind the glass. The air inside the museum was cooler, filled with the subtle scent of age and history. Old papers, polished wood, and faintly musty velvet ropes from dusty exhibits filled her scenes. The museum was charming, full of colorful displays of the town's Wild West days, the legend of the Silver Vein Mine, rusty tools, and tintype photographs of town residents. Rue rounded a corner and stopped short, nearly colliding with the inquisitive goat.

A woman in her thirties, dressed in a vintage red and brown dress with matching embroidered gloves, was in the middle of a low-key whispered argument. Her sparring partner, an older, bald man in a sharp gray suit, sweated bullets and waved his hands in the air. The woman kept her voice low and calm while the older man's words were sharp.

The man reared back when he spotted Rue and Nacho clacking around on the polished wood floor. He practically hissed out loud when he spied the goat. He snapped at the woman next to him, "You deal with that four-legged vermin in the museum. The mayor would use the animal as an excuse to close us down permanently if she saw it." He pointed dramatically at Nacho, then stormed off, muttering about *liability* and *no respect for historical preservation.*

The woman adjusted her gloves and faced Rue with a warm, apologetic smile. "I'm so sorry about that. Mr. Evans is the museum curator and currently...extremely stressed." She winced. "Normally we don't allow goats in the building but..." She bent and patted Nacho fondly on the head "This one tends to sneak in no matter what we do. The whole town has adopted him." She gave him one last scratch before she straightened.

Rue shook her head as she watched Nacho sniff, then lick the glass of a display about mining lanterns.

The woman offered her hand. "I'm Isla Gray. I work here at the museum. I assume you're our newest saloon bookshop owner?"

Rue took her hand and nodded, trying not to be distracted by the feel of gloves, not skin, on the woman's hand. Wearing elaborate gloves these days wasn't a normal daily requirement, but it suited Isla. She appeared as if she'd stepped out of one of her own museum displays, an elegant brunette with perfectly styled hair, and a welcoming smile.

"Nacho," Rue hissed. "Stop that." The goat continued his licking spree on any reflective surface he could find. She drew her thoughts back on target and dropped the woman's hand after a brief squeeze. Then she gave a weak smile. "Yeah...that's me. Rue Maddox. Sorry about the goat again."

Isla let out a surprisingly girlish giggle. "We're used to him. Our cleaning service is here twice a day now. He does like the glass for some reason. And you don't need to apologize. You just arrived in town."

Rue sighed. "I guess my reputation got here before I did."

Isla smiled politely and held up a hand. "The town likes to talk about those who are different. I wear gloves because of a skin condition. You can imagine what the residents thought of that." She shared a commiserating glance with Rue. "It's a small town. Gossip spreads faster than wildfire. And you found the body of the most hated man in Silver... sorry, *Ghost* Vein." She tilted her head. "So, yes. You're news."

"For the record, I didn't kill him."

Isla patted her on the shoulder. "There are at least a

dozen people who would've gladly taken out Tobias. You're just the unlucky person who found him first."

Before she could respond, Isla linked arms with her, expertly directing her past some mining exhibits. She paused in front of a display of dusty tools and a glass case of ore samples.

"Silver Vein, aka Ghost Vein, was founded in eighteen fifty," Isla said with a practiced lilt to her voice. "The entire town was built around the mine. It started with silver, of course. But there were rumors that Elias Grimshaw, the owner of the mine, struck gold deep beneath the primary shafts. Supposedly, he and eight hand-picked miners dug out a rich vein. The miners and the gold were never seen again. Grimshaw disappeared a few days later."

"What happened to the miners?"

"All accounts say they just disappeared like magic. All eight of them. No bodies. No trace. Just gone."

A chill prickled Rue's spine. "What do you think?"

"Honestly, I think they ran off with the gold. But there was outrage and accusations documented in the town at that time. And then Elias Grimshaw vanished. One day he was here, the next...poof." She gestured at a nearby wall of black-and-white old fashioned photographs, most of them faded and grim. A stern family portrait took pride of place in the center of the display, an image captured of a man, his young wife, and a little boy. "His wife and son left shortly after. Packed up and left in the middle of the night."

Rue eyed the photograph. "They don't exactly look happy." The older man with a receding hairline had a glare that could melt metal. He sat next to a younger woman wearing a full-length, puffy gown. Her hair was smoothed back into a bun and parted in the middle. A small broach sat at the base of her throat. Her blank expression offset her husband's glower. A little boy around three or four sat at their feet playing with a small ball, his hair parted down the middle and slicked flat. The boy defied tradition and grinned, a distinctive diagonal crease at the corner of his mouth, and his nose had the same straight aquiline edge as his father's did. Rue's gaze was drawn back to the man. She shivered at his expression. That was a man who took no prisoners. "He definitely looks like he'd sacrifice anyone for wealth and power."

"It's all conjecture. We have no concrete evidence either way that he killed the miners. His wife and son left shortly after he disappeared. Since then, any trace of Elias Grimshaw's descendants has vanished." Isla drew Rue away from the photographs and paused in front of an exhibit featuring a piece of raw gold sitting under protective glass.

Rue leaned in, eyes narrowed. It wasn't flashy like the fake gold in the shops. It looked dull, jagged, and pitted with age. But the second she saw it, her stomach flipped.

That's it.

A similar rock to the one Tobias held. A shiver worked its way along her spine.

Nacho bleated loudly and butted Isla's leg, apparently tired of being ignored.

"Sorry." Rue grinned. "He's basically a walking stomach. He's probably looking for snacks, and no one wants a hangry goat around."

Isla chuckled. "You're not wrong. Everyone in town feeds him. I'm surprised he's not overweight. Technically, he belongs to Delilah from the general store, but he goes where he pleases. The town's unofficial mascot." She looked down at the goat fondly. "Josiah, our lovely curator, hates him. But then I guess he hates most people right now."

"Why? Hating most people, I mean," Rue added.

"He's been under pressure trying to secure funding for a museum expansion. He's stressed. Yelling at everyone. I saw him arguing with Tobias a few days ago, very secretive. I asked what it was about, and Josiah snapped that it wasn't my business and stormed off."

"Friendly," Rue murmured.

Isla winced. "He means well. He's just focused on the museum, and he's on edge. He argued with the mayor as well."

A voice suddenly cut in from behind them, nasal and theatrical.

"Or maybe it isn't stress but rage caused by *demonic energy*."

Startled, Rue turned. A younger, skinny woman with platinum-blonde hair, too much eyeliner, and a brightly colored scarf knotted around her throat stood nearby, filming them with her phone. She turned her back slightly so her viewers couldn't see their faces, only hear Rue and Isla's voices.

"I mean, look at the energy all around this town," she said to her invisible audience. "The mine closing after a series of accidents. Miners vanishing and now a murder? *Classic signs of a long-buried curse or excess demonic energy*."

Isla gazed up at the museum's ceiling. "Here we go."

The woman didn't stop. "My name is Maribel Knox," she announced, turning to face Rue. "I host the *Spirits, Secrets and History* podcast. I travel around the country uncovering secrets and paranormal mysteries." She held her phone up like a torch, blue eyes wide and gleaming with barely contained glee.

"I...um..." Rue ground to a halt, unsure what to say.

Maribel ignored Rue's awkwardness and turned the

phone toward a nearby rusted metal object on display. "Now *this* could be an ancient ritual artifact. Possibly inscribed with blood runes or used in demonic summoning. See the sigils?" She pointed her phone toward the end of the object where shapes appeared.

Isla cleared her throat. "It's a branding iron, Maribel. It's engraved with the Silver Vein Mine logo and Elias Grimshaw's initials. They used it to mark mine property. Not demonic. Just *corporate*."

Maribel stopped recording, put a hand on her hip, and pouted at the women. "Work with me, Isla. You're always so literal. I'm trying to boost my viewing numbers here." Her pale-blue eyes flicked to Rue. "I'll swing by the saloon later for an interview. Murders are a hit with my audience." With a smirk, she waggled her fingers in farewell and sauntered off toward another display.

Isla exhaled. "Kids these days."

Rue stared after the younger woman, still processing. "I'm definitely *not* giving an interview to anyone. Especially not someone who thinks the murder was caused by demonic energy."

"Good call." Isla offered a sympathetic smile. "Anyway, if you ever want a proper tour, minus the theatrics, come by anytime. But for now..." She glanced around. "I should get back to work before Josiah realizes I'm letting goats roam the museum again."

Rue chuckled. "Thanks for the history lesson."

Giving a graceful nod, Isla disappeared down a side hallway.

"Come on, Nacho. I'm sure it's snack time somewhere." Rue headed to the front door and stepped out into the morning sun of Silver Vein, blinking at the bright light. It wasn't particularly strong, but it warmed her just enough to make her sigh. She turned her face up to the sky, eyes closed, trying to soak in the light and the quiet peace, however temporary.

Nacho bleated softly, pressing against Rue.

Smiling she scratched the back of his neck, burrowing her fingers into the softer down under the course outer layer of hair. "At least *you* don't think I'm a murderer. I'm just your snack giver."

The goat leaned into her hand hard, almost knocking Rue over.

"Okay, okay. We'll go find your mom and maybe a second breakfast for you. I have no idea if goats get hangry, but I'm not taking chances. My PR is bad enough in this town." Rue squared her shoulders, took a deep breath, and started down the street. "Fake it till you make it, Rue girl," she muttered.

Especially when the town thinks you're public enemy number one.

SIX

The general store sat at the corner of Main Street and Hex Lane. Rue wrinkled her nose. She guessed in a supernatural town, streets named after people and businesses were normal. But still, Hex Lane had an ominous feel to it.

Nacho distracted Rue as he bounded onto the wooden boardwalk, where a building with a wooden slatted awning and a creaking swinging door carried a sign that read "Boone's General Store" in faded hand-painted script.

Rue couldn't get over how much the residents had embraced the wild West aesthetic. Then again, this had been a real rough and tumble mining town once upon a time.

Unbothered by history, murder investigations, or Rue's tangled nerves, Nacho trotted toward the open door without looking back.

"Thanks, buddy. I guess your loyalty goes to anyone who feeds you. I might as well adopt a cat." Forgetting her worry for a moment, Rue stepped inside and let the ambiance wash over her. She closed her eyes for a few seconds and inhaled. The interior smelled of floor wax and old wood. Rue opened her eyes and took in Boone's General Store. Wooden shelves filled the floor in organized aisles. Stock from canned peaches to locally made soaps and beauty potions. A display of enamel mugs with a slogan of "I brake for ghosts" scrawled on the side sat right beside an old bottle of homemade taffy. She'd stepped back in time. She expected an old cowboy or miner to pop up and accuse her of claim jumping. She quickly grabbed a handful of groceries as she wandered around the store. Rue spotted a tall, sturdy, older woman with a long, silver braid hanging over one shoulder stacking tins of green beans. The woman's sharp hazel eyes flicked toward her.

"Hi." Rue pasted on her best *please-don't-hate-me* smile. "I'm Rue Maddox. I inherited the Silver Tongue Saloon Bookshop and Café. Nacho keeps wandering over to visit, and he followed me into the museum this morning. He may have upset the curator. Thought I'd return him before something drastic happened," Rue babbled as the woman's gaze pinned her in place.

The old woman didn't answer immediately. Instead, she stopped stacking her cans and took in Rue, from her stained tennis shoes to her messy, auburn ponytail. She frowned and grunted, "Hmmph."

That didn't sound promising. Rue shuffled her feet. She felt like she was back in school getting a lecture from her teacher.

"Delilah Boone. This here is my general store. That goat"—she jabbed a thumb toward Nacho, who was busy licking a bottle of peanut brittle—"is a pain in my patootie, but he's mine."

An older man behind the counter gave a hearty wave. His long salt-and-pepper hair looked like it'd had a fight with a tumbleweed and lost. But his blue eyes twinkled in direct opposition to his wife's no-nonsense, sharp gaze.

"That's my husband, Hiram," Delilah added. "Don't let the long hair fool you. He's the friendly one." Her faded, gray brows beetled as she frowned at Rue again.

Rue managed a nervous laugh. Then she spotted movement out of the corner of her eye. A woman hovered awkwardly down one of the aisles nearby. In her late fifties or sixties, the woman's gray hair was slicked into a bun so tight Rue winced in sympathy. Shoulder pads, a power pantsuit, and turquoise glasses completed her image along with multiple silver and turquoise rings decorating her stubby fingers. The woman seemed to be trying hard not to appear as if she was eavesdropping but canned peas were *not* that interesting.

Delilah coughed sharply, dragging Rue's attention back. "You bringing Nacho back is probably the first smart thing you've done today."

"Thanks. I'll take that as a compliment." *Talk about being damned by faint praise.*

"Don't."

The eavesdropper abandoned all pretense and strode forward like a woman on a mission. "Delilah," the woman said curtly. "We all know the real draw for this town is the mine. Not your wandering pet."

"The curse is bad publicity," Delilah snapped. "The goat, on the other hand, is great PR. The town loves him."

"That's where you're wrong. All our tourism surveys suggest that the goat's likeability is way down on their priority list." The woman, in her eighties' pantsuit, sniffed. "But if you truly were an invested business owner, you'd know that."

Rue's eyes ping-ponged between the two women. The enmity between them was obvious.

"Mayor Agnes Flint." The suited woman turned her full attention on Rue and shoved her hand out. Her handshake was firm.

Rue hid her wince. Was the mayor some kind of secret weightlifter? "Rue Maddox. I'm new in town."

"I've heard of you."

"Wonderful. Let me guess. Small town. Fast gossip. Murder in the back alley. I'm probably one headline away from a collectible mug."

Agnes didn't crack a smile at Rue's awkward joke. "It's not exactly the start most people hope for."

So much for using humor to lighten the vibe. "No. Not the best impression." Rue agreed.

Delilah crossed her arms and shot Agnes a withering look. "The only person making a bad impression around here is you, Aggie."

"It's Mayor Flint," Agnes snapped. "I was duly elected."

"Only because you bribed the voters with cinnamon rolls you didn't even make yourself," Delilah muttered.

Agnes' cheeks flared red. "At least I'm doing something to benefit and modernize this town. You're still ringing up orders on that ancient till like it's the eighteen hundreds."

"You leave Hiram's till out of this. It's his pride and joy," Delilah said, talking about the cash register like it was his beloved child. "It's more reliable than any of your newfangled nonsense. And it doesn't need a Wi-Fi signal or your endless interference to work."

Opening her mouth to say something to calm the choppy waters, Rue decided to hold her tongue. Her momma would say it was wiser to shut your mouth than add to the verbal garbage around you.

Thankfully, Nacho picked that moment to provide a distraction by sneezing onto a display of licorice ropes.

Agnes flicked a disgusted look at the goat and then at Rue. "That goat is just as disturbing as a murder in your back alley."

Wow. She really went there. "I'm of the feeling that murder trumps wandering goats."

"A murder in *your* alley." Agnes speared Rue with a pointed stare. "I'm watching how this situation unfolds, Maddox. Closely."

"Great." Rue smiled with gritted teeth. "Mayoral surveillance will hopefully scare off Tobias' murderer."

Agnes smoothed her suit jacket. "Murder has consequences. And a town like ours doesn't need *any* bad press that might affect our tourism."

"Oh, for heaven's sake, woman." Delilah threw up her hands. "She didn't murder anyone, Aggie. She found the body. And she's barely been here long enough to find decent coffee, let alone a murder weapon."

"Tea."

"Excuse me?" Delilah frowned at Rue.

"Tea drinker, not coffee," Rue offered.

"I'm simply saying," Agnes replied coolly, ignoring Rue's interruption, "that perception matters to the public."

Rue snorted. "Tell that to the podcaster filming rusty historic mine tools and thinking the murder was caused by demonic energy."

That cracked a smile from Delilah. "Maribel Knox is a mosquito with a microphone. Don't let her get under your skin."

"She already tried. Apparently murder ups her ratings or some babble like that."

Straightening, Agnes pointed a finger at Rue, all icy

authority. "Well, I *hope* you plan to behave, Ms. Maddox. We have enough drama in this town without bookstore wannabe witches adding to it."

"Now, now, Aggie." Delilah grinned. "Don't go insulting witches. It's bad luck."

Agnes's expression tightened. "Enjoy your visit, Miss Maddox. And don't give any formal interviews. Ghost Vein thrives on tourism. Sightseeing tourists, treasure and ghost hunters, even mouthy podcasters. A murder is not good for business." She jabbed a finger at Rue's chest. "Keep a lid on it, and don't go finding any more dead bodies."

Rue stared. "Are you telling me to stop finding murder victims?"

"I'm telling you not to be the kind of person who stumbles across them. I'm not going to let one wide-eyed newcomer ruin my hard work."

"Oh, for pity' sake, Aggie. No one else shuts their mouth in this town. Why should she?" Delilah smirked.

"We'll see how funny you find it when your store gets written up in some online gossip column."

"If I had a nickel for every time some big city blogger said nasty things about me, I'd be rich," Delilah replied sweetly. "Now scoot. You're scaring my goat." She walked toward the mayor and flapped her hands, shooing her to the front of the store.

Aggie hissed. "If you weren't the only general store in town, I'd take my business elsewhere."

"Feel free. I think my business will survive." Delilah curled her lip as the mayor threw her a vitriolic glare and stomped outside, slamming the door behind her.

"Was that normal?" Rue loosened her tight grip on her shopping basket.

Delilah gave a noncommittal grunt. "That's Aggie on a good day."

"I get the feeling she thinks I'm a murder magnet." Frankly, how did that work when the count of bodies she'd found was exactly...one? Or did she expect Rue to find more?

"She blames everyone for something. Except herself." Delilah picked up a cloth and wiped her hands after giving Rue a critical once over. "Ignore Aggie. Do what you want. This town has stood through flood, fire, and more than one suspicious death. It'll weather this as well."

"Suspicious death or disappearances?"

"It's an old mining town. Most deaths were suspicious back then. But you're really asking about the missing miners from the old story, aren't you?"

Rue nodded. "It's obviously a big part of Ghost Vein's history. Tobias spoke about it on his last ghost tour before he died. And I saw the exhibits at the museum before Nacho got us kicked out."

"Guff and nonsense." Delilah muttered. "Fantasy stories spun into legend by bored men and women who have nothing better to do than gossip. I don't hold with it. But your aunt Ruth..." She trailed off, jaw tightening.

Rue's curiosity spiked. "Taz told me about her. That she was a curse-breaker witch."

Delilah's eyes snapped to Rue's, sharp and hard. "Your great aunt was obsessed with that mine. With the curse. She poked and prodded, upset half the town. Ruffled feathers that didn't need ruffling." She dropped the cloth on a shelf. "People don't like their family skeletons dragged out of the closets for everyone to see. Especially when it's an outsider doing the dragging."

"My mom...she didn't talk much about Ruth or

anything supernatural. I had to move out to even speak to someone about magic. Mom was more of the 'if you can't explain it, ignore it' school of thought."

Giving a dry, mirthless chuckle, Delilah nodded. "You'd be surprised how many people share that opinion. I remember Ruth talking about your mom. She wasn't impressed by your great aunt's so-called gifts. Called them delusions and forced your father to step back from his family."

"Yeah, I just discussed this with my mom recently." Rue set down the basket, slid her hands into her jeans' pockets and hunched her shoulders. She still couldn't believe her mom had blackmailed her dad.

"Let me give you some advice, Ms. Maddox," Delilah said, voice low. "Don't go digging. Don't go looking for what Ruth left behind. It won't end well."

Nacho let out a soft *baaa*, as if punctuating Delilah's warning as she spun and stomped off.

Rue blinked, stunned at the woman's warning. A warm chuckle drew her attention to the counter.

"Don't mind her. She gets in moods. And Aggie is normally the one who upsets her." The older man behind the counter winked. "Delilah has a bark louder than a hellhound with a stubbed toe."

Huffing out a surprised laugh, Rue approached the counter with her half-filled grocery basket in hand. "You're Delilah's husband?"

"Hiram Boone, long-suffering husband to hurricane Delilah."

"Rue Maddox. And I think I upset your wife."

Hiram snorted as he processed the groceries. "That was Aggie. She's not really mad at you. More like sad," he told her gently. "Sad and angry that she didn't get the chance to make peace with Ruthie. They fought like cats and dogs, but they were two peas in a pod. The same stubborn pod. Delilah figured there would be plenty of time to fix it. But life doesn't wait for apologies."

She gave him a soft smile. "Thanks for telling me that. It helps."

He bagged Rue's groceries and tipped an imaginary hat. "You take care of yourself, Ms. Maddox."

With a wave to Hiram and Nacho, Rue stepped out onto the sun-bleached boardwalk. The late morning sun glinted off dusty windows, its warmth brushing against her skin. Delilah's words echoed in her head. *"Don't go digging. Don't go looking for what Ruth left behind. It never ends well."* Rue winced. Just what she needed. A grim, ominous warning on top of a possible murder charge.

"Fantastic," she muttered. "The whole town thinks I'm a murderer, a curse magnet, or some kind of witchy meddler-in-training. Perfect."

Nacho trotted out from the general store and gave an encouraging *baaa.*

"Don't suppose you've got any helpful insights, oh wise bleater of the desert?"

Nacho cocked his fuzzy head, listening to Rue.

"Should I pack up and leave before anyone else dies mysteriously? Or just wait until the townsfolk chase me out with pitchforks and branding irons?"

The goat responded by ramming his head gently into her thigh, then trying to eat a stray flyer stuck to the general store's noticeboard.

Rue sighed. "Excellent. My emotional support goat is also a paper shredder."

She leaned against the wooden beam just outside the store's false front and let her gaze wander over the street. It was quiet for the moment, just a handful of tourists wandering past in wide-brimmed western hats, their sneakers crunching on gravel as they snapped pictures of shopfronts and mannequins dressed like old-fashioned cowboys and miners.

Everyone else seemed to belong here. Even the weird ones. But her? She felt like a puzzle piece from a different box, jammed into place by someone too impatient to take the time to figure the puzzle out. Rue glanced down at Nacho, who'd somehow managed to pick up a glittery sticker from the sidewalk and was now wearing it on his forehead like a proud badge of honor. It read *"Ask me about ghost tours."*

Rue snorted and laughed, half-delirious, half-genuine. "Well, I guess you've got your own branding going on."

Nacho bleated in agreement and tried to nibble her laces.

"Okay, message received. Food first, emotional crisis later." She straightened her spine, gave the goat a pat, and took a deep breath of crisp, high-desert air. Turning, she froze when she spotted the mayor. The woman in her red power pantsuit stood near the edge of the general store building. Half turned from view, the mayor was clearly unaware that Rue watched her.

"I said no," she hissed. "We aren't expanding. I don't care what the council thinks. I'm the mayor. I *am* the council." She paused to listen. "Focus on the real history, not that nonsense about curses and ghostly miners. The town's had enough drama."

Rue froze, curiosity building. The mayor was the one who had reinvented Silver Vein. The one who pushed the curse and ghostly miner campaign to beef up tourism. So, why pull back now? It didn't make sense.

"Over my dead body is your expansion application going through," Agnes snarled. "Focus on finding your lost gold. That's what matters, Josiah."

Wasn't Josiah the first name of the museum curator, Isla's boss? Maybe the lost gold the mayor referred to was the gold Tobias had when he died. Had he stolen it from the museum? Rue's brain scrambled. So many questions and hardly any answers.

Agnes ended the call with a muttered curse, turned, and spotted Rue watching.

For a long, tense few seconds, they stared at each other. Then Agnes lifted her chin and stomped off without a word.

Rue exhaled. This town had more twists and turns than an Agatha Christie novel. She had the feeling she'd walked into the middle of something she wasn't meant to see. Rue didn't have a clue what any of this meant, but Taz might.

Turning on her heel, Rue hurried back to the saloon, groceries in hand and mind racing. The swinging saloon doors creaked as she pushed her way inside. They still had a closed sign up, but Taz had left the front doors unlocked for her. Rue shut and locked the door behind her and dumped her groceries on a table.

A now familiar sight hit her, the gleam of polished wood, the scent of fresh lemon cleaner, and her two employees wiping the counter in a war against Nevada dust. "You guys missed all the fun," Rue announced, dodging as Nacho nearly tripped her bolting for the kitchen and more snacks.

Cassie stopped wiping, eyes wide. "Did someone else die?"

"Not yet." Rue winced. "I mean, no. I did not find a body, but the mayor might kill *me*. Does that count?"

That earned a snort from Taz. "Doesn't count. The mayor always has someone on her hit list. What happened?"

Settling onto a stool at the café's counter, Rue relayed everything. Delilah Boone's snark-off with the mayor, her conversation about Ruth's curse obsession, and the mayor's veiled warnings about opening her mouth. Not to mention the phone call she'd overheard with the phrase "over my dead body." By the time she got to the part about the mayor's refusal to fund the museum expansion, both women had frozen mid-clean.

"All that in one single outing to find peace and relaxation?" Taz shook her head. "I think we need to call you Sherlock, not Maddox. You have a nose for investigation."

"Or for gossip and dirt on people." Cassie snickered.

"That too," Taz agreed but looked puzzled. "Still doesn't make sense why the mayor's shutting down the museum expansion. That kind of thing usually brings more tourists, not less."

"Exactly, and she wants the curator to focus on history and not the lost gold. Oh, and I met Isla at the museum. And a pushy woman called Maribel, who wants an interview on the murder." Rue rolled her eyes. "I hate to agree with the mayor, but I'd rather keep my mouth shut too."

"Isla's a gem. How she puts up with Josiah Evans as a boss, I have no idea." Taz bustled, hiding cleaning products out of sight under the counter.

"Maribel Knox is a spooky history podcaster." Cassie curled her flip. "She has a rep for supernatural heavy stories, and she's not always truthful. She likes drama even if she has to invent it, and she's nosy."

Rue mulled over everything she'd heard, but her mind kept going back to one thing. "The mayor also told the curator to focus on his lost gold." Rue drummed her fingers on the gleaming counter. "I wonder if she's talking about Tobias' disappearing gold? Did he steal it from the museum first before someone stole it from him?"

"After they killed him first," Taz pointed out. "Pretty strong motive for someone to take him out. Gold fever has always caused crazy, murderous behavior."

Cassie stiffened "Wait. I saw Tobias having a full-blown shouting match with the mayor a few days ago. He wanted money to expand his ghost tours. Said he had new material. The mayor was having none of it. There was a lot of arm waving and threats."

Rue's eyes widened. "That sounds like a motive, and add in the strange phone call I overheard? The mayor's at the top of my suspect list now."

"You need to tell the sheriff what you heard, Cassie." Taz spun and pointed at Rue. "And you need to tell Cole about the phone call. It might help get you off his suspect list."

"I guess it's nice to be wanted, but being number one suspect isn't really what I had in mind." Rue stood and grabbed her groceries. She stared pointedly at the goat. "You're staying down here, Nacho. I'd like to take a shower in peace, without having to worry about a hangry goat." Giving the girls a dramatic salute, she headed upstairs.

Her apartment, still warm from the morning sun, welcomed her in. Rue dumped the bag of groceries on her kitchen counter. She unpacked it absentmindedly, her brain buzzing with curses, gold, ghosts, and small-town politics. Sighing, Rue buried her questions at the back of her mind and opted instead for a calming, unending, hot shower.

Thanks to her great aunt Ruth's heated water spell, for ten whole minutes, no goats, ghosts, or murder, just steamy, watery bliss. Rue was starting to think that alone might be worth staying in town for. She knew she had to decide what she wanted to do with the saloon, but she wanted to experience life in Ghost Vein first. She let the hot water melt away the day's weirdness but eventually had to turn the shower off or face a day of pruny skin.

Shivering, she stepped out into a room full of steam. The mirror was fogged, the glass opaque. Rue swiped at it with a towel, but as the condensation thinned, words shimmered into view.

Don't trust the gold.

She froze before grabbing a towel and wrapping it around her. The words were traced in the condensation. Deliberate, slanted slightly, as if they had been written by a shaking finger. Rue tried the door, still locked. No one else could have been in here. Except...

A ghost.

Her heart slammed against her ribs. "Ruth?" she asked the air around her. "If that's you, I appreciate the warning, but *maybe* next time pick a less naked moment?"

Silence.

Nothing moved.

"Please be Aunt Ruth," Rue muttered, voice shaky but hopeful. "Please don't be creepy guide, Tobias. I am not emotionally equipped to deal with ghostly perverts today."

Rue waited, but no more messages appeared. She padded into her bedroom, squeaking as she nearly tripped over a slumbering Nacho. She looked down at him. "Seriously? I left you downstairs and now you're back for naptime?"

Nacho failed to move and instead snored with delicate little huffs.

She was positive she'd locked the apartment, so how did

Houdini goat get in? "Delilah's going to accuse me of goat-napping," Rue muttered, yanking on sweatpants. "Or tell people I've got snacks hidden in my bra." She crept into the living room to check her locks and stopped dead.

The front door was wide open.

Rue slammed it shut and locked it, leaning back against the wood. Silver Vein—no, *Ghost Vein*—wasn't just a town with secrets. It was a freaking haunted puzzle. She didn't know what kind of ghostly nonsense was happening here. She didn't know why the mayor was shutting things down or who Tobias had annoyed enough to murder him. But she did know one immutable thing.

She was going to find out all the answers to her questions. Even if it meant unraveling the town's dirty secrets and ghostly mysteries.

Even if she had to kick some floaty paranormal butt to do it. Because no one interrupted her shower time...

No one.

SEVEN

Sweat tracked down the back of Rue's neck as she stepped out onto the boardwalk. She lifted her face and breathed in the dry air and...a mouthful of dust. Coughing, she thumped her chest multiple times. "Stick to sleuthing, Rue. You'll never make it as a meditation expert." Sighing, Rue consulted the brochure map Taz had shoved into her hand the other day.

She had questions and everything revolved around the mine. Dusty, cursed, and probably haunted, it called her name. Time for a visit. Unfortunately, her car was still having a prolonged visit at Jesse the mechanic's garage. She needed to see if it was ready or use Ghost Vein's public transport. Rue laughed out loud to herself. This was Silver Vein. Public transport probably meant borrowing a mule or finding a mythical unicorn shifter willing to drop her off at a haunted mine. Likelihood? *Non-existent.* Jesse, the mechanic, it was.

Taz pointed her down the street and told her his garage was just past the coffee shop with the upside-down cactus sign...because of course it was.

Which explained why Rue found herself walking past sun-bleached storefronts, dodging aggressive cowboy-costumed tourists and handsy miners' ghosts. Taking a step around the upside-down cactus, Rue squinted at a plain wooden and tin building with a crooked, hand-painted sign that proclaimed *Jesse's Garage – No Possessions, Poltergeists, or Payment Plans.*

"Possessions?" Rue murmured. "Is he expecting a possessed car or an unhappy ghostly customer?" She stepped into a concrete workshop area.

A lanky, muscled man with a worn ball cap that had *"Ghosts are my people"* embroidered on the back stood hunched over the open hood of a truck. A radio played a classic rock station just loud enough to probably ward off ghosts—or grumpy sheriffs.

"Morning." Rue called. She spotted her sweet little car tucked into a corner with its hood open. "Do I take it if the hood is open, it's a good sign?"

Jesse looked up and grinned. He wiped his hands on a rag that had seen better days. "Hey there, Miss Book Saloon girl. Come to rescue your poor little car?"

"Depends. Is she still flatlined?"

"Still waiting for a part, unfortunately. Some cosmic force really doesn't want you behind the wheel. But it shouldn't be much longer."

Rue crossed her arms. "I've met the sheriff. I'm not convinced the cosmic force isn't just him in disguise. Although, he'd probably want me driving out of town, so maybe not."

He laughed, his expression softer. "For what it's worth, I'm sorry you were the one who found Tobias. He wasn't exactly a little ray of sunshine, but no one deserves to die like that."

"I didn't kill him." Rue sobered. She still couldn't forget the sight of the poor man laid out on the ground...or the blood on her hands.

Jesse held up both hands and warded Rue off as if she'd offered him a lit stick of dynamite. "Not my business. That's Cole's job to figure out. And I'd rather not hear any admissions. If you say too much, I might have to pass it along."

His tone was matter of fact but not unkind. Rue appreciated that. At least one person wasn't quick to point fingers or whisper behind her back.

"You seem like a good person...just with bad luck. And I'm sure certain *other* people...might eventually notice that too." He waggled his eyebrows.

Rue barked a sharp laugh. "Doubt it. Sheriff Muscles seems to think my presence is an inconvenience the town has to endure."

"Sheriff Muscles, huh?" Jesse snickered. "He'll love hearing that."

"He hasn't exactly been rolling out the welcome mat." Rue curled her lip. "And please don't tell him I called him that. He doesn't need a bigger ego than he has now."

Jesse changed the subject, grinning. "So, what's the rest of your day look like? Are you prowling around town with your goat minion or shaking down tourists for answers?"

"Actually, I was hoping to go out to the mine. Thought I'd look at the place. See if it stirs up anything."

"Bold move." Jesse whistled. "Wish your car was ready, but lucky for you, Ghost Vein Taxi Services is fully operational." He fished a card from his pocket. Slightly smudged, but still legible, it read *"Jesse R. Carter. Mechanic and Taxi services."* A phone number was listed on the other side of the card.

"I'll drop you off at the mine, and you can call me when you're ready to head back. I'll swing out and grab you."

Rue took the card and read it. A smile tugged at her lips. "Thanks, Jesse. That's really kind of you."

He spluttered. "Kind? No guy wants to be known by that tag. Haven't you heard? Nice guys finish last. Besides, I'm just a sucker for girls with haunted saloon bookshops."

Laughing, Rue pocketed the card. Ghost Vein might have a killer on the loose and have a bubbling underbelly of secrets and lies, but at least she had a ride. And the phone number of a handsome man. She definitely *did not* let her thoughts wander to Sheriff Grumpy's arms. Or his low, serious voice. Or the way he looked at her as if she were a puzzle to solve.

Nope. She was a grown woman. Fully capable of focusing on cursed gold and mysterious murder without being distracted by biceps and a husky voice...

Probably.

Jesse saluted Rue with a lazy grin as he pulled into the dusty parking lot. "Give me a call when you're done with your mine sleuthing. Or if you get possessed by a grumpy miner."

Chuckling, Rue waved as he pulled away in his truck, a puff of desert dust trailing behind him. It was nice to spend time with someone light-hearted and non-judgmental, unlike a sheriff she wouldn't mention. She turned toward the mine with a deep breath, hands on her jeans-clad hips.

Wind ruffled her shoulder length, frizzy, auburn hair. She'd let it out of its normal messy ponytail for once. "All right. Let's see what secrets you're hiding, Silver Vein."

The Silver Vein Mine Tourist Park had seen better days. Nestled against the rocky hillside, the mine's entrance yawned open, framed by weather-worn timbers. A small bench seat sat next to it. A crooked sign swung above it, cheerfully declaring, *"Ghost Vein Mine. Formerly known as Silver Vein. Est Eighteen Fifty-Nine. Tours Every Hour. Spirits May Be Included."*

"Subtle." Rue shook her head. She still couldn't get used to the casual way people in town referred to the supernatural. Her mother would have run back to Florida, screeching hysterically. Stepping forward, Rue scrutinized the tourist park. Multiple wood and tin buildings stood over to one side, including the public bathroom, gift shop, museum, and storage buildings.

Rusted ore carts sat frozen on bent tracks, and a mannequin, dressed as an old-fashioned miner, listed to one side and clutched a plastic lantern and pickaxe. Visitors milled around, dodging ancient mining equipment that looked more discarded than historic. Faux tumbleweeds dotted the gravel path and the front of the gift shop.

At the mine entrance, a young brunette woman in overalls and a miner's helmet directed people toward the shop. The woman kept shuffling away from the shadowed mouth of the mine every few minutes with an accompanied look over her shoulder.

Rue couldn't blame her as she spotted a ghostly miner's figure, in tattered, dirt covered clothing, flickering in and out of sight. A low mutter reached her ears of *"Dang new safety rules."* Most tourists glanced away from the ghost, although a few tried to take pictures before the employee moved them on.

Rue shivered. "Get a grip, Maddox. Ghosts are normal, everyday occurrences. Saddle up. You've got a job to do."

She forced herself to walk forward and averted her eyes from the safety-obsessed ghost miner. "Still not going to be used to that anytime soon." Rue veered toward the building with a sign announcing Tickets & Authentic Sarsaparilla. She ducked into the gift shop with the vague hope of answers. Inside, it smelled like lemon scented industrial cleaner and dust. Shelves were covered with mine, ghost, and gold-themed cheesy souvenirs. From plastic pickaxes and tiny glass bottles of fake gold dust glitter to cowboy shot glasses shaped like boots.

Beyond the clutter, a small museum space branched off a back wall, and from what Rue could glimpse, featured faded photos, old crumbling maps, and a few glass display cases of tools. She wandered across, unsure if she wanted to do a tour or just get an idea of the mine's atmosphere.

A low argument caught her ear, and she spotted an older man in a bright orange staff vest standing toe-to-toe with another man in khakis and a stiff button-down shirt. The way the older guide hunched forward made him seem anxious and frustrated. Rue got the sense the other man might be management, maybe even the owner. She tilted her head and examined a fake bottle of gold before she drifted forward, her gaze focused on a blurry photo featuring a grizzled old miner. She kept her eyes on the display while her ears locked onto the voices.

"I don't care if the council's dragging their feet," the man in khakis snapped. "The ghost tours make bank. Even if Tobias was a pain in my butt, he brought in cash. We need someone to take over...*fast*."

The older man's jaw clenched. "It's not safe. The weird stuff in the mine's been increasing. Lights flickering, shadows that don't line up, cold spots in the wrong places. Tobias stirred it all up. All those solo trips into the tunnels, poking around where he shouldn't. I don't want any part of that."

Rue's eyebrows shot up. *Solo trips?* Why was Tobias going into the mine alone? And more importantly...what was he *looking for?* She waited for the arguing to fizzle out, and within a few seconds, the men stomped off in opposite directions. Casually, Rue made her way back to the main shop area, where a bored young woman rearranged plastic pickaxe magnets by the register.

"Hi there." Rue channeled her best clueless tourist energy with a wide, vacant smile. "Just wondering about the tours?"

The woman perked up. "Sure. We've got the traditional mine tour that runs every hour. It's about forty-five minutes, includes a flashlight and helmet, and there's a waiver to sign in case the mine ghosts get sassy."

"What about the ghost tours? I heard those were a thing?"

The girl's cheer faltered. "Oh. Yeah, uh...those aren't running right now. The guide...Tobias? He um...passed away recently. Kinda tragic."

"Oh wow." Rue feigned surprise. "That's awful. I think I heard something about someone dying behind the bookstore the other day...that was *him?*"

"Yup." The girl nodded solemnly, then leaned in. "And let me tell you, he was...weird. Obsessed with this place. Always coming in alone, late hours, poking around where he wasn't supposed to. He kind of had a reputation with women as well. Either that or..."

"Or?"

"The ghosts got him for messing around in the mine and stealing their stuff." The girl let her words explode out, then sat back with a satisfied smile, waiting for Rue's reaction.

Rue played along and gasped, hands to her chest. "Ghosts? You mean the miners who disappeared along with the gold? Like in the old story of the mine?"

"Exactly." The girl nodded. "Maybe it was the curse and the ghost? Could have been both. But the new bookstore owner kicked him out the same day he died. My cousin works across the street and swears the new owner had words with him. Loud ones."

Why did gossip get more dramatic and further away from the truth every time it got repeated? Rue stiffened, but her smile didn't waver. "That's horrible. Ghost towns. Expect the unexpected, am I right?"

The woman chuckled. "Spot on. Still, it's sad. Even if he was a pain." She sobered and cleared her throat.

Rue nodded, her expression faintly thoughtful as she handed over her card. "Yeah. Things don't always turn out like you expect. I'll take a ticket for the regular tour, please. Might as well get the full experience."

"Sure thing. You can wait by the main gate outside. There's a big sign with the rules." The girl checked her phone. "The tour starts in five minutes, so the guide should be out shortly."

Rue thanked her and stepped outside, nerves prickling. She didn't know exactly what Tobias had been looking for in those tunnels, but she was beginning to think someone hadn't wanted him to find the gold. The question was... curse or human killer?

The wind caught Rue's heavy auburn hair as she stepped up to the wooden gate near the mine's entrance. The gate, slightly ajar, swung on its hinges. The young employee who had stood guard near the mine had moved to the gate, speaking to tourists. A handful of people dressed in dusty denim and wide-brimmed cowboy hats clustered together. Low murmurs that included the words *"tour guide,"* *"death,"* and *"murdered"* bounced around.

One woman, sipping from a metal mine cup, whispered to her male companion, "I heard he was just *found* in the alley. No one even knows what happened?"

Her companion nodded. "Murder. That's what happened. I heard it might be caused by demonic energy."

Rue cleared her throat, not-so-subtly, and the couple fell awkwardly silent. Just then, the older guide from inside the museum rushed over, his long, gray, stringy hair flapping behind him.

"We're here for the *historical* tour. Not gossip. Let's keep it factual and respectful." His voice carried a no-nonsense bite. He adjusted his staff vest and snatched a miner's helmet off his younger counterpart.

The group quieted down.

The tour guide stood straight and launched into a practiced spiel. "The Silver Vein Mine, not the so-called Ghost Vein Mine"—he glared around the group as though daring anyone to comment before he continued—"was established in eighteen fifty-nine, with a brief but profitable run before it closed in somewhat tragic circumstances. This front portion of the mine has been reinforced and cleared for tours, but most of it remains unstable and off-limits." The guide motioned for the group to follow.

They descended into the mine. The temperature dropped fast. The harsh sunlight outside gave way to dim artificial lamps affixed to reinforced wooden beams. The tunnel floor had been neatly swept for tourists and the non-historical steel support beams looked newish.

But beneath it all was a pressure, a heavy weight of something older.

Something waiting.

Rue shivered and pulled her senses back to the tour guide. Just her overactive imagination. Nothing waited, ready to pounce. They were in an empty mine. Nothing else, she kept telling herself firmly.

They turned a corner into a larger cavern where rusted ore carts lay abandoned. The guide's voice echoed against the stone walls as he continued. "Obviously, everyone has heard the stories, of course," he said with a stiff smile. "Accidents. Disappearances. The stories say Elias Grimshaw, the mine's owner, performed blood magic to protect his gold and sacrificed the miners to hide it. Personally? Sounds like tall tales to me. But folks say their granddaddies heard voices down here. Chanting. Ghosts. Whispers. Flickering lights. Me? I'm here for the real history. The rest is just noise."

Rue tilted her head, gaze sweeping the shadowed corners. "What about the cursed gold? Does it exist?"

The guide frowned. "Rumor. Legend. No historical evidence. Probably invented to scare off looters."

"But there *was* an incident, right? The miners who disappeared?" Rue pressed. "Something that got the mine shut down?"

He sighed like he'd spoken of this too many times to count. "There was a collapse. A bad one. And several miners did indeed disappear. Their absence is historical record. Grimshaw vanished shortly after, and the mine was sealed. That's as much as I'll say on *that*."

Cold crawled up Rue's spine. She hugged herself, rubbing her arms. "Normal reaction to being underground. I'm just cold," she muttered to herself.

A few tourists standing next to Rue shot her confused glances and shuffled a few steps away. That's when she heard it...a low hum, a chant.

Rhythmic.

Repetitive.

Rue turned, heart thudding. She scanned the cavern, and her eyes caught movement in the far corner of the chamber.

A man stood there. An old miner, his beard thick and tangled, eyes sunken and glassy. His stained and tattered shirt hung off an almost skeletal frame. One arm hung limp by his side, and his chest, visible through the torn shirt, failed to rise and fall. Like he no longer needed to breathe.

He watched her. Not the group. Just Rue...and no one else could see him. Her breath caught in her throat. "No," she whispered, backing up. "Nope, no..." Her legs threatened to buckle, and her vision pinched at the edges as panic gripped her chest. Ghost. She was actually seeing a ghost. Okay, so she'd already caught a glimpse of a miner's ghost when she'd first arrived, but something about this one freaked her out. Was this one of the miners who had disappeared?

"Miss?" the tour guide called out, but his voice sounded garbled.

Rue wavered on her feet, dizzy. Her eyes locked on the ghostly figure as everything tilted sideways.

"Quick. Grab her," the tour guide barked as everything went dark.

She came back to herself as the guide propped her up on a stone bench outside the mine entrance. Sunlight, harsh and too bright after the darkness, almost blinded Rue as she cracked her eyes open an inch. Her hands shook as her breath came fast.

"Here," a voice said gently, pressing a bottle of water into her hand.

Blinking multiple times to focus, Rue finally managed

to keep her eyes open for longer than a few seconds. She finally realized the guide from the mine tour knelt next to her.

"I'm Arnold. You're okay. That mine...it gets under your skin sometimes."

"I saw...him. A miner. Covered in blood. And I heard voices chanting. I thought...I don't know what I thought. I guess I thought it was all fake."

Arnold nodded. "You're not the first. Some people see him, but most don't." He sat beside her on the bench, his gnarled hands folded in his lap. "It's been worse lately. Ever since that dang Tobias started the ghost tours. He stirred things up, poking around where he shouldn't. Even went to the council on his own, pushing for more money to expand into sealed areas. The owner backed him. Money talks. But the mayor shut it down hard."

Rue's fingers tightened on the water bottle. "Did Tobias mention if he found any gold?"

The guide let out a bark of laughter, but his gaze slid sideways, avoiding Rue. "He asked a lot of questions. Pointed ones. He thought he could find the gold no one else could and get rich. I know he was selling off anything he found. I reported it to the owner and the mayor. But nothing happened."

"Do *you* believe in the cursed vault?"

"I believe Grimshaw didn't just walk away and leave behind that much gold without a reason. But it's best not to talk about it. No good comes from digging too deep. Not in Ghost Vein."

Rue's voice dropped as she processed his words. "Is the mine really unstable? Why would Tobias risk getting killed if the gold wasn't real?"

Arnold gave her a look. "Parts of the mine, I wouldn't go

in. I told Tobias to be careful, not to go in alone, but he never listened. He wanted to map out new areas for his tours, supposedly. I told him to talk to Letty Navarro first, but I don't know if he ever did."

"Who's Letty Navarro?"

"At the library."

"The librarian?"

He nodded. "Yup. She's got the blueprints and old maps of the tunnels. Could've helped him avoid the bad spots."

Her thoughts whirled as Arnold stood and dusted off his knees. He looked like he wanted to say more but instead, offered a tight smile.

"You'll be all right. But take my advice and stay out of the mine. Some truths are buried for a reason." He waited for Rue to stand and then led her back to the gift shop. "Gotta get back to my tour. The other guide's good, but she tends to skip the historical facts. Younger generation." He shook his head and left.

Rue pulled out the business card Jesse had given her and tapped in the number with still shaking fingers. He answered on the second ring.

"Already done flirting with ghosts?" he teased.

Rue let out a shaky breath. "Can you come get me?"

There was a pause, then Jesse replied, all joking absent from his voice. "Be there in five."

Exactly five minutes and forty seconds later, Jesse's pickup rolled into the parking lot in a cloud of dust. He barely parked before hopping out, eyes narrowing the second he saw her pale face. "What happened?"

She tried to wave him off, but it ended up looking more like a failed high-five. "I'm fine. Just had a bit of a moment."

Jesse grabbed a flannel blanket from behind his seat and

wrapped it around her shoulders before pulling her into a solid, warm hug for a few seconds.

She hadn't realized she needed a hug until right then. He smelled of motor oil and wet fur. Fleetingly she wondered what a grumpy sheriff's hug would feel like. Rue pulled away and offered a wobbly smile. "Thanks."

"All part of the service." He helped her into the passenger seat and turned the heater on high. "Okay, what happened? Cole would have my hide if you got hurt. You look like you saw a ghost."

"I did," she muttered, staring out the window. "Beard. Ripped shirt. Blood. Chanting voices. The normal for Ghost Vein, I guess." She let out a choked, bitten off laugh.

He gave a low whistle. "You got the full Ghost Vein welcome package."

Rue shot him a look. "Does everyone just *accept* the weird stuff around town as normal?"

"Locals avoid the mine unless they have no choice. It gives residents the creeps. Always has. Most of us grew up on stories about Elias Grimshaw and the missing miners."

"Arnold, the tour guide, said there was a rumor Grimshaw used blood magic. Sacrificed the miners to protect the gold. I don't think he believes it, but he did mention it."

"Yeah, that story's been around forever." He navigated the roads carefully, one eye on Rue. "My grandma used to say Grimshaw was hungry for power and didn't care who he stepped on or buried to get it." He shifted gears smoothly as the truck reached the outskirts of town.

"You grew up in Ghost Vein?" For some reason, Rue assumed he and Cole had met in the army and then both moved here for jobs.

"I moved here when I was a kid. My grandma raised

me. Then I joined the army and met Cole. We got out around the same time. I opened my garage and Cole became the sheriff." He smiled. "Digging for dirt on the sheriff?"

"What? No..." Rue spluttered then glared at Jesse. "It's the gold. That's what I want details on. Not Sheriff Grumpy."

"Hoo." Jesse hooted. "Me thinks she doth protest too much. But if it's information you want, I can tell you what Gran saw."

"And?"

"Grimshaw was a wealth and power obsessed opportunist. He vanished not long after the miners did. His family left town fast. Didn't even hold a memorial, just packed up and disappeared. Real shady."

"Is this a story your gran had passed down to her? She couldn't have seen it happened, otherwise she couldn't have raised you."

Jesse shot Rue a considering look before answering. "Gran used to clean Grimshaw's house. She liked his wife and the kid, but she hated Grimshaw."

What? "How could your grandmother have raised you? She had to be at least a teenager to clean someone's house. And that was in eighteen fifty-nine. That's like a hundred and sixty-six years ago. It's not possible."

"Let's just say my family is long-lived." Jesse refused to look at Rue and his hands tightened on the steering wheel.

Huh. Jesse's family had to be paranormal, and he didn't want to tell her. Rue tried to lighten the mood. "You're a bunny shifter...right?" She twisted in her seat to stare at him. The corner of his mouth twitched. "Ha. I'm right." She fist-pumped into the air, surprising a chuckle from him.

"I'm not telling you what kind of paranormal flavor I am, but it definitely isn't a bunny."

Rue pouted. "Bunnies are cute."

"Bunnies are food and nothing else." A twinkle appeared in his eyes and his hands relaxed. "Keep guessing, and I might eventually tell you if you hit on it."

Giggling, Rue turned back to the staring out the window. "I'll have to have a think. Make sure I choose the right answer." She changed the subject. "Do you think the Grimshaws were hiding something nefarious?"

"I think that poor woman took the first chance to run with her kid. That doesn't exactly scream Elias Grimshaw's innocence."

They rolled to a stop outside the Silver Tongue, and Jesse turned to her with a grin. "Stay safe and avoid ghosts, or the grumpy sheriff might come knocking. And trust me, he doesn't deliver flowers."

Rue groaned. "Ugh. Please no. I've hit my broody lawman quota for the week. Thanks for picking me up, Jesse."

He winked. "You're welcome for the rescue. Call me if any more spirits want to chat."

Shaking her head, Rue discarded the blanket and slipped out of the pickup. She waved as Jesse headed back to his garage. The last thing she needed was another chat with a ghost or a visit from Cole Dawson. The less she had to do with the sheriff, the better...

EIGHT

Rue entered the Silver Tongue and joined Taz in the kitchen. "Well, that didn't go exactly as planned."

Taz stopped unpacking the latest delivery of baked goods. "What happened? Tell me it wasn't another body?"

"I swear everyone thinks I'm a body magnet. This time, there wasn't a body attached. At least, not a physical one."

"Ah." Taz nodded. "You saw a ghost. They always swarmed Ruth when she visited."

A commotion outside drew them out to the front window where two tourists on the boardwalk were arguing over spilled sarsaparilla.

"Ever since Tobias started the ghost tours, everything has been out of whack here. Ruth was positive it was the cursed gold. Maybe if you find it and break the curse, the town will go back to normal?"

"Even if I found the gold, I have no clue how to do Ruth's curse-breaking mojo."

"Ruth left notes, boxes of them in the basement." Taz dropped her voice. "If she was hiding anything witchy, it's most likely there."

Rue squared her shoulders. "Basement it is."

In the basement, Rue found a cluster of old boxes lined up against the far wall. She headed across and grabbed one. A faint click sounded and something behind the boxes shifted.

"*No way...*" Excited, she shoved the rest of the boxes aside and discovered a portion of the wall had swung open a few inches. "A secret room. Well, how about that." She opened the door wide, revealing a small room.

It smelled of lavender, candle wax, and dust. There were shelves filled with old books and scarred journals. Against a wall was a desk with the witchy equipment she'd expected. Candles, crystals, small bundles of dried herbs, and an old map pinned to the wall with red thread criss-crossing over the town's landmarks.

Pinned above the map was a single sheet of paper with thick writing in black marker... *The truth is buried. Trust no one.* Rue's blood chilled.

A sudden gust of lavender-scented wind slammed the door shut with a resounding bang. Rue's eyes widened, then she lunged at the door. She yanked on the brass handle. It was solid, unmoving. She slammed her palms against the wood and shoved. "Hello?" she shouted, heart pounding like a jackhammer. "Taz?" Rue screeched again.

Nothing. Only her own breath coming faster and faster. "You have *got* to be kidding. I'm locked in a secret witch bunker, and the only witness to the fact I'm down here is unpacking baked goods upstairs."

She slapped at the door again. "Open up, will you? This is getting old fast."

Rue checked her phone. No cell reception. She kicked the door, cursing. She tried to use her body weight to force it open. It wouldn't budge. A thump sounded outside, and she placed her ear to the door, hoping to hear Taz. Instead, she heard heavy footsteps and a creak as the door opened. Framed in the doorway was a confused Sheriff Cole Dawson.

Without thinking, Rue launched herself at him. "Thank you," she gasped, burying her face against his shoulder. "I thought I'd end up suffocating to death in there." Rue jerked away when she remembered who she was hugging and nearly fell back into the secret room. "I didn't think anyone but Taz knew I was down here. Then the door blew shut, and I thought I was trapped and..." She narrowed her eyes. "Hang on. Was that *you?* Was this a prank? Did you pretend there was a draft and slam the door shut to scare me?"

"What? No. I just got here. Taz mentioned you were in the basement. I came down and heard you yell."

"There was wind." She snapped, pointing at the door. "It blew shut and trapped me."

He raised a brow. "We're in a basement. Inside a building made of stone and timber. No windows. No breeze. Unless you installed a fan in the last ten minutes..."

Rue propped hands on her hips. "Then how do you explain the *door slamming?*"

"It's Ghost Vein. Some days, logic just doesn't apply." He peeked into the room and let out a low whistle. "So, this is Ruth's setup, huh?"

"You knew she had a hidden witchy lair?"

"Never seen it, but I knew she had to have a working space away from prying eyes. I didn't expect it to be hidden behind a secret door, but that's Ruth for you."

"You knew she was a witch? A curse-breaker?"

Cole met her gaze without flinching. "I've seen weird things. In the military, in this town. I've watched things happen that shouldn't be possible. Ruth was the real deal. It made people nervous." He leaned against the doorway. "She broke hexes. Unraveled nasty stuff. That made enemies. Folks blamed her for the things she exposed. But I can tell you her death was natural. Heart attack. Nothing sinister. No matter what anyone whispers."

Rue stared at him, uncertain. "What about Tobias? Was his death natural? Or was it caused by the cursed gold?"

Cole's jaw tightened. "Plain old murder. Nothing supernatural involved."

She pressed on. "What about the gold I saw him holding? Did you find it?"

He hesitated. "Still looking. And even if he had it, that doesn't explain who wanted it bad enough to kill for it. He had enemies, but you need to stay out of this."

"You still think I'm a suspect."

"I think you're snooping," Cole uttered calmly. "And you're not trained. This isn't a game. It's dangerous. If you keep inserting yourself into this like Ruth used to, someone's going to take that pretty nose of yours and do something with it."

"Is that a threat, Sheriff?"

Cole groaned and rubbed the back of his neck. "I'm trying to tell you how dangerous this investigation is. Stay out of police business or I'll arrest you."

His words weren't bullying, but they landed hard. Hard enough to leave Rue momentarily stunned.

They stared at each other, the silence stretching. Tension snapped between them, charged and heated words unspoken.

Her heart thudded. She hated that he might be right. Hated that his arms had made her feel safe. She hated the way his eyes softened when he looked at her. Like she wasn't a suspect but someone worth worrying about.

More than anything, she hated the flicker of warmth in her chest at the thought he might not see her as just a problem to manage.

He opened his mouth to say something else, but instead, he stepped into the room. Grabbing a stack of dusty boxes, he motioned with his head. "Let's go. I'll help you bring these up."

Just like that, their shared moment cracked and fell apart. Rue followed Cole in silence as he led the way upstairs.

He dumped the boxes in the spare room and gave her another warning. "Focus on the Silver Tongue. Clean your own house before you go messing in other people's."

Before Rue could bite back, the overhead lights flickered, and a series of soft thumps sounded.

They both stiffened.

Cole looked around the small apartment. "Was that...?"

"That's probably Ruth. I don't think she likes us arguing."

He didn't comment. Instead, he turned and walked out.

Staring at his annoying, attractive, retreating back, Rue realized she was frustrated and grumpy. Also...a little warm. She fanned her pink cheeks. He had rescued her from potential suffocation and endured her hysterical hug. She should be equal amounts thankful for his rescue and annoyed at his warnings. Instead, she just felt...*warm.*

A thump sounded again, and one of Ruth's boxes fell on its side. "Fine," Rue grumbled. "I heard you the first time. Stick to the investigation. I got it." But as she stared at the dusty boxes, her mood shifted. She wasn't a child to be maneuvered or controlled.

If Cole didn't want her involved...*tough*. She had a plan. Next stop, Letty Navarro.

Rue had just started digging out the truth. Cole Dawson better get out of her way because she wasn't stopping her truth-seeking for anyone...

NINE

The scent of fresh cinnamon rolls hit Rue the moment she stepped into the kitchen the next morning. Taz and Cassie already bustled around the café and the kitchen, sleeves rolled up and spirits high.

Cassie waved as she spotted Rue. "Hey, boss. How's your investigation going? Any breaks yet?"

"Not yet. I feel like I'm missing a piece of the puzzle. That's why I'm heading out to track down Letty Navarro this morning. Her name keeps coming up, and she has maps of the mine. Might be worth a look."

Taz barely looked up from loading scrolls. "Not this morning, sweetie."

"Sorry?" Taz normally supported her sleuthing, so to hear a no was a surprise.

"We open back up this morning. Remember?" Taz pointed to the still closed saloon doors. "Sheriff Grumpy shut us down, and we're finally allowed to open back up today. Ruth's pride and joy needs her new boss front and center, at least for a while."

Rue groaned. She was such a bad owner. She had

completely forgotten about the Silver Tongue reopening. She had a creeping feeling she was letting her great aunt down. "Right. The re-opening."

"You forgot, didn't you?"

"Maybe? I just sort of re-prioritized the sleuthing. Solving a murder is important."

"You're also trying to reopen your aunt's business. This morning, you need to move the Silver Tongue to the top of your to-do list."

"I know. I'll help but..." Rue groaned. "I sound ungrateful and I'm really not. But I haven't worked in a bookshop since...well, never. I've only shelved books in a library. I have no clue what I'm doing." She nibbled on the corner of her lip. Rue didn't want to let anyone down, but right now she felt like a juggler who couldn't catch the balls.

"Hold that thought." Cassie winked at Rue before disappearing into the kitchen. She returned a few moments later, dragging a lanky young man with curly, ginger hair. Halfway through munching on a roll, he went wide-eyed at the sight of Rue.

"Ta da." Cassie jazz handed. "This is Thomas Reynard." Cassie slapped him on the back hard enough to make him cough as he tried to swallow his mouthful. Ignoring the choking, Cassie beamed. "Thomas helped Ruth out in the bookshop. He's your secret weapon."

Thomas wiped his crumb-covered hand on his jeans and stuck it out in greeting. "Hi, Ms. Maddox. Sorry about the crumbs."

Rue shook his hand, already charmed. "Hi. I'm Rue. And I don't know what I'm doing."

He grinned. "Perfect. Ruth said that every time we had to stock displays or order books."

She laughed. "I shelved books at my local library. That's the bookwormiest job I've ever had."

"You'll be fine. Most of it's automated—inventory, payment, all the back-end stuff with cataloguing. Ruth bought new accounting software just before she died." He faltered for a few seconds before rallying. "I can show you how it all works."

Exhaling in relief, Rue nodded. "Numbers make my brain melt. I'm all words, no math."

"I *love* numbers." Thomas beamed, practically vibrating. "I'm saving to do an accounting degree. But college is expensive, so I've been working here and doing all of Ruth's accounting."

"So, how about you help me keep this place running, and I'll write you a glowing college recommendation?"

"Would you? That'd be great."

Cassie whooped and slapped his back again. "See? Nothing to worry about."

And it meant that Thomas could help her when she needed to investigate.

"I know what you're thinking, Rue Maddox." Taz smirked. "But before you sneak off to play wild west Miss Marple, you're going to learn the bookshop ropes."

Rue placed her hand over her heart. "I am deeply committed to the success of the Silver Tongue Bookshop and Café. So, I have no idea what you're talking about."

Thomas grinned. "Ruth would have loved you."

Something twinged in Rue's chest. She rubbed at the tiny, strange warmth that bubbled under her hand. She was part of a team with support and back-up. It had been a long time since anyone offered to stand beside her in anything. She smiled and put her sleuthing away for the moment. "Okay. Let's get to it."

Taz waved them off toward the bookshop. "Go. Inventory waits for no witch."

"Tour time." Thomas rubbed his hands together and gestured for Rue to follow. His tour of the Silver Tongue bookshop took about ten minutes. By the end of it, Rue's brain buzzed. So many new things to learn. She just hoped she could get the hang of it.

"Okay." Thomas pointed to the sleek little till system and laptop on the counter at the back of the store. "The touchscreen laptop's super easy to use. You log in and hit the sales app, then you scan the barcode on the back of the product. You hit sell on the app, then pick cash or card. It tells you the change if it's cash, or you swipe if it's a card or phone they use to pay. Gift bags are under the counter. Print a receipt and you're done."

He moved, ignoring Rue's anxious expression. She followed close behind as he flung open a door to an office. "This is Ruth's office, if you need to hide in peace." He spun and opened another door opposite the office. "This is our prep room where we get the stock ready for sale and catalogued." He pointed to an older desktop computer on a small desk. "I'd been trying to convince Ruth to update our stock computer, but she never got round to it." He shot Rue a pleading glance under his ginger fringe.

"I'll look into it," Rue promised.

Beaming, he pointed out the organized shelves on the far wall and a scarred wooden table. "This is where we log our new inventory, stamp our logo on the back, and add a barcode. We then scan it into our digital system, add the book's description, and...boom. Ready for the shelves. We can have breaks in here as well, but I normally spend mine with Cassie." He looked anxious for a few seconds.

"Don't worry, that's fine. I don't want to change anything. My dad always said if it isn't broke, don't fix it."

"Yeah, Ruth used to say the same thing."

Rue blew out a breath. "I won't lie. I'm nervous."

He winked. "You'll be fine. I'll stick around and make sure you've got the hang of it. Mornings are usually busiest. After lunch, it's dead quiet." He cleared his throat. "Which is when Ruth would head out on her, uh...snooping missions." He waggled his eyebrows.

"That's good to know." She offered a weak smile. "I just don't want to mess up the shop. It's her legacy."

Before Thomas could answer, a soft *tap-tap-tap* echoed from the shelves. It sounded again. Frowning, Rue stepped out into the main area where all the bookshelves sat. Books rustled as if someone had walked by, brushing their fingers along the spines. A lavender-scented breeze tugged gently at Rue's green-colored bookshop apron. She stilled, eyes wide.

Thomas grinned. "I think that's Ruth's way of telling you you're doing fine."

Rue laughed, a little shaky but warmed by it anyway. "That or she's demanding better shelf dusting."

From the café, Taz's voice rang out. "All hands on deck."

"Showtime." Thomas straightened his matching apron and drew Rue over to the counter at the back of the shop.

For the next hour, the shop was bookish chaos. Fumbling at first, Rue got the hang of it eventually. She pressed the wrong buttons, double-charged a woman for a cactus bookmark, and scanned her own hand more than once. Thomas quickly stepped in and fixed her mistakes, gently cheering her every victory.

By the time the morning rush died down, Rue fanned

herself with a promotional flyer on an upcoming midlife country hoedown.

Thomas leaned on the counter beside her. "You nailed it. Ruth would be proud."

Red bloomed in her cheeks at the compliment. "I thought I'd end up breaking something, but after a while it got easier."

"See?" Thomas winked at his boss. "You're a natural."

Rue waved the compliment away. "My mom didn't do praise. She was more *a why-can't-you-get-it-right-the-first-time* person."

Thomas gave a sympathetic wince. "Ruth was really patient. I just try to act the way she would have."

"If I could get a handle on the witchy stuff and the murder investigation, I'd feel halfway competent."

As if summoned by Rue's words, a thin blue book slid from a nearby shelf and landed at her feet with a *thump*.

Thomas picked it up and handed it to Rue. "I think this is meant for you."

Scanning the title, Rue looked up and stared at Thomas. *"Witch Hexes and Curse-Breaking for Intermediate Practitioners?"*

"Ruth's answer to everything. Read a book. Learn something. And you might want to listen to her. Ghosts get cranky when you don't listen to them."

"My mom is like that too. But less ghosts and the paranormal." She toyed with her apron strings. "This is probably rude, but you don't seem stressed about the ghost stuff."

He shrugged. "Mom's a hedge witch. Her nan was a Scottish witch and my dad's a fox shifter. I didn't get their powers, just the red hair and skin that burns at the sight of sunlight." He rolled his eyes. "It's fine though. I've got math skills. Numbers are my magic."

"Spoken like a true spreadsheet wizard."

Thomas waved her off toward the café. "Go take a break. I've got this."

"You sure?"

"Get sugared up and you can sleuth away this afternoon."

Not having to be told twice, Rue whipped off her apron and headed for the cinnamon scrolls. The café buzzed with chatter and caffeine. Rue joined the end of the line and scanned the pastry case when a low voice caught her attention. Two locals were deep in conversation at a table behind Rue.

"I'm tellin' ya, I heard him at The Hole." The man lowered his voice. "Blathering on to the bartender. Said he had something to sell. Somethin' *big*."

Rue's ears perked up. Could they be talking about Tobias?

"He always talked big, then he died. I figure some tourist's husband got wind of his antics and offed him."

Definitely Tobias. She shuffled her feet and pretended to stare at the pastries and scrolls.

The woman shot a glance at Rue and nudged her companion under the table. They stopped talking and stood. Then with a sharp backward glance, they left, taking the mystery with them.

Rue stared at the door, brain racing. The Hole? What kind of name was that? Obviously, a bar since a bartender was mentioned. And selling? Maybe Tobias tried to sell the gold he'd been holding when he died. Questions spun around her brain, but she didn't get long to think about it before the doors blew open with a bang. Maribel Knox strutted in, dressed in a tiny little denim mini skirt and top and a bedazzled cowboy hat.

Her phone was lifted high, already recording. "Buckle up, witches. It's gonna be a *bumpy ride,*" she cackled. "I'm standing in the infamous Silver Tongue bookshop and cafe, where a certain *tour guide* met his *gruesome* end after being *cruelly evicted...*"

Rue froze mid-step, jaw tightening. Before she could think too hard about it, she stalked over and tapped Maribel on the shoulder. She kept her face angled away from the camera. With her luck, her mom would see the footage and never let her hear the end of it. "I'm sorry, but you have to stop filming. You're welcome to stay, but not if you're recording." Rue gritted her teeth, hoping that Maribel would leave without any drama...a faint hope.

Maribel gasped theatrically. "You hear that, viewers? *Suppression of the press.*" She swung her phone toward Rue. "What do you say to the fans about this violation of my rights?"

Plastering on her most graceful, *I-will-handle-you-politely* smile, Rue continued. "You can record outside. But inside, this is private property. I'm not suppressing *your* rights; I'm protecting *mine* and my customers'. And as the owner, I can refuse service."

Maribel leaned in closer. "Just like you *refused* to serve the dead guy? Sounds suspicious to me. Did the cursed gold or demonic energy cause it? My viewers would like to know."

Rue's jaw clenched. "I had *nothing* to do with the murder. And the idea of demonic energy is ridiculous."

With a huff, Maribel finally ended the recording and lowered her phone. "Ugh. You're a *terrible* interview subject."

"I'm not an interview subject at *all,*" Rue snapped.

"And if my face shows up on your channel, I'll sue. You do *not* have my permission."

Maribel's smirk faded. She sniffed, spun on her heel, and flounced out.

The tension in the room snapped with an almost audible pop. Some of the café goers erupted into spontaneous clapping.

Rue barely heard it. She had murder on her mind and way too many questions. What had Tobias been trying to sell? And why couldn't she shake the annoying Maribel? Forgoing her break, Rue headed back to work. She'd just finished wiping down some bookshelves when a scuffle broke out in the doorway of the saloon.

Two older women were wedged in the doorway, shoulders bumping as they argued over who should enter first. One wore a black button-up blouse tucked into a long black skirt, her straight, jet-black hair streaked with silver and pulled into a tight bun. The other sported loose silvery curls and a swirling tie-dyed dress.

"Lynette, you walk like a drunken squirrel," the black-haired woman snapped. "Just move out of the way."

"I *was* moving, Wynona," Lynette shot back. "You're the aggressive one with the pointy elbows."

"I was born with them. You know it's a family thing."

Taz sighed and massaged her forehead. "Not again."

The two women's voices rose as a full-on elbow-swinging, hip-checking, squabbling match broke out at the entrance.

Rue and Taz rushed over to intervene, trying to separate them without copping a whack in return.

"Ladies..." Rue started, placing a hand on the tie-dyed woman's arm.

The woman, Lynette, snatched her arm back and

pointed a finger at Rue. "Ruth kept the peace around here. If she were still alive, this wouldn't be happening. You need to step up and do your job." She shoved the rest of her way into the café, the other woman following close behind.

Do her job? She'd been working at the bookshop all morning. Or did the woman mean the witchy side of Ruth's inheritance?

The other woman, Wynona, scoffed. "Ruth was nothing but a meddler who didn't know when to keep her nose to herself. If you're anything like her, you'll do more harm than good. Best if you stay out of things."

Rue reared back, not sure what to say to the sudden verbal attack. "Look, I'm not sure what…"

"Leave it, sweetie. We don't care," Wynona sneered.

A voice cut across the café like a knife. "That's enough." Cole stood in the doorway, arms folded, his expression forged in steel.

Tension drained from her spine. Rue hated how safe he made her feel. Hated it…mostly.

Both customers spun and faced the sheriff, glaring. Wynona's eyes narrowed, but Lynette had the grace to look embarrassed.

"I'm sorry," Lynette apologized to Rue. "Wynona just knows how to push my buttons."

Wynona cackled. "Weak personalities blame outside influences for their shortcomings."

They muttered under their breath and glared at each other again.

Cole's voice dropped a notch. "*Enough.* You're family. Act like it."

"Family?" Rue whispered to Taz.

Taz gave a nod. "Sisters. Witches but in competing

covens. Think Hatfields and McCoys but with tarot cards and curses."

Cole pointed to the door. "Cool off. Outside. Don't make me drag your cauldrons to opposite ends of town again."

Growling and cursing, both women stomped outside and stormed off in opposite directions.

Cole made his way toward Rue, and the teasing warmth in his eyes caught her completely off guard. "They're relatively harmless." He tilted his head toward the door. "As long as you don't take sides or get involved in their squabbles, you're fine."

"Is that your professional advice, Sheriff?" Rue found her voice. It was easier to ignore his grouchy charm if she kept talking.

He shot Rue a lazy smirk and it came with dimples. *Actual dimples*. Rue forgot how to swallow.

"Professional and personal."

Taz let out a tiny honking *snort* behind them.

Breathing just became optional. Rue was too busy trying to decide if she'd overheated and her face had melted to reply. She fanned herself with the café's menu.

Cole glanced at Taz, who hadn't bothered to hide her amusement. He sighed. "And *you*, stop making fun of me. I can flirt."

"Can you though?" Taz teased.

A strangled laugh escaped Rue. She covered her face with the menu, giving up on subtle.

Reaching over, Cole tweaked the menu to one side, revealing Rue's beet-red face. He gave her a crooked smile that did *nothing* to help her blood pressure. "Stay out of trouble, Rue."

And just like that, he prowled out, boots loud on the old wood floor.

"He's so...confusing. Talk about emotional whiplash. I need a neck brace." She hadn't realized she'd spoken out loud until Taz burst out laughing.

"You two are hilarious." Taz wiped her hands on a dish towel. "But also kind of cute. You're awkward, and he's trying desperately to flirt. It's hilarious."

"It's like watching a rom com movie. We just need popcorn." Cassie popped in from the kitchen.

"He's grumpy." Rue frowned. Was she that awkward around Cole? Maybe she needed a flirting course refresh.

"He's grumpy because he *cares*." Taz waggled both eyebrows suggestively. "For you, in case you were wondering."

"He gets grumpy because he's awake," Rue corrected her friend. But her protest was weak. Because he had been caring. Protective. Charming, even.

And those dimples...

Taz poked Rue in the ribs. "You need a break. A girls' night out."

Rue groaned. "Do I have to put make-up on?"

"Yup. You can survive one night of socializing. Think of it as distraction therapy. Plus..." Taz added with a knowing gleam, "...you might find a bartender worth questioning."

"You know everything, don't you?" Rue pretended to pout.

"Nope, but I overheard that couple too. And I'm beginning to figure out how your mind works."

"Maybe you're psychic?"

"Ha. I wish." Taz giggled. "If I make it a girls' night and invite others when you go sleuthing, I'll have someone to dance with."

"I can multitask. Dancing and sleuthing." Rue grinned wickedly. She turned toward the bookshop and whispered under her breath, "Take that, Sheriff Grouchy with the sweet dimples. I'm one step ahead of the law for once."

And she was starting to *like* it.

TEN

"Are you sure we aren't in the wrong place?" Rue stood outside a creaky wooden building on its last legs. A hand-painted wooden sign hung crookedly above the door and had "The Hole" printed on it. Below, someone with a thick, black marker had scrawled, *"get in, get out or get burned."*

"Comforting."

Next to her, Taz fluffed her dark brown, curly hair. "Don't let the décor fool you. The nachos here are a religious experience. Just don't ask for a ghost-tini."

"Why? Will the ghostbusters pop up?" Rue giggled at her own joke before trailing off when Taz gave her a side eye. "Hey, that was funny."

"Not so much."

"The bartender doesn't do touristy stuff. He threw a fit when someone asked for a drink with an umbrella in it. This is a no tourist, no frills bar." Bonnie, Cassie's mom, adjusted her sparkly, tight black top.

"That feels a bit like an overreaction. Sometimes a girl needs a tiny umbrella in her drink." Even if it was soda. Rue had given up alcohol when she was younger. One whiff of it, and she ended up with a flaming red face. Being auburn haired, it wasn't a great look on her.

"Not here, you don't." Taz grinned. "Besides, you haven't met the bartender yet." She winked, and Bonnie burst into giggles.

"I am so going to regret this night. I can feel it." Rue shook her head and pushed the rickety bar door open. A wave of noise washed over her as she stepped inside. Locals filled darkened booths that rimmed the outside of the room. Battered tables and chairs sat around a scuffed-up dance floor in the center of the room. Boots stomped in time to the whine of a steel guitar. The band, *The Dustbiters*, howled and screeched from a raised stage, framed by partially working fairy lights.

The band was a chaotic, musical mess of banjo twangs, fiddle screeches, and an overly hairy lead singer with flickering yellow eyes...make that one eye. His other was so swollen he could barely see out of it. In fact, he looked like he'd fought a raccoon and lost. Rue made a mental note to ask Taz what yellow eyes meant in Silver Vein. The fairy lights fizzled and sparked. Talk about a death trap waiting to happen. "Do the lights always do that?"

"Every Thursday, ladies' night. Sometimes we even get electrical shocks or a small fire. It's a game of chicken to see who gets zapped first."

"Delightful," Rue muttered.

The wooden floor beneath her booted feet groaned with every step. The boards were warped and worn smooth by decades of boots, spurs, and bar brawls. Rue tilted her head back to see wagon-wheel chandeliers twinkling overhead, casting flickering shadows against scarred, dark-paneled walls.

At the bar, Rue scanned the chalkboard menu. *Barstool*

Nachos. Ghost Vein Chili. Deep Fried Pickaxe Fries. Dynamite Dogs. Silver Vein Beef Sliders. "Wait. Where's the drink menu?"

"Don't need one. It's whiskey, wine, beer, or soda. That's it." Taz pointed to another sign. *No cocktails. No bubbles. No ghost puns.*

Rue giggled at the sign. Half the time, she wasn't sure if Ghost Vein residents were joking or serious. But it was entertaining.

Taz elbowed Rue. "It's serious. Order a witch-tini, and they'll salt the floor under your stool. Trust me, the bartender has a temper, so don't push it."

Speaking of the bartender... Behind the scarred and dented wooden bar, *he* stood with arms crossed, watching them. Black shirt. Black jeans. Muscles too big for his ego. Shoulder-length, oily brown hair tucked behind one ear. And hazel eyes that definitely thought he was too cool for Ghost Vein.

Catching Rue's gaze, he sauntered over. "Ladies." He stared straight at Rue.

Rue wasn't sure if he was trying to flirt or challenging her to a staring contest.

Giving him her brightest smile, Taz gave her drink order. "Two beers and a lemonade."

His eyes still on Rue, he nodded. "You legal?"

"I'm twenty-eight years old." Rue gave an internal grimace. Taz teased her about her own flirting, but at least she and Cole weren't creepy like this guy.

He grunted and finally broke eye contact with Rue as he filled their drink order.

"Is he real, or did someone hex a romance book cover and drop it in a vat of smug and arrogant?"

Bonnie cackled. "He likes to think he's Ghost Vein's

answer to a male supermodel, but only the tourists go for him. None of us local gals are that stupid."

He definitely wasn't all that. An image of Cole and his dimples flashed into her head before Rue pushed it away. She kept an eye on the bartender as he poured drinks with more flex than finesse. She wasn't here for flirting with creepy guys. She was here for the murder. For answers...and maybe some Ghost Vein Chili.

Grabbing their drinks, the women settled into a booth. Rue scanned the bar, trying to remember the face of the man who'd been gossiping in the café earlier that day.

Her attention was drawn to the dance area, packed with bodies. Two steppers, slow dancers swaying cheek to cheek, and a group of boot-scooters creating weird line dancing patterns on the floor. The room buzzed with heat, conversation, laughter, and the smack of chairs being dragged. And over it all, the twang of banjo and off-key music, and the occasional lightbulb above the dance floor sparking with mischief.

"It's great, isn't it?" Taz bopped around on her side of the booth. "Take your mind off a certain flirty sheriff?"

"Oooh. I heard the big guy had finally fallen." Bonnie giggled and took a swig of her beer. "For the last two years, he's dodged every invitation, every casserole dish brought by matchmaking mommas. Now here he is, flirting with our own Maddox. It's fate."

Spluttering, Rue wiped soda from her emerald-green, silky top. She'd paired it with tight black jeans and high heeled boots. "He thinks I'm suspect number one. That's all."

"Please." Taz rolled her electric-colored, eyeshadowed eyes. "That's long over. He's warm for your form."

"How old are you? Can we change the subject, please?

I'm supposed to forget him, remember?" Rue leaned back, trying to relax in the battered booth. She let her gaze roam the room and spotted Isla bobbing her head in time with the music. The museum assistant chatted animatedly to an older man in plaid. Rue gave a wave when Isla caught her watching. A few booths down, Maribel held court dressed in a tiny red leather top and mini skirt with matching boots. Surrounded by wide-eyed males, she brandished her rhinestone bedazzled phone like a wand.

"Place is packed." Rue raised her voice over the music.

"Thursday's ladies' night. Bad music, bad beer, and bad choices." Taz waggled her eyebrows. "There will be some heavy heads tomorrow."

Bonnie giggled. "And your therapy just walked through the door."

"What therapy?" Girls' night out was beginning to look like trouble if Rue couldn't keep up with the conversation this early in the night.

"Sheriff Smolder and Deputy Dreamboat just walked in wearing tight jeans."

Rue made a show of not turning around and took a long sip of lemonade. "Not interested."

Bonnie grinned. "Cassie's told me all about it. She said the flirting is a hooooot." Bonnie drew the word out.

"He has not... We aren't..." Rue stuttered, heat flooding her face.

"Oh, he *definitely* has." Taz counted off her fingers. "Grumpy smirks? Check. Random appearances? Check. Carrying boxes up and down stairs? Triple check. And don't forget about those dimples."

Groaning, Rue sank lower in her seat. "Don't talk about the dimples. Besides, I'm a murder suspect. Cops don't flirt with suspects."

"It's different here in Ghost Vein," Bonnie muttered into her beer.

Rue laughed, surprising herself by how warm their teasing made her feel. It had been so long since she'd had people who cared. Friends who called her out while smiling.

Her gaze drifted again. Maribel had sauntered over to the bar and turned up the flirt. Smiling. Tilting her head. Lightly touching the bartender's arm. The man looked unimpressed and shook off her hand.

Making a snap decision, Rue drained her lemonade and stood. "Time for another round, ladies? My treat."

"That code for snooping?" Taz eyed Rue over the rim of her glass.

"Yep. That's code."

Taz elbowed Bonnie. "She's going in. Operation eavesdrop has commenced."

"This is so exciting." Bonnie wiggled in her seat.

Rue made her way to the bar, stopping just far enough away so she could watch Maribel crash and burn in her flirt attempt but not look like she was eavesdropping.

Maribel leaned in again, lips moving. Rue couldn't hear her words, but her body language screamed attempted seduction. He gave her a tight smile and said something that had her pulling back. With an offended huff, Maribel flounced away, her boots clicking like tiny angry hooves. The bartender had already moved down the bar, organizing glasses and wiping the counter.

Rue slid onto a stool, her fingers drumming casually against the bar.

He glanced her way. "Beer or lemonade?"

"Lemonade and two beers for my friends, please." She smiled sweetly. "I'm the responsible one."

Grunting, he filled her glass and slid it over to her.

Smiling her thanks, Rue handed over cash for the drinks and waited as he grabbed the beers. She glanced toward the dance floor where Maribel now held court. "Is she always that subtle?"

The bartender snorted. "Maribel's about as subtle as dynamite and does as much damage."

"She didn't get her way, huh?"

"Not even close." Jackson leaned one elbow on the bar. "She wanted a *date* or some dirt. Maybe both."

"What did she get?"

"A bar tab. People don't always get what they want here." He smirked at Rue.

"Did Tobias get what he wanted? I heard he liked to come in and do some buying and selling"

His smirk faded. A wave of yellow swam over his eyes before disappearing. "Tobias had a mouth, and he talked big. That's all. Why do you want to know?"

"I just moved here. Seemed like a quiet place until the murder. Now all you hear about is Tobias and his schemes." Rue didn't have to fake the shudder that rolled through her at the memory of Tobias in the alley.

He relaxed and gave a lazy shrug. "Mining towns aren't exactly strangers to death. Especially when the one stirring up trouble is a pushy tour guide who doesn't know when to quit."

"I heard he was selling stuff under the table. And that he believed all that stuff he said on his tours. But did he really find anything?"

The bartender's posture tightened, his hands stilled for a beat too long. A few seconds later, he went back to wiping the counter. "The guy came in a few times. Kept trying to sell junk he found in the mine. Personally, I wouldn't touch it. Who knows what kind of bad karma's attached to that old stuff."

"Sounds dangerous. What kind of stuff?"

"A few old coins, rusted miners' gear. Thought he was going to make a fortune."

Rue feigned outrage. "Seriously? Selling stuff from those poor miners who disappeared? Isn't that illegal or something?"

"Depends on who's buying. The museum guy had a couple of meetings with him. And the librarian's a history nut. I heard her basement is full of weird old stuff. She might have bought from him too."

That was multiple times Letty Navarro's name had come up. Rue really needed to track the librarian down. "And gold? How much did he sell that for?"

Yellow flashed over his eyes again, the same eerie, unnatural glint she'd seen before. The same kind of glow a predator's eyes had at night when the light caught them. Rue didn't blink or let her expression show any unease.

"Why do you say that?" His jaw ticked.

She rolled her eyes "Because it's a cursed mine with a cursed gold legend. Not exactly a wild leap."

He relaxed and nodded. "Fair. But no. He never mentioned gold, at least not to me. What's it to you?"

"Just curious."

A smirk flirted with his mouth as he leaned close. "Look, why don't I show you around town? Since you're new and all."

Rue didn't answer. Mostly because a wall of heated, solid muscle appeared at her back. She didn't even need to look as her breath caught, and her cheeks flared hot.

"That won't be necessary. She's already got someone for that."

The bartender raised his hands and stepped back. "Hey. No problem, Sheriff."

He turned away to serve another customer, but Rue didn't miss the flicker of amusement behind his eyes. She wrinkled her nose. She bet the story of Cole interrupting would be around Ghost Vein before the end of the night.

Cole leaned against the bar, next to Rue. His gaze flicked to the lemonade in her hand. "Didn't realize chatting with the bartender was part of your girls' night itinerary."

"What can I say? I'm full of surprises." Rue gritted her teeth as his voice caused a tingle to spark along her spine.

His arm nudged hers. "You're also not good at laying low and staying out of my investigation."

Her heart thudded and she fought for composure. She pretended casualness. "You keeping tabs on me, Sheriff?"

"Maybe." His lips twitched.

Their eyes locked. The air between them thickened, and the bar noise around them receded. Her brain short-circuited, logic scattering. He made her feel seen. Even when she wasn't sure she could trust it. *Just why does he have to be so infuriating?*

"Your drinks are getting warm." Cole broke the moment. "Maybe you should slow down. You might go on a sugar bender."

Rue took a sip, hiding the way her hands trembled. *Yup. She was absolutely doomed.*

The bartender slid a slideways glance at Rue before heading to the other end of the bar. There went her intel-gathering mission. Still, she'd gotten something. Letty Navaro's name had popped up again, as had the museum curator. Rue took a breath to steady herself, forcing her mind back to sleuthing instead of Sheriff Dimples. She turned to unleash some well-earned snark... only to find his stupidly handsome, faintly stubbled face *way* too close. His dark eyes sparkled. Rue gritted her teeth. That wasn't fair. He was a lawman. He should sparkle less.

"I'm surprised to see you in here."

She sniffed, ignoring her sweaty palms. "It's girls' night out. And I'm appropriately attired for once, thank you very much."

Cole glanced over Rue's emerald-green, silky shirt and her tight jeans. "In my professional opinion, you're wearing *entirely* appropriate clothing. You fit in just fine." He winked and grabbed the others' beers with one hand.

Rue's face went up in flames. Cole didn't need to practice his flirting at all. He was a natural. She was the awkward one. She fanned herself with her free hand. "Is it hot in here?"

He gave her a small, maddening smirk. "Maybe it's just you."

Did he just...was that... Did he just say she was hot? Or did he mean it was hot in the room? Rue's brain short-circuited, and she opted for the easy way out...head back to her table and let Taz laugh at her. Rue grabbed her drink. "Uh huh. I'll just head back to the girls then." She made for the booth, with Cole following close behind.

Jesse already leaned against the booth, flirting with both Taz and Bonnie. The girls giggled and lapped it up.

Cole placed the beers on the table and brushed against Rue. Just a quick, casual pass of warmth and muscle.

She shivered. *Get a grip, Rue. He's just a man in tight jeans.* A man in tight, perfectly worn, pale-blue jeans that hugged his thighs and should be illegal. *Criminal. Absolutely criminal.* She fought a whimper. Maybe the bar hadn't been a good idea. Before she could combust entirely, movement in the corner of her eye caught her attention. Maribel. Scuttling toward the side exit, looking like she followed someone else out of the bar. Had Maribel found someone to take her home? Rue's mystery senses tingled, which was better than admitting other parts of her senses tingled because of the sheriff and his tight jeans. She turned to Taz. "Bathroom break. Back soon."

Taz frowned but nodded, and Bonnie made a kissy face behind her beer.

Ignoring their antics, Rue took a few steps and melted into the crowd, ducking past dancers and heading toward the side door. She almost made it.

A warm hand wrapped around Rue's arm just before she reached the partially open door.

"That's not the way to the bathroom. But it *is* the way outside. If you were, say, following someone who just slipped out."

Curses. Foiled again by Mr. Tight Jeans. Rue looked up at Cole and pretended she had no clue what he was talking about. "I...that's not the way to the bathroom?"

"Don't lie," he said gently. "I know that look. It's the same one you get when you poke your nose into my investigation."

She opened her mouth, but what could she say? The bathroom excuse had packed its bags and fled town.

"I'm just making sure you're not about to do something dangerous. I'd prefer not to find you in a ditch. Or worse."

His hand was still on her arm. Warm. Steady. Strong. "I'm not a child," Rue muttered.

"No. You're a stubborn woman with a nose for trouble."

Rue huffed. "I was just going to see where Maribel went."

"Exactly. Nose for trouble." He released her arm and

bopped said nose. The warmth of his hand lingered on her skin.

"You going to arrest me for needing some fresh air?"

Cole smiled, dimples on show. "Not unless you're trespassing while you do it."

Curse those evil dimples. They canceled out his grumpiness. So unfair.

"I'm serious, Rue," he said. "I don't want you getting hurt."

Her heart twisted. She wanted to storm away but instead stood there, a little breathless, wondering what to say next. "Fine. But I still have to pee."

He chuckled. "This way, then."

Before they could move, a scream sliced through the music and chatter. From outside. Where Maribel had just disappeared to.

Cole and Rue shared a look before pushing through the open door into the dark.

Maribel was sprawled on the ground near the edge of the street. Hair mussed, her leather outfit askew, one boot half-off. Her bedazzled phone lay nearby, its screen a spiderweb of cracks.

"Are you okay?"

Maribel looked up at Rue with wide, watery eyes. "Someone rushed me. Knocked me down and tried to take my phone."

"Weren't you with someone?"

"One, that's none of your business. Two, I wasn't with anyone. I was just heading back to my B&B."

Rue *swore* she'd seen Maribel following someone out here. She wasn't crazy. *Right?*

Cole crouched beside Maribel, checking for injuries. "You hurt anywhere?"

"Just my pride." Maribel placed a delicate hand on his arm and let out a tiny sob.

Of course she did. Rue gritted her teeth. Maybe she should give the woman the benefit of the doubt. She had just been knocked over. Anyone would be upset...wouldn't they?

Maribel, ever the drama queen, slumped against the sheriff as he helped her stand. "I'm fine. No need to make a thing of it."

The sheriff didn't budge. "It's getting reported. If you're filing insurance on the phone, we need a statement."

Pouting, Maribel gave in with a dramatic sigh. "Whatever you say, Sheriff." She fluttered her long, fake eyelashes at him.

Rue rolled her eyes so hard she thought she might have sprained them.

Taz and Bonnie rushed out, followed by Jesse, concern painted across their faces.

"What happened?" Taz asked, breathless.

Rue gave them the quick version. Maribel, attempted mugging, no witnesses.

Jesse glanced at Cole. "Want me to hang around until Mayhew gets here?"

He nodded, already on the phone. "Appreciate it."

Jesse tipped his chin to the girls, then grimaced. "You should head out. This might take a while."

Maribel gave a sugary little wave. "Bye, Rue."

Cole waved distractedly while still speaking on the phone to his deputy.

Scowling, Rue turned on her heel, boots crunching on gravel as she and Taz headed home. Bonnie peeled away toward her own place, muttering something about needing a long bath and stronger beer.

Taz gave Rue a sidelong glance as they walked. "You go off to snoop, and we find you with Ms. Drama Llama *and* tall, dark, and grumpy?"

Rue groaned. "I was at the bar to get information, then Sherriff Grumpy turned up and scared off my source. I followed Maribel, and Cole busted me

"Uh huh." Taz sounded unconvinced. "And the arm touching and display of machismo at the bar?"

"There was no macho activity at the bar, or flirting. Strictly information gathering."

"I didn't mention flirting. Guilty conscience maybe?" Taz teased.

They reached the saloon, the comforting creak of the old porch steps grounding Rue a little. As they stepped inside, she told Taz about her conversation with the bartender. "He said Tobias was selling old mine gear, including coins. He mentioned the museum guy had meetings with Tobias. And Letty might have been a buyer too."

"And let me guess. Maribel's 'attack' was perfectly timed to drag Cole away from you." Taz curled her lip. "That woman is so predictable."

"Doesn't matter. I was working."

"Uh-huh. We could see your red face from the other side of the room." Rue made a strangled noise and opened the door to her apartment. "Goodnight, Taz."

"Sweet dreams of tight jeans," Taz called as she disappeared down the stairs.

"Everyone's a comedian." Rue sighed and stepped into her dark apartment, closing and locking the door behind her. The only sound was the soft hum of the fridge. She headed to the bathroom, peeling off her boots with a sigh. She flipped on the light and...froze. Across the bathroom mirror, in bright red lipstick, were three chilling words:

"Watch. Your. Back."

Her breath caught. She stepped closer, heart thudding painfully against her ribcage. Rue stared at the shaky writing. "Is this about the investigation? Or Maribel?"

No one answered.

"Ruth, If this is your idea of ghostly encouragement, we're gonna have words."

The silence stretched on.

Giving up, Rue grabbed a makeup wipe and scrubbed the message off. The tension didn't leave her shoulders. She'd gone out for questions and a girls' night and come back with threats, flirting, and a lipstick warning from the beyond. Ghost Vein wasn't just menaced by ghosts. It was haunted by secrets...

And I'm right in the middle of it all.

ELEVEN

"The gold's not cursed. *I* am." Rue scowled at the closed sign stuck on the front door of the Ghost Vein Public Library. Its very presence mocked her.

Rue had showed up like an eager beaver only to find the library shut up tight. She was beginning to take it personally. With a long-suffering sigh, Rue dug into the little leather backpack she'd grabbed before leaving. Amidst lip balm, crumpled tissues, mints, and her emergency chocolate stash, she fished out one of the Silver Tongue's business cards.

On the back, she scribbled a short message...

Letty. I'd love to chat. Heard you know a thing or two about Ghost Vein. Call me. Rue, Silver Tongue Bookstore & Café

She bent down and slid the card under the door. Straightening, she slipped her pen away. "Please be the type of person who actually looks down and checks your door mat."

The spring morning had begun to warm, and the dusty boardwalk already creaked and groaned under the sun's glare. Rue scuffed her boots as she headed back toward the Silver Tongue, dragging her feet just enough to match her mood...frustrated. She grumbled about her bad luck and cursed her timing when she ran directly into a muscled wall scented with stale beer, cigarettes, and sour musk. Gagging, Rue reared back on reflex and wavered on her feet.

Strong hands caught Rue before she tumbled to the boardwalk. She looked up into the grinning, sleep-deprived face of the dodgy bartender from last night's escapade at The Hole.

"Well, hey there, sugar," he drawled, righting her. "You always fall this hard for a man before lunch, or am I just lucky?"

"You're definitely *something*." Rue fought her instinctive recoil. The long-haired, muscled bartender might be someone's idea of sexy, but it definitely wasn't hers.

He winked at her, unfazed by her snarky comment. "Looks like manners don't show up until lunch either."

"Thanks," Rue muttered and stepped sideways to pass him.

But the bartender slid in front of her again, arm casually extended to block her path. "Now, now," he mock-scolded. "I *did* save you from eating the boardwalk. Nasty injury, that. Could've got a splinter in your lip." He pretended to shudder.

"You're right." Rue smiled sweetly. "Thank you so much for saving me from the deadly menace of *wooden planks*. I'll alert the media to your heroic actions."

He pressed a dramatic hand to his black-T-shirt-clad chest. "Ah, sarcasm. My favorite language. You're a riot, sweetheart." He leaned closer. "Two things. One, what's your name? And two, how about that drink I mentioned last night?"

Rue leaned away from him. Not only did he stink, but she realized he was wearing the same outfit. It didn't look like the good ole bartender had made it home last night. Not even long enough for a shower or to brush his teeth. She wrinkled her nose in disgust. Rue checked her phone for the time and looked up, incredulous. "It's nine a.m."

"Eh." He shrugged. "It's five o'clock somewhere."

"Not in *Ghost Vein*, it's not."

"How about a name, sweetheart?"

Maybe if she gave him her name, he'd leave her alone. "Rue Maddox. And I'm not interested in a drink. Satisfied?"

Something flickered behind his eyes. A thin yellow sheen pulsed over his irises before clearing. "Jackson Malone, at your service. Didn't peg you for a *judgmental* type." He crowded in, towering over Rue, his breath sour.

Rue's irritation curled into a hard ball in her chest. She opened her mouth to blast the creepy, persistent man into space when someone moved in beside her.

Solid.

Quiet.

Cole.

"Is there a problem here?" Cole's voice sliced like cold steel.

Jackson shuffled back and held up his hands in mock innocence. "Nope. Just saying good morning. Thought the lady might want to grab a drink after being so friendly last night." He shrugged and stuffed his hands into his jeans' pockets. "*Girls, right?* No harm, no foul." Just like that, he continued down the street, whistling offkey, not a care in the world.

"Ugh. *What a douchebag.*" Rue stared after him, jaw clenched.

"You okay?"

"Fine. Dodging creeps, you know. Just a normal day." Rue smoothed her shirt and let out a breath. "No. Really, I'm fine. He just wouldn't take no for an answer."

Cole's lips twitched like he *might* have smiled but thought better of it. "Last night?"

"At the bar, I tried to interview him. He thought I was interested, I guess." Rue grimaced. "For the record, I wasn't. Definitely not my type."

"I'd like to ask what your type is, but right now I'm more interested in why you were interrogating him?"

"I had a tip." Rue coughed and tugged her backpack tighter on her shoulder. "Someone mentioned Tobias tried to sell old miners' gear to the bartender. I wanted to find out what kind of gear."

He sighed and ran a hand through his short-cropped hair. "And? What'd you learn?"

"Apparently it was just old mining junk and a few coins. Jackson looked squirrely when I mentioned gold, but he told me he didn't buy anything. Said he saw Tobias and the museum curator meet up. He told me to talk to Letty Navarro, the librarian." Rue huffed. "She's hard to pin down."

"Makes sense. Letty's got a whole archive in the basement, and the curator has a museum of miners' artifacts. Those two would be top of my list if you wanted to buy or sell historic mine artifacts."

"Why does Letty have a miners' archive in her basement?"

"One of the missing miners was a family member. She's always had an interest. If someone in this town wants an artifact dated, appraised, or just identified, she's the go-to."

"I really need to speak to her," Rue grumbled as they walked in tandem down the boardwalk. Cole's leg brushed against hers every time he subtly moved away from passing pedestrians. She told herself the red heat creeping up the back of her neck was from the spring morning sun, not Cole. *Focus. Mining gear. Librarian.* Not Sheriff Dimples and his citrusy, fresh cologne.

"You're sure about your information?"

"Bartender seemed pretty sure. Especially about Tobias and the curator. Multiple meetings in a quiet booth at The Hole."

Cole cleared his throat. "Good work," he said, sounding almost reluctant to admit it.

Ha, Rue crowed silently. "Bet that hurt Sheriff Grumpy to admit." She surprised herself and winked at Cole.

A twinkle appeared in his eyes, but before he could say anything, a cloud of pastel silk and heavy perfume descended on them.

"Cole, sweetie," Maribel trilled, fluttering around the sheriff. She pressed a manicured hand to his chest. "Thank you again for being such a gentleman last night," she cooed, batting her lashes. "It was so late, or maybe that's early, when you left." Maribel giggled.

Rue arched a brow and turned to Cole, who blushed furiously and tried to peel Maribel off him. "Oh, always such a gentleman. So *sweet.*"

"Just doing my job."

"Excuse me." Rue gave the sheriff a tight, saccharine-sweet smile. "I have to go actually *work.* At least *some* of us do." She stomped inside the café without a backward glance. The door slammed behind her, cutting off Cole's protest.

Taz glanced up from behind the counter, eyebrows lifting as Rue marched up. "What's got your goat?"

Rue dropped her bag on a stool and crossed her arms.

"Maribel," she snapped. Just the one word, but it was enough.

"Oh, yeah. She was in here earlier looking for Cole. Said she wanted to thank him for walking her home."

"She *thanked* him, all right. Outside. With hands on."

Taz wiped her eyes, laughing. "You do know he dragged Jesse with him when he took her home, right? She scares the heck outta him."

"Wait, what? I thought it was just the two of them? She said he left her place sometime this morning."

"He had to wait for Deputy Mayhew to turn up, take her statement, and get cleared by the paramedics before Cole took her home. So, yeah, it probably would have been early this morning," Taz said. "Cole didn't want to be alone with her. Jesse said she was all handsy and dramatic, like escorting a drunk octopus."

That was not what she'd expected...at all. Now she felt horrible for her hissy fit. She stared at her dusty boots. "I just assumed she was his type."

"Cole? Not a chance. He hasn't dated anyone since he moved here, and that includes Maribel. Pretty sure he's waiting for someone *specific*."

Rue looked up just in time to see Taz watching her with an infuriatingly smug glint in her eye. "Oh, no. Don't start with your matchmaking. He probably won't even talk to me after my fit outside."

Taz smirked. "Maybe that certain someone specific should stop dithering and ask the man out instead."

"I do *not*...I mean...I don't have flirting skills. I have *awkward silence* skills. I have *trip over my own tongue* skills. My entire romantic history can be summed up in one sentence."

"Sounds like you're due for some luck, then. Good thing you came to Ghost Vein."

"Nope." Rue backed away. "I do not ask anyone out. I barely make eye contact with my bookshop customers."

"Awkward is cute. It's your love language," Taz said sweetly.

"I *hate* you."

"Good. I'm doing my job as your girl-Friday then." Taz slapped a plastic cupcake container onto the counter. "Now take your romantic angst and sleuthing nose and deliver these to the mine gift shop. Arnold the tour guide ordered a bunch for some employee birthday thing. The mine doesn't open for another hour or two, but he'll probably be lurking around the gift shop or museum."

Scowling, Rue grabbed the container and turned to leave, only to be stopped by Taz dangling a set of keys in front of her.

"You forget you still don't have a car? Can't exactly walk to the mine."

Groaning, Rue snatched the keys. "What am I driving? A goat-drawn sled?"

"Such a comedian. Try Cassie's *Red Demon*." Taz pointed outside.

Rue's gaze followed her finger and landed on the *shiniest, lipstick-red scooter*. She'd completely missed it in all the Maribel-draped-over-Cole drama outside.

"She offered it, so you can get around snooping while she's working."

Rue leaned toward the kitchen and hollered, "Thanks, Cassie. You're a goddess."

The teenager popped her head out of the kitchen. "You break it, you bought it. Otherwise, have fun." She waved at her boss and disappeared back into the kitchen.

"Now get out and drive safely." Taz waggled a finger. "Nothing kills the romance vibe faster than a speeding ticket from the guy you're crushing on."

"Stop matchmaking."

"Never," Taz sang. "Have fun."

Shaking her head, Rue stomped outside, cupcakes in hand, trying very hard *not* to think about Cole or Maribel's claws on his chest. The morning air wrapped around her, and she decided maybe the breeze would clear her head. She slung the cupcake container into the scooter storage compartment and slid on Cassie's pink helmet. Then she revved the scooter's engine. "Let's go, Red Demon. Take me to the haunted mine so I can deliver sugary birthday carbs."

The scooter belched a cheery little roar, and Rue peeled away from the boardwalk, Sheriff Cole Dawson firmly in the back of her mind...for now.

Rue zipped into the gravel lot outside the gift shop at the mine. Cassie's red demon sputtered dramatically before coming to a stop. She yanked off the helmet and breathed in the crisp morning air. "Okay, *fine*. The scooter's awesome. Taz was right." Stowing the helmet, she grabbed the container of food and headed inside.

"Arnold?" she called as she entered, but the gift shop stayed quiet, not even a faint hum from a vending machine or the creak of floorboards. Frowning, Rue wandered through the shop and the museum. Still no sign of Arnold. Just a big ol' bucket of nothing.

"This is weird, even for Ghost Vein. Why order birthday cupcakes if you aren't even here to pick them up?" Rue headed back outside. Her boots crunched over gravel as unease scratched at the base of her spine. The mine didn't open for another hour or two, but someone should be here. The gift shop didn't just run itself. Where was everyone? "Arnold?" Rue called out, slowly turning in a circle, trying to spot someone. A small sound like a moan or a groan came from the direction of a small shed at the back of the public bathroom.

Faint but distinct, the noise came again. Her nerves tightened. Clutching the container to her chest, Rue crept around the side of the building and ground to a halt.

Arnold lay sprawled in the dirt, head bleeding, eyes open and unfocused. A rusted piece of metal that looked strangely familiar lay beside him.

"No, no, no," Rue whispered, panicked. She dropped the container and crouched next to him.

A low, tiny groan sounded again and Arnold's eyes flickered. "It's okay. You're alive," Rue breathed and fumbled for her phone, jabbing at the screen. "Cole," she barked into the phone when he answered. "I just found the tour guide, Arnold, hurt. He has a head wound. He's alive but not moving much. He's behind the public bathroom."

"Stay there. I'm sending the paramedics and Doc Halliday. I'm on my way."

The line went dead, and Rue turned back to Arnold, whose blood-matted hair made her stomach churn. "You'll be okay."

A scuffing noise behind her made Rue spin. "Who's there?" she called out, brandishing her phone like a sword.

Nothing. Just silence, except for the reassuring sound of Arnold's harsh, ragged breathing.

The sound vanished, leaving Rue's adrenaline pumping. She scooted closer to Arnold. "No one's getting you, I swear." Rue patted him on the arm, eliciting a faint groan.

What felt like a lifetime later, Doc Halliday and the paramedics came skidding onto the scene.

"We *have* to stop meeting like this." Doc knelt next to Arnold, her tone dry but her movements brisk as she assessed the victim.

Rue let out a shaky laugh. "Right? Maybe I need a bingo card. One more meet up, and I got a free cookie. Sorry. I use inappropriate humor when I'm stressed."

"Normal reaction." Doc flashed a brief smile before returning to her job. She and the paramedics worked fast, checking Arnold's vitals and securing a neck brace.

The mine owner and a few employees rushed over, faces pale. They stayed on the fringes watching.

Cole arrived seconds later, barking orders and directing the owner and staff to wait in the break room. Suddenly he popped up beside Rue, pulling her into a tight hug that made her knees go soft and squishy.

"You okay?"

Too flustered to respond immediately, she nodded into his shoulder. "Shaky but...yeah. I'm okay. I just hope Arnold is too."

He stepped back, concern creasing his brow. "What were you doing out here?"

"Delivery for the gift shop." She pointed to the upended cupcake container. "Arnold placed an order for someone's birthday. I couldn't find anyone. I heard groaning and found him."

"Did you see anyone?"

"No." She shook her head. "I thought I heard someone nearby after I found him, but...no, I didn't see anyone."

Cole's jaw tightened. "You're lucky. This isn't a game, Rue. I don't care if it was business. You need to stay away from the mine."

And just like that, Sheriff Hug Mode had been swapped for Sheriff Grumpy Mode. Rue pushed away from Cole and folded her arms. "Now I'm banned from delivering baked goods?"

Before he could answer, Mayor Agnes Flint stormed up. "He's right. You need to stay away from the mine. And while we're at it, why is it *always* you who finds the bodies?"

"Because I was literally delivering cupcakes?" She scanned the mayor, who'd appeared so fast on the scene. The bottom of her power pantsuit was covered in the same dust Rue had on her jeans from kneeling next to Arnold. *Interesting.* "How'd you get here so fast?" Rue asked, her voice casual but sharp.

"Excuse me?"

"You showed up *real* quick. I mean, even the sheriff only arrived a minute or two before you."

Mayor Flint cleared her throat. "Not that it's any of your business, but I had a meeting scheduled. With Arnold."

"With the *tour guide*? Not the mine's owner?"

"Yes, Arnold. He had concerns about upcoming tours."

Very interesting...

Cole cut into the conversation. "Rue, I need you to go back to the café. I'll take your statement there." He captured her gaze. "Be careful."

"I will." She grabbed the container of cupcakes and started toward Cassie's scooter.

"*Ms. Maddox,*" the mayor barked. "Don't leave town."

The words echoed in her mind like a threat as Rue swung a leg over Cassie's red demon and zoomed back to town with red dust on her jeans and way too many questions in her head.

The ride back to the café felt longer than usual. Rue clung to the scooter handlebars with tense fingers, glancing over her shoulder every so often. The back of her neck prickled the whole way, like someone or *something* was watching her. She passed a stray coyote on the side of the road near Jesse's garage. It watched her with an unnerving intensity but melted away when she noticed it. By the time she pulled up at the Silver Tongue, her nerves were frayed. Rue grabbed the container and stowed the helmet away before heading inside.

The café hummed with mid-morning chatter and the clink of coffee cups. She waited for a lull in the rush, then herded Taz, Thomas, and Cassie into a quiet corner booth. "The gift shop was empty. I found Arnold behind the bathrooms, head bleeding and barely conscious. Someone had hit him over the head with a piece of metal. I swear I've seen it before, but I can't remember where."

Taz gasped and Cassie paled. Thomas laid an arm around Cassie's shoulders and gave her a gentle squeeze.

Rue pushed on. "And get this, the *mayor* showed up out of nowhere, only a few minutes after Cole did. Claimed she had a meeting scheduled with Arnold. Not the mine owner."

"That's weird." Taz frowned. "You'd think she'd speak to the owner, not a tour guide."

"Exactly. And she was covered in the same dust that Arnold and I were. If she'd just turned up, why would she already be covered in the dust?"

"You think she's lying?" Cassie whispered.

"I think she's shady. She told me not to leave town. Even if I'm off Cole's suspect list, I'm on her murder bingo card." She handed the slightly squished cupcake container to Taz. "Sorry I didn't deliver these to Arnold."

Taz took the container. "Pretty sure he wasn't in the mood for baked goods."

A loud crash sounded from the kitchen. "Not another body," Rue squeaked.

But instead of a killer, *Nacho* trotted out, proud as a goat could be, with a stolen blueberry muffin clamped in his mouth and his entire face dusted in flour.

"I think you need to take a breath, sweetie." Taz patted Rue on the shoulder. "I'm more worried about the mess that dang goat left on the floor."

The group watched as Nacho trotted proudly around the café, leaving tiny white hoofprints across the floor like a goat crime scene.

Rue sagged and massaged her forehead. "We need a new rule of no goat-caused jump scares. My nerves will never recover otherwise."

"Cassie and I will cover the café and bookshop. You two go and check flourgeddon." Thomas pushed Cassie gently toward the café counter before heading to the bookshop side of the saloon.

Rue and Taz headed for the kitchen, only to stop short at the door. Flour canisters had toppled, spilling a flour miniature blizzard across the floor. White dust swirled lazily in the sunlight streaming through the window.

"Oh, *Nacho*," Taz groaned. "You're cut off. No more snacks and treats." She drifted forward, then pointed. "Look."

In the thickest patch of flour, words had been etched in white. *The vault is not the prize. It's the prison.*

Jerking back, Rue snapped, "Come on, Ruth. Stop with the ghostly riddles and *just haunt me like a normal dead relative.*"

Nacho bleated his agreement and scampered from

behind them, prancing through the flour, nearly wiping out the message with his enthusiastic hooves.

Taz knelt beside what was left of the message. "Ruth's trying to warn you about the vault."

"Maybe she shouldn't be so cryptic. She's doing a bang-up job of annoying and scaring me."

"She's worried for you."

Rue stared at the partial words until they blurred. "The murder, Arnold's attack. It's all connected."

"And we need to figure it out...*fast*."

A loud clatter made Taz twitch. Nacho had knocked over a box of Ruth's things in the corner, sending old files and loose papers fluttering across the floor. Taz bent to gather them up, then gasped. She held up a small journal, battered and dusty, and a cluster of folded notes. Taz flicked through them, a frown growing more pronounced the longer she read. "Rue...I think this is one of Ruth's journals."

"What's in it?"

"Looks like notes on the mine. A list of dates. Ghost sightings. Mine-related incidents. And these..." She held up the separate papers. "I only had a quick look, but one of the pages mentions wards, stay away hexes, suppression. I don't think Ruth was breaking the curse."

"But why not?"

Taz chewed her lip. "I don't know. I don't even know if I'm right. But I think you need to talk to Wynona. She knows more about hexes and ward magic than anyone. She'll know what this stuff means." She handed Rue the slightly flour-dusted cupcake container. "Use the cupcakes to bribe her. Wynona's got a sugar obsession. Might loosen her tongue."

Rue gave her a look. "Hope you're right. Because it feels like I'm one step away from stumbling onto another corpse."

Taz winced. "Let's not say that out loud."

Nacho, still playing in the flour, snorted in agreement.

Rue stared at the ghost-written message one more time. *The vault is not the prize, it's the prison.* What had Ruth been mixed up in before she died?

And now I'm right in the middle of it...

TWELVE

Rue's nerves hadn't improved since stumbling over Arnold bleeding in the dirt. Anxiety clung to her, itchy and impossible to ignore. Borrowing Cassie's scooter again helped a little. What she really needed was answers.

She cut the engine in front of Wynona's house and stared. The place had crawled out of a Gothic fairytale, a rickety old Victorian once painted black but now faded and in need of a new coat. Peeling trim and sagging porch boards that Rue doubted would even hold her weight completed the image. Clutching the plastic container of cupcakes, Rue braved the porch and rapped on the door. "If I end up hexed, I'm blaming you, Taz."

The front door banged open and framed a scowling Wynona, a dark silhouette in black clothing, with her sharp chin, hawkish nose, and dark gray, streaked hair. The woman needed only a pointed hat and a broom to complete the Wicked Witch look.

Rue swallowed, already regretting this.

"Standing around on the porch like a stray cat, are you?"

Wynona snapped, her eyes narrowing. Then her gaze flicked down to the cupcakes. Interest sparked.

"I have a few questions to ask."

"*Hmph.* Well, hurry up. Either get inside or quit loitering. You'll drag my reputation down, letting the sheriff's new sweetie linger outside. No one wants their nefarious activities ruined."

The *sheriff's new sweetie* comment hung in the air. *Great. Just great.* She wasn't even dating Cole, and already the town had her married off and responsible for tarnishing the criminal underworld's campaigns.

Wynona whirled and disappeared inside, leaving the door open. Rue exhaled shakily, squared her shoulders, and stepped in.

The air wasn't dank with old herbs and candle smoke as she'd expected. Instead, it smelled faintly of citrus and lavender polish. The foyer glowed with soft light bouncing off pale walls, floral curtains fluttered in a gentle breeze, and the furniture was cozy. *Inviting.* This was not the lair of a hex-slinging witch. It was the kind of place you'd expect your favorite aunt to own. Assuming your aunt didn't happen to sell hexes and curses.

"Stop snooping," Wynona barked from deeper inside. "Kitchen. Now."

Rue nearly dropped the cupcakes. "Friendly as ever." She trudged toward the voice. The kitchen made her stop dead. Gleaming white stone counters, polished silver appliances, and a centerpiece vase full of cheerful daisies. Rue stared, gobsmacked. This was less hag hut and more glossy home magazine.

Wynona snatched the container from Rue's hands, popped the lid, and plucked out a slightly squashed cupcake with blue icing. In loopy, slightly smudged letters, it read

Happy Birthday. She arched a brow. "Desperate, are we? Regifting sad cupcakes in exchange for gossip?"

"They're not sad, they're..." Rue cut herself off. Taz had specifically instructed her to play nice, even if Wynona ate her alive. "Look, I wasn't trying to bribe you. Not exactly."

Wynona bit into the cupcake anyway. "Obviously you want something. Spit it out."

Rue swallowed, nerves pricking her skin. "I was up at the mine to deliver something to one of the guides. But when I got there...I found him. Hurt. Someone attacked him."

The older witch froze mid-bite. Her dark eyes widened, then narrowed again. "Who?"

"Arnold. The older tour guide."

The cupcake dropped back into its wrapper as Wynona's face went chalky. Then the color flared back, hot with fury. "That old fool. I told him it was time to retire, but no...he can't stay away from that cursed hole in the earth." She spat a string of curses sharp enough to peel paint. "Is he..." Her voice cracked, then steadied. "Is he alive?"

Rue nodded quickly. "Doc got to him fast. But it looked bad. I think someone jumped him. Hit him with something heavy, maybe from the mine."

Wynona swore again, pacing the spotless tiles. Finally, she let out a gusty sigh and dropped into a chair. "He's got a hard head. He'll live. But fools like him don't deserve the second chances they keep getting." She pulled two more cupcakes from the container and slid them onto plates. One she pushed toward Rue. "Eat. If you're going to darken my doorstep with gossip and doom, you can at least share the sugar."

Rue sat, peeling the wrapper with shaky fingers. She and Wynona chewed in silence, the soft crunch of sprinkles and the muffled hum of the fridge the only sounds in the bright kitchen.

Wynona dusted off her hands. Her sharp gaze cut back to Rue. "All right, girl. Ask your questions. Maybe I'll answer, maybe I won't."

That was almost polite for Wynona. She wasn't snapping like the other day. "Uh..." She shifted in her chair. Where did you even start with a woman who could probably hex your toenails off for fun?

"Spit it out," Wynona barked.

"Fine." Rue inhaled and let the words tumble before she chickened out. "I found Ruth's notes. And some journals. And, uh...a witchy room."

The hex witch snorted so hard it could've doubled as a foghorn. "Of course you did. Ruth loved her little theatrics. But her so-called 'curse-breaking' skills were a mess. Half the time, she made more work for the rest of us. Didn't make her popular around here."

Bristling, Rue glared. Ruth might not have been perfect, but she was *hers*. "Well, her 'theatrics' left me with messages on a mirror. Things like *keep it buried, don't trust the gold, watch your back, don't trust anyone.* That, plus a bunch of notes about suppression, barriers, forcing people away..."

That got Wynona's attention. Her head tilted, eyes narrowing in a calculating way. "That doesn't sound like Ruth trying to break a curse. Sounds like she was protecting something. Scaring others off. Warding, not unraveling. Not her normal style."

Rue's throat went dry. "You're saying she wasn't just poking at old curses?"

"I'm saying she must have had her reasons." Wynona leaned back in her chair. "But don't go thinking she and I got along. I found her arrogant. And I'd wager she thought the same of me."

Rue almost smiled at that. It was the most honest thing Wynona had said.

"And yes," Wynona went on. "I sell the odd hex on the witch black market. No sense pretending otherwise. Ruth would break them whenever she sniffed one out. Then some anonymous tattletale would report me." Her mouth twisted. "Not hard to trace a hex back to its maker. She knew it. And I'd bet my left eye my goody-two-shoes sister, Lynette, tattled plenty too. Those two were as thick as thieves, especially after Ruth fell out with Delilah."

Letting that sink in, Rue risked another question. "What about the cursed gold? Do you think it's real?"

That earned her a belly laugh so loud it rattled the daisy vase on the counter. "You've got gold fever, don't you?"

"I couldn't care less about the gold. But it keeps coming up."

Wynona's mirth faded, replaced by a grim look. "I think it's real, yes. And I think Grimshaw sacrificed the miners who dug the vault to protect it. Blood magic at its nastiest. He silenced them and sealed the vault with their deaths."

Rue's skin crawled. She couldn't imagine how horrific it would be to be sealed away. Unknown and missed.

"I don't dabble in blood. But a few witches who did around that time packed up and left Nevada right before Grimshaw vanished. *Cowards.* But it probably saved their skins. He had a reputation for being ruthless. If he thought they'd open their mouths, he'd have killed them, too."

"Do you think there are Grimshaw descendants?"

"No clue." Wynona shrugged. "If there are, they'd be fools to come back to Ghost Vein. This town doesn't forgive. Doesn't forget. And some of those who disappeared back then still have family here." She hesitated. "I did hear a rumor his wife and kid headed east. Boston, maybe. After that? No idea."

Rue's stomach tightened. More puzzle pieces and none of them fit neatly. "What about Tobias, the tour guide who died? Did he come here asking for hexes?

That drew a sour face. Wynona leaned closer, voice dropping. "He came to me, bought some hexes. Said he wanted to keep certain people away from sealed areas of the mine...especially Arnold." She flushed faintly, pink rising in her pale cheeks. "I made sure nothing I gave him would touch Arnold. I...adjusted things."

Rue nearly choked on her own spit. Wynona, Ghost Vein's resident hex-dealer, was sweet on crusty old Arnold.

"He wasn't the only one sniffing around either," Wynona continued briskly. "That annoying phone girl wanted to interview me. Ask questions about the cursed gold. I shut her down. I don't need that type of attention. But she was pushy."

Maribel. The only pushy, annoying, phone girl Rue knew currently. "Anyone else?"

"Josiah Evans had made some noise about buying some hexes to protect the museum's displays. He was worried about some important artifact going missing. And the mayor has been leaving messages lately." Wynona made a face. "I try to avoid law enforcement and the council. Both are bad news."

All her suspects. What a surprise. At least Letty Navarro's name wasn't mentioned this time. Rue wondered if the important artifact Josiah had been worried about was the old piece of paper and the gold Tobias had been holding when he died. "Thanks, Wynona. I appreciate it."

"Don't take appreciation, but the sugar paid your tab."

Wynona nodded at the cupcakes. "Now, you gotta leave. I got a client coming, and he doesn't want anyone knowing he does business with me." She stood, showing Rue to a side door.

"Would I recognize your client?"

"Well, now. You might if you hung around until the coast is clear." Wynona gave an exaggerated wink, then shoved Rue out the side door.

Rue crept around the side of Wynona's house, pressing herself against the weathered boards. She leaned out just enough to see who Wynona's mysterious client was.

The man on the porch tugged the brim of his hat low, head ducked as though he hoped the shadows might swallow him whole.

Rue's eyes widened. *Josiah Evans?* The museum curator. Another neat little checkmark on her growing list of suspects. Wynona had mentioned him earlier, but this was concrete confirmation that he was dabbling in something dodgy.

Her father's voice echoed in her head. *Curious and curiouser, Rue-girl. When men hide their errands, the errands are worth knowing.*

And Josiah was *definitely* hiding. The way he shuffled inside, almost hugging the doorframe, screamed *don't see me.* Which only guaranteed Rue was going to obsess about it later. Why did Ghost Vein's most buttoned-up man need Wynona's hexes? And why keep it a secret?

When the door shut behind him, Rue exhaled and darted back toward Cassie's scooter. She kicked it into life and took off, heart skipping with the kind of adrenaline that was half triumph, half panic.

The Silver Tongue was warm and bright when she slid back inside. For a blissful moment, she almost felt normal again. Then Rue spotted Jesse leaning across the counter from Taz, his grin turned up to full wattage.

"Seriously?" Rue muttered.

Jesse glanced up at Rue, lazy charm dripping from his smile. "Well, if it isn't our intrepid sleuth. How's my favorite trouble magnet?"

"Pretty sure that title comes with a death wish." Rue slipped onto a stool. "What are you doing here, Jesse? Run out of engines to flirt with?"

"Garage is clear. Except for your sweet car." Jesse shrugged. "Still waiting on a part, but I thought I'd check in. Make sure you're okay after...y'know? Arnold."

Rue's chest tightened. "I'm managing. Have you heard anything about his condition?"

"As far as I know, he's holding on. Cole would have more information. Meanwhile you can update me on your snooping."

"I thought you didn't want details. So you wouldn't have to spill to Sheriff Grumpy."

Jesse spread his hands, feigning innocence. "Doesn't mean I'm not curious. Watching you two work the same case but from different angles? Better than Netflix. Besides...when you're not driving me nuts, you're entertaining."

"You mean when I'm not driving *Sheriff Grumpy* nuts."

Taz smacked Jesse's arm before he could retort. "Don't encourage her." She made cutting motions to her throat before her hand dropped away.

Rubbing her temple, Rue was suddenly aware how wide Taz's eyes were and how big the grin Jesse sported. "He's behind me, isn't he?"

"Yes," came the deep rumble. "Sheriff Grumpy is."

Rue twisted around. Cole stood just inside the door, wearing plain jeans and a fitted shirt instead of his uniform, which somehow made him look both less official and more... dangerous. A smile tugged at the corner of his mouth.

Rue's cheeks burned. "Just be glad I didn't call you Sheriff Dimples." Their last interaction and how she'd stormed off in a huff played through her head. She should probably apologize, but honestly, she had no clue how to broach the subject without looking like an awkward idiot.

His smirk widened.

Fantastic. He's going to file that new nickname away and whip it out the second I let my guard down.

"I hope you're not investigating. Finding Arnold was enough excitement for you," Cole muttered.

She attempted her most innocent expression. Unfortunately, Rue's face felt stiff, and Jesse burst out laughing.

"She looks constipated."

Taz groaned. "Would you *stop*."

Rue ignored them, clinging to the only thing that mattered. "Arnold? Please tell me you have an update."

Cole's smile faded, replaced by a sober steadiness. "He's in a serious condition. Alive, but hasn't woken up yet. I'll let you know when I hear more."

Rue nodded, throat tight. The words sat heavy between them.

Taz dived in to fill the awkward silence. "Maybe Rue needs a distraction. Tomorrow's Saturday..." She darted a speaking look at Jesse.

Jesse perked up like she'd handed him a challenge. "The reenactment in the square. Cole can take you. Keep your spirits up."

Rue felt her face ignite. "Excuse me...what..."

Clearly thrown, for a moment Cole looked flustered. Then his jaw squared, sheriff-stubbornness in full effect. "Come with me to the reenactment. It'll be fun. And the mayor's making some kind of announcement."

Rue's mouth opened. Closed. Opened again. *Abort, abort, abort.*

"C'mon," Jesse coaxed, his grin positively wicked. "Think of all the clues you might nose out while you're there."

The sheriff shot him a glare that promised retribution. "Stop helping."

Rue blurted, "Fine. I'll go."

Cole's expression flickered with satisfaction before he carefully tucked it away. "You'll enjoy it. As long as you keep out of trouble."

Rue growled under her breath.

Taz shoved Jesse toward Cole. "Enough. Before you both put your feet so far in your mouths you choke."

They stumbled outside, and Cole immediately hooked Jesse in a headlock. They scuffled their way along the boardwalk, Jesse yelping as Cole mussed up his hair.

Taz shook her head as if she couldn't believe either of them had survived this long. "It's a wonder those two get dates."

Dates.

The word ricocheted through Rue's brain. Her eyes widened. Oh no. She'd just agreed to a date with Sheriff Dimples.

And she didn't know which was scarier...chasing a murderer or going on a date.

THIRTEEN

A date. With Cole Dawson. Sheriff Dimples himself.

The next afternoon, Rue stood frozen in front of her wardrobe.

Her night had been one long, restless loop filled with dreams of Arnold lying pale and still. Nightmares of hands dragging her down into the mine. Then jolting awake to worry about what on earth she'd wear.

She flipped through her clothing, muttering, "Nope. Too funeral. Too librarian. Too *I-have-no-clue-what-to-wear-so-let's-throw-this-on...*" As if on cue, the hangers rattled softly. A soft *shuff-shuff-shuff* of fabric brushed her hands. One sleeve dropped, then another. Before she could react, the wardrobe doors creaked, then slammed shut with a decisive thump.

Rue yelped, spinning around. When she turned back, a neat little pile had been laid out on the bed. Dark jeans, a fitted dark blue, long-sleeved shirt, a cute brown leather jacket, and ankle boots to match. "Ruth?"

The air shifted, cool with a lavender scent.

Rue grinned despite herself. "Thanks, Aunt Ruth. I

could get used to having a ghostly fashion consultant." She ran her fingers over the clothes. "Pretty sure that creepy tour guide isn't the ghost picking out my ankle boots. So, thanks again, Aunt Ruth."

She pulled the outfit closer, shaking her head. Only a few weeks ago, the idea of a ghost in her apartment would've sent her bolting for the door. Now she was basically trading wardrobe tips with one. Her mother would be horrified. Her father, on the other hand, would've been delighted.

The thought made her throat tighten. She made a mental note to try calling her mom again. Maybe enough time had passed since her move to Ghost Vein for her mother to pick up the phone. *Maybe.* Rue took a steadying breath, changed, and headed downstairs.

The Silver Tongue smelled of lemon cleaner as she stepped into the café. The afternoon light slanted across the polished tables where Taz, Cassie, and Thomas were tidying up.

Cassie looked up and let out a long, appreciative whistle. "Well, well. Look at the boss. You're smokin', Rue."

Thomas went pink, trying to focus on wiping a table instead of looking at her.

Taz smiled warmly. "You look lovely. I'll see you there. Just want to finish up here first, then I'll head over."

Rue felt a stab of guilt. "You sure? I feel bad leaving you to clean up while I...y'know?"

Cassie rolled her eyes so hard Rue thought they might stick. "This is a *big* thing. Sheriff Dateless hasn't so much as let the matchmaking mamas corner him at a bake sale in two years. And you?" She grinned like a loon. "You've snatched him out from under their noses. This is epic."

Rue narrowed her eyes. "You're all going to keep an eye on us, aren't you?"

All three nodded in unison.

"And laugh?" Rue added.

Taz smirked. "Lots and lots of laughing."

Rue sneered at her employees but couldn't quite suppress a smile. She smoothed her shirt. "Like my shirt? Ruth picked it out."

"She did?" Taz's face lit up. "That's so exciting. It means she's getting stronger. Maybe soon we'll actually be able to see her."

"Even if it freaks me out, I'd rather see her than find cryptic stalker messages on my mirror," Rue admitted.

The group chuckled, but Rue felt a flicker of warmth beneath the nerves. Maybe, just maybe, she wasn't completely alone in this.

A firm knock rattled the saloon door. Before Rue could move, Cassie darted across and swung it open.

Cole and Jesse stood framed in the doorway, both looking faintly impatient.

Cassie, however, dissolved into giggles.

The men exchanged a wary glance. "What?" Jesse asked.

"Oh, nothing. Just picturing all the town's matchmaking mamas crying into their potluck dishes when they see you two together today." Cassie's grin widened.

Cole's jaw tightened, and Rue's stomach did a nervous drop.

Before Cassie could keep teasing, Taz swooped in, grabbed her by the elbow, and herded both her and Thomas toward the kitchen. "Out. Finish cleaning, then you can go too. Shoo."

Cassie cackled all the way down the hall with Thomas following close behind.

Rue rubbed her sweaty palms against her jeans, only to stiffen when Jesse leaned in with a conspiratorial wink.

"Don't worry, I'm not horning in on your date. I'm just going to keep Taz in line."

"Ha," Taz snorted. "You wish. You couldn't handle me."

Both Rue and Cole paled at the word *date*.

Taz cooed at their expressions. "Awwww. How sweet."

Jesse barked out a laugh. "I doubt the criminals Cole drags in think he's sweet."

"Those are completely separate things," Taz snapped. "Right now, they're sweet." She flapped her hands at them, an impatient mother hen. "Now, go. Out. Before Jesse makes it worse."

Cole gave Jesse a long-suffering look before gently steering Rue toward the door.

Outside, the air was crisp with the faint smell of kettle corn drifting along Main Street. Cole shoved his hands in his pockets. "It's not far. Just a short walk, if you don't mind."

She managed a smile. "That's fine." *Maybe I should nix the idea of dating, focus on sleuthing.*

They started off walking side by side, both stiff with awkwardness. Gaps opened in the conversation, silence stretched. Rue fiddled with her jacket zipper, while Cole glanced at passing windows like he'd never seen them before.

Finally, he cleared his throat and began pointing out landmarks, as if giving a mini tour might patch the holes. "That bakery's been here since the eighteen-eighties. And over there's the old assay office. Tourists love it."

Rue nodded, clutching at normalcy until a sudden draft

teased across the back of her legs. She slapped both hands protectively over her backside.

Cole stared, baffled. "What are you doing?"

Rue straightened, cheeks flaming. "When I first moved here, one of the miner ghosts pinched my butt. So, anytime I feel wind and there's no actual wind, I…uh…cover my bases."

His lips twitched, then Cole chuckled. The sound rolled through Rue, melting the tension.

They walked closer after that, and the words came easier.

"The reenactment's in front of the library," Cole said.

Rue perked up. "I've been trying to track the librarian down, but she's impossible to pin."

He shot her a knowing look. "Letty avoids people when she knows they want something. Especially if it's about the cursed gold."

Rue spluttered, then laughed. "Fine. Guilty. It's about the gold."

They passed the general store, where Delilah leaned in the doorway, smirking at them. Before Rue could retort, a small clatter sounded, and Nacho the goat trotted out, bleating merrily as he fell into step behind them like an unofficial chaperone.

Rue's pulse stuttered when Cole reached down and laced his fingers through hers. She nearly tripped. *Please don't let my hands still be sweaty*, she chanted mentally. Rue shot him a sideways glance, half-panicked, half-thrilled.

He gave her a small smile and tightened his grip.

Rue gulped and focused on the street ahead, where the crowd thickened near the library. Tourists jostled for space, craning necks as reenactors set their stage. Amidst the bustle, Rue spotted Maribel Knox.

The podcaster stood near the library steps, talking to someone cloaked in the shadows of the library.

A prickle slid down Rue's spine. She hated the fact that Maribel always seemed to be looming wherever she ended up. Of course, that could also be the way the annoying woman flirted with a certain someone.

Rue edged through the crowd, letting Cole lead. The smell of fried dough mixed with the chatter of tourists. Main Street buzzed. Booths along the boardwalk sold kettle corn and candied nuts. Kids darted around with paper hats and wooden toy guns, while two men in dusters argued loudly about historical accuracy. It seemed Ghost Vein loved a spectacle, especially if it involved the cursed mine.

"Don't look like you're going to your own execution."

She nearly jumped out of her boots. Cole had stopped beside her, a questioning look on his face.

Her mouth went dry. Out of uniform, with the afternoon light catching his dark hair and those aggravating dimples threatening at the corners of his mouth, he looked far too human and far too handsome for her peace of mind.

"Execution feels about right," Rue muttered. "Half the town is watching."

"They're always watching. Small town people have nothing to do but gossip." Cole lips twitched. "You just notice it more because you think they care."

"Gee, thanks," Rue deadpanned.

From across the square, Cassie waved both arms like an overexcited kid. Taz stood beside her, mouthing *have fun* with exaggerated eyebrow wiggles. Thomas gave an awkward thumbs-up. Jesse just stood grinning at their antics.

Rue groaned. "I should've worn a disguise."

"Relax." Cole steered her toward the library where the

crowd was thickest. "All you have to do is stand there, smile occasionally, and don't trip over any cowboys."

"Easy for you to say. You don't have Cassie betting I'll fall on my face before the mayor finishes her speech."

His smirk widened. "How much is the pot up to?"

"I heard fifty bucks."

Cole chuckled, the sound low and warm enough Rue's stomach did a flip.

They wove through the throng toward an open stretch of boardwalk. "Here's good." He positioned her so she faced the front of the library.

"Good for what? You still haven't told me exactly what the reenactment is."

"You need to experience Ghost Vein in its glory. In other words, stand back and enjoy the show. We just have to get through the mayor's announcement first."

Rue squeezed his hand and settled in to enjoy the moment. For once, sleuthing and the investigation didn't top her list.

Mayor Flint stood at the top of the library steps, a vision in a pressed peach-colored suit with square shoulder pads and the kind of slick smile that looked like she'd practiced in front of a mirror for hours. The mayor lifted both hands. "Citizens of Ghost Vein, if I could have your attention."

The crowd silenced...mostly. A few tourists kept chatting, but locals leaned forward, expectant.

"I'm Mayor Agnes Flint, and I'm here to support this fine town of ours."

Applause thundered, whistles rising above the clapping.

The mayor waited, then spread her hands again. "History is the lifeblood of Ghost Vein. Without it, we would not stand here today. So, in honor of that history, the council has decided to award a renovation grant to upgrade our beloved library's archives."

A murmur rippled through the crowd.

"The archives will be temporarily closing," Mayor Flint continued. "But only until the work is complete. Then the library will reopen, stronger and more accessible than ever."

From somewhere in the back came a hiss. Then a curse. Rue spun, scanning faces, but whoever it was had already ducked out of sight. Her skin prickled. Someone wasn't impressed with the library getting an upgrade. Or was it the fact that the archives had to close during the renovation?

"And," the mayor pressed on, "this festival weekend celebrating our heritage is officially open." She gave a bright, brittle smile as people tried to shout questions. But she ignored them, already edging backward.

A roar broke out from the edge of the square. "This is favoritism." Josiah Evans, the museum curator, was red-faced and shouting. A young woman clutched at his sleeve, trying to pull him back, but he dug in his heels. "The museum deserves that grant, not the library. What does the librarian have on you?"

Gasps rippled through the crowd.

The mayor's jaw tightened. She stepped forward again, chin lifted. "The funding must be distributed fairly. The museum has already received more than its share. Now it is the library's turn."

Boos and claps collided in a messy storm of opinion.

Mayor Flint stepped down, conferring with a short, silver-haired woman in the crowd.

Rue elbowed Cole. "Who's that?"

He frowned. "That's Letty Navarro. The librarian. And I'll admit, this isn't the move I expected. The library was just renovated a year ago. Why funnel more money to the archives?" He shook his head. "Doesn't sit right."

Her thoughts whirled. Maybe it wasn't about fairness. Maybe it was about keeping things buried. What was in those archives the mayor didn't want people finding? "Guess I'll have to step up my librarian stalking before they lock those doors."

Cole gave her a sidelong glance. "If we bump into her, I'll introduce you."

Rue was about to answer when a commotion rolled down the street.

His posture straightened and a grin tugged his mouth as he turned Rue toward the noise.

Two men staggered into view, one dressed as a miner, the other as a cowboy. Their voices rose in a booming, exaggerated argument. The cowboy slapped his thigh. The miner pulled out an old pistol and swayed dramatically, taking a swig from a battered whiskey bottle.

"How accurate is this supposed to be?"

"More accurate than the council would like." Cole's grin widened. "Drinking and gunfights were daily events around here."

Before Rue could reply, a soft body pressed against her leg. She looked down to find Nacho, Ghost Vein's resident goat menace, sidling up against her. She sighed. "I really need to start carrying snacks." Across the street, she spotted Taz, Cassie, Thomas, and Jesse weaving through the crowd, all waving when they caught her eye. Rue lifted a hand, just as a sudden gust of wind spiraled into a dust devil, stinging her eyes. She covered her face. When she blinked the grit away, she heard Cole curse.

The miner staggered, this time for real. His arm flailed

and his pistol clattered onto the street. He stumbled over a horse trough and crashed down hard.

The crowd gasped.

Cole swore again, brushing Rue's arm. "Stay here." Then he shoved through the gathering bodies, his tall frame disappearing in a swell of onlookers.

Rue waited, craning for a glimpse, her nerves jangling. After a few restless minutes, she decided to use the chaos. Maybe she could track down Letty...

"Howdy, Rue."

She turned and nearly tripped over Maribel Knox, who appeared with her phone raised high, filming the whole thing. Her glossy smile beamed as she aimed the camera at herself and Rue in quick succession.

"Isn't this incredible?" Maribel gushed. "So authentic. Almost too authentic, don't you think?" She turned her lens on Rue. "And there's my good friend, Rue. Always in the middle of the action."

Rue forced a tight smile. *Friend, my foot.*

Maribel tittered. "Thanks again for your help at the bar the other night. Cole was such a gentleman, wasn't he?" Her smile sharpened. "And your saloon looks so much better now that you've taken over."

"Excuse me?"

"Oh, I just meant it looks...livelier. Ruth had her charm, of course. But you've really spruced the place up."

Condescending. Backhanded. Rue's blood boiled. "Ruth did a good job."

Batting her lashes, Maribel shrugged. "Take it however you want, darling."

The girl radiated *mean girl vibes* like no one's business. Rue wrinkled her nose. She thought she'd left this kind of behavior back at school.

"And I couldn't help noticing..." Maribel leaned closer. "Were you and the sheriff walking up together? Was it a date?"

Rue opened her mouth, but Maribel steamrolled right over her.

"Oh, poor thing. Left all alone already? Guess work is more important to him." She winked and flounced off, murmuring into her phone.

Speechless, Rue stared after her. How could anyone be that condescending with a straight face? She'd just decided to march up to the library when a familiar shadow loomed beside her.

Cole.

"Sorry," he said, voice low. "Got pulled in longer than I wanted. You okay?"

Rue waved it off, swallowing the sting Maribel had left behind. "I'm fine. How's the miner?"

"Doc just arrived. I'm going to see what she says. If I have to help get him settled, I might have to reschedule our date."

Her cheeks flamed at the word. *Date.* Still terrifying. "That's fine," she blurted, trying to sound casual and failing miserably. "I'll...wander. Find Taz. Don't worry."

Relief softened his shoulders. "Thanks." He gave her a nod and vanished back into the crowd.

Exhaling hard, Rue pushed through clusters of tourists until she edged near the library. Voices drifted from the shadows of the side alley near the building. She stopped, ears straining.

Josiah Evans again, his tone sharp, desperate. "This isn't fair, Agnes. You promised funding for the expansion."

The mayor's clipped reply floated out, cool as iced tea.

"The archives are overdue. It's their turn. This is a council decision."

"That's rubbish," Josiah spat. "The council is led by *you*. The cursed gold is the town's biggest draw. It's historically important, and it should be exploited. Think of the revenue."

"The gold may be important, but chasing childish treasure maps is not. Throwing money away on a missing map helps no one."

"That's not fair. It's not what you told me when I first approached you."

The mayor's voice dropped, low and pointed. "If you find the complete map...then we might talk."

Rue leaned closer, listening hard.

Mayor Flint spotted Rue and cut the conversation short, heels clicking as she swept away.

Josiah cursed under his breath, then stormed in the opposite direction.

A treasure map? Rue's thoughts whirled. Her mind flashed to Tobias in the alley, clutching that torn, tattered paper with the nugget of gold. She'd nearly forgotten it in the chaos of finding Arnold. But what if that scrap had been part of something bigger? A map? A clue to Grimshaw's hidden stash? Definitely worth killing for. The mayor's name kept cropping up. Just like Letty's. And neither one sat right in Rue's gut. She kept moving, weaving through knots of townsfolk until she almost collided with a familiar figure.

Isla. Today she wore jeans and a flowery rust-colored shirt, her gloves a perfect match. "Sorry. I'm not the most coordinated on my feet. Especially in a crowd."

"Fancy seeing you here," Isla chirped, falling into step beside Rue. They paused just outside the library doors. "It gets busy because of the tourists. They love the western reenactments."

Rue opened her mouth to ask a question, but Isla beat her to it, her smile sly.

"Before you ask, there's no treasure map."

"Excuse me?"

"I heard them too." Isla's tone was casual, but her eyes glinted with amusement. "The rumors are wrong. There was never a treasure map. Not really. What Grimshaw commissioned was a map of the mine. A complete, accurate, working map. It's been missing since he vanished."

Rue nodded.

"The story is Grimshaw memorized it." Isla lowered her voice. "And then cut it into pieces. Supposedly he hid them all over town, just in case. Rumors, of course."

Rue's mind flashed back to Tobias's scrap of paper. Torn edges. Jagged lines. Could that piece have been from Grimshaw's map? Her stomach churned. "Thanks." Rue forced her voice to steady. "Anyone else sniffing around for it?"

Isla tilted her head thoughtfully. "The tour guide. He was always at the museum, pestering Josiah. Taking photos of the displays. Honestly, it seemed like Tobias was pressuring him. I had the feeling they were up to something shady. No proof, of course. Just a hunch."

Suspicions rumbled around Rue's head. *Tobias and Josiah.* Secret meetings. Artifacts changing hands. And maybe pieces of a map hidden in plain sight. If Josiah kept records, and of course he would, they'd be in a ledger or a catalogue somewhere. She just needed to track it down. "Appreciate you talking to me, Isla."

Isla beamed. "Need anything else, just let me know." She gave a wave and disappeared into the tourist crowd.

Rue turned, lost in thought until Cole popped up beside her. She yelped, staggering back. "I thought you were with the doc?"

Cole steadied her by the elbows, his eyes searching her face. "Doc's got it handled. The miner will pull through. I can walk you back to the saloon, if you want."

Relief loosened Rue's shoulders. "That'd be nice. I'm glad the miner wasn't hurt."

"Not hurt unless you count breaking his whiskey bottle. Apparently, the fool thought he should be authentic. He's as drunk as a skunk." They fell into step together, the crowd thinning as they left the library behind. Cole's jaw ticked. "I'm sorry our date got..." He hesitated. "Our afternoon got interrupted. But it's the job."

Rue waved a hand, trying not to think about how nice it sounded when he said *our*. "Don't worry about it. It wasn't really a date anyway. Jesse kind of shoved us into it."

Cole's mouth curved. "Then I'll just have to do better next time."

Rue's heart skipped, then Nacho the goat barreled between them like a furry wrecking ball. Yelping, Rue stumbled. Her hands shot out and grabbed the only solid thing in reach...*Cole*.

He caught her, strong arms circling her waist as her boots slid across the wood of the boardwalk. Rue clutched his shirt, pulse hammering. "Well," she blurted, cheeks burning. "Guess I'm falling for you. Or maybe falling on you? At least it was a goat this time, not a ghost pinching my butt." Her laugh came out nervous, too loud. "Goats and ghosts might be better company than some people." Rue tried not to grimace. She really needed to stop talking. As soon as she got nervous, she babbled. Not a great date impression.

Cole didn't answer. His gaze had locked on hers, steady and intense. His arms still wrapped around Rue, the warmth of him radiating through her jacket. The world narrowed down to the faint scuff of his boots and the rough whisper of her own breath.

"Rue," he murmured.

She froze, holding her breath as he leaned in. The air between them sizzled, something unspoken...

And then a gaggle of rowdy tourists shoved past, jostling them apart.

Rue stumbled back, cheeks blazing. Wow, her date skills were worse than she originally thought. She cleared her throat a few times.

Cole stepped away, his hands falling to his sides. "You okay?"

"Fine." Rue's voice squeaked. She coughed. "Thanks for...catching me."

His smile was slow, deliberate. "I'll always catch you."

Her stomach flipped, traitorous and giddy. Cole definitely didn't need any dating practice. He had it down pat.

They walked the rest of the way in silence, tension still buzzing between them, until the Silver Tongue came into view.

Rue stopped at the steps, fiddling with her sleeve. "Thanks. For taking me to the reenactment. Even if it wasn't a normal date."

Cole's mouth tugged at the corner, almost a smile. "Hopefully it will be better next time. Stay safe, Rue."

And before she could answer, he was already striding down the street, muttering to himself. Rue stared after him, speechless. *Next time?*

Nacho bleated and head-butted her hip. The miniature goat had followed them from the library. Rue sighed, rubbing the goat's ears. "You're right. Sheriff Dimples is not the point. Dating him would just be a distraction I don't need." She glanced once more at Cole's retreating figure, her chest tight.

"What I *want*," Rue told the goat softly, "is another matter."

FOURTEEN

The saloon was shut tight for the day, which normally meant Rue would be holed up inside trying to learn how to run the Silver Tongue or trying to figure out her curse-breaking. Instead, Taz had declared it a mission day.

"Why are we here?" Rue stared at the small hospital as they headed inside. She was surprised a place as tiny as Ghost Vein had one, but with all the tourists it was probably a necessity.

"I baked." Taz thrust a plastic container of cupcakes under Rue's nose. "We're going to see Arnold."

"I thought you didn't bake?"

"I told you. I don't bake for the café. But that doesn't mean I can't bake." Taz tapped the cupcake container Rue held. "I thought Arnold might like the cupcakes he missed out on when he was attacked. And you can ask him some questions." Taz nudged her friend.

"You are a very smart woman."

"I know. That's why you're giving me a raise." Taz smiled sweetly at her boss.

"Let's discuss that later. When we aren't snooping. I say

we should've brought coffee," Rue muttered, eyes flicking toward the busy nurses' station. "Cupcakes are a breakfast food in some cultures. And a good bribe. If Cole catches us here, he isn't going to be impressed."

"Never underestimate the power of bribery," Taz replied cheerfully.

They were halfway through explaining themselves to a pleasant-looking nurse when trouble walked in wearing a badge.

Deputy Mayhew.

Cole's deputy was all sour-faced suspicion wrapped in a law enforcement uniform that looked a bit tighter than it should be. Cole radiated stoic cowboy lawman energy. Mayhew gave off mall-cop-in-a-bad-mood vibes. His pale blond hair receded, and his once-fit frame had turned into what Rue kindly dubbed stress belly.

"Visiting hours aren't for nosy civilians with an axe to grind," Mayhew snapped, glaring at them.

"I'm not here to grind any axes. Or swing them. Unless provoked."

"You're not funny, Ms. Maddox. And you're not welcome here. Arnold Granger is a victim of a crime. You've got no business trying to benefit from his pain."

Rue's mouth dropped open. "Excuse me? I found him. I'm not benefiting. I'm worried. And I have cupcakes for him." She held the cupcake container up to Mayhew's face. "See? Cupcakes. Baked this morning."

Mayhew crossed his arms. "Right. And how many bodies have you tripped over since you arrived in town? Either you're a magnet for trouble, or you're making it."

It took a full beat for Rue's brain to catch up. Did he just imply she was some kind of killer groupie? *Speechless.*

Completely speechless. Rue Maddox, awkward and mouthy, had nothing.

"You absolute meathead," Taz snapped, stepping between Rue and Mayhew. "You've got some nerve accusing her. You think murder makes for a good hobby?"

Mayhew looked startled for half a second, then narrowed his eyes. "Should've figured you'd defend your boss, Moreno. Looking out for your job, I guess."

"Oh, and you were always a class-A jack—"

"Enough."

Cole's voice cut through the tension. He strode down the hallway, boots quiet but his presence loud. His badge glinted under the harsh lights, but there was no warmth in his eyes. Not like last night.

Cold.

Distant.

Sheriff Mode: Activated.

He didn't greet Rue. Didn't even look at her. He stepped between them all, nodding once at the nurse who wisely found somewhere else to be.

"Deputy, take a walk."

Mayhew opened his mouth to protest.

"Now." Cole's tone iced over.

With a last scowl and a mumbled insult Rue couldn't quite catch, Mayhew stalked off.

Rue turned to Cole. "What is that guy's problem with me?"

Cole didn't answer right away. Instead, he folded his arms, his posture stiff. "What are you doing here?"

"Taz brought cupcakes. We wanted to check on Arnold."

"He paid for the cupcakes but never got them," Taz

added. "We're just delivering them. That's not illegal, right?"

For a second, it looked like Cole might argue. But then something in his shoulders relaxed a touch. "Fine. Five minutes. No questions. He's still recovering."

He moved aside, and Rue brushed past him, the chill of his mood clinging to her skin. He didn't look at her. And after their almost-kiss, the cold stung.

Inside the room, Arnold was propped up on pillows, watching daytime TV. His face lit up when he saw them and his gaze fastened on the cake container.

"Hey. Did you bring the ones with lemon frosting?"

"Of course I did," Taz said with a grin, setting the container on his bed.

Rue gave him a small wave. "Glad you're awake, Arnold."

"Glad you're not another hallucination." He squinted at Rue. "The last one was a goat in a nurse's uniform."

Taz snorted.

Rue tried to smile, but her heart wasn't in it.

Cole stood in the doorway like a statue, checking his phone. Then, as if on cue, it rang.

He stepped into the hallway to take the call but turned back for a moment. "Do not question the victim. I'll be back in two minutes to walk you out."

Rue watched him leave, confusion and frustration tangling in her chest.

Last night, he'd stared at her as if she mattered. Today, he wouldn't even look her in the eye. She refused to dwell on whatever was going on in the sheriff's mind and focused on her snooping. Rue waited until Cole's heavy boots faded down the hallway and the door clicked shut behind him.

She turned to Arnold, who was licking lemon frosting off his thumb.

"Hey, can I ask you something?"

Arnold's eyes twinkled. "Only if I get to finish this cupcake."

"You drive a hard bargain." Rue pulled up a chair. "What do you remember about the attack?"

Arnold frowned. "Not much. It's all fuzzy. I remember walking out of the mine...and then—wham—something slams into my head. But after that..." His gaze shifted to her. "I remember you."

"Me?"

"You were talking to me. Telling me I'd be okay. I think I thought you were an angel at first. Then you said something about hitting someone with a phone. So, I figured you probably weren't."

Taz snorted.

Heat rose in Rue's cheeks. "Well, I guess a temper rules out an angel."

He grinned crookedly. "I'll take your help instead."

"Do you remember anything else? Anything weird that happened at work that day?"

He scratched the side of his head, careful to avoid the thick white bandage. "I was supposed to meet with the mayor. That much I know. But I don't remember why. I remember hearing a noise...like someone kicking gravel. I turned and then I blacked out. Nothing until your voice pulled me back."

Rue sat back. "You don't remember what hit you?"

"Sheriff said it was some kind of iron thing from the mine, I think."

Her spine went ramrod straight. "Wait. Iron thing, like a branding iron?"

Arnold's brows lifted. "That's what he said. A Silver Vein Mine branding iron."

Her breath caught. *That's why it looked familiar.* "I've seen one of those before. At the museum. It was in one of the Grimshaw displays behind glass. Could it be the same one?"

Arnold's face creased with thought. "Maybe. We've got another one in the mine museum too. Well, had. There's been...some stuff disappearing lately."

Rue's brows shot up. "Disappearing?"

"Tools, trinkets, old rusted equipment, little things at first. We thought the things were just misplaced. Then we figured maybe someone was helping themselves after hours."

"That's two museums with things going missing now."

"And a branding iron turning up as a weapon," Taz agreed with Rue.

"Do you think the thief could be the same person as the attacker?" Rue asked the old guide.

Arnold frowned. "Could be. Or maybe they're covering their tracks. People have been poking around the mine lately. Asking questions. Looking for...something."

"Like what?"

"I don't know," he said. "I thought it was just the usual ghost chasers and treasure hunters, but maybe not. That day, the mayor said she wanted to talk in person about something. I don't remember much more. Just that she called me, said she wanted to meet. And then..." He gestured vaguely toward his bandaged head.

"Hang on." Rue frowned. "You said the mayor called you for the meeting, not you contacting her?"

"She wanted the meeting with me. I thought it was weird. I'm only a tour guide. But she was pretty adamant."

Huh? Interesting lie the mayor just got caught out in. "And you have no idea what she wanted to talk about?"

He shook his head, then winced. "Just...the mine. She said it was important. But I didn't think anything was out of place that day. Nothing strange, aside from the usual town weirdness."

"Well, it's a short list of answers," Rue muttered. "And an even shorter one if Cole finds out I was asking questions."

Right on cue, the door creaked open.

Cole stepped in, phone still in hand, brows drawn together in mild suspicion. "Everything good in here?"

Rue flashed her most innocent smile. "Just cupcake delivery and small talk."

Arnold, ever the gentleman, held up his cupcake. "Just two pretty girls keeping an old man company with lemon frosted cupcakes. Can't a guy enjoy his cake in peace?"

Cole didn't quite smile, but his jaw unclenched. "Let's go. Before I get accused of playing favorites."

As they stepped into the hallway, Rue felt the cold close in again. She didn't even try to make conversation. Cole kept his gaze forward, his expression unreadable.

He didn't speak until they reached the front doors. "Next time, don't go behind my back."

Rue stopped short. "Excuse me? Next time, don't make me feel like a criminal for caring."

He didn't respond, just pushed open the door and held it for them.

Taz marched through with a huff.

Rue followed, fighting the instinct to spin around and demand answers. But what was the point? Hot and cold. Flirty one night, frosty the next. The emotional whiplash was getting exhausting.

By the time they stepped out into the crisp sunlight, Rue's jaw clenched tight. "Well, I guess I should be grateful he saved me from a second date worse than the first."

Taz snorted. "Don't mind him. He's just worried about you."

"Probably." Rue deflated a little. "Still sucks, though. And we didn't get much out of Arnold."

"Maybe not. But we've got another potential source we can tap."

Rue narrowed her eyes. "You mean Jesse?"

Taz grinned wickedly. "Nope. I mean downtown. Where all the good gossip and bad decisions live and die."

Rue raised an eyebrow. "Are you suggesting we go flirt with bartenders for information?"

"Why do you go straight to the bar? You don't even drink." Taz shook her head. "Nope, I'm talking about the woman who hears all, Doc Halliday."

Taz bumped her shoulder lightly against Rue's as they walked toward the clinic. "Don't take Cole's behavior too personally. He's just got his game face on."

Rue snorted. "His game face could make ice."

"He's under pressure. The mayor's breathing down his neck, the town's on edge, and now Mayhew's stomping around like a troll with a clipboard."

Rue sighed. "I know, I *know*. It still stings, though. Last night he was all warm and sweet and now..."

"And yet," Taz said slyly, "we still managed to get a few crumbs from Arnold."

"Not enough."

Taz steered them off Main Street toward a squat, tan

brick building nestled between the bank and a stationery shop. The sign above read *Dr. L. Halliday, GP* in faded gold paint. A short gravel path next to the building veered off to a gate, leading to a cozy cottage behind it.

"She lives out the back. Clinic up front, parties out the back when she's in the mood."

A sleepy looking receptionist waved them through with a bored "Heya," and they made their way to the break room. Dr. Halliday sat at a small round table, legs crossed, sipping tea. A plate of cookies sat untouched beside her.

"Girls," Doc Halliday greeted them, beaming. "Come in, come in. Ignore the biscuits, they taste like cardboard. Tea?"

"We're good, thanks. We just wanted to check on Arnold's progress. We saw him at the hospital, and he looks great, but we thought we'd ask the expert."

"Ah, the tough old guy." Halliday set her mug down and waved at the seats across from her. "He's doing fine and healing well. A little grumpy but that's his default. No signs of complications. So he should be released soon."

"What about his memory?" Rue asked. "Is it normal to not remember anything? Will it come back?"

"It's not uncommon. Head injuries are tricky. He may never get the full day back. Or it might trickle in with a dream. Brains are weird. But he's stable, lucid, and strong enough to complain, which is always a good sign. I'll send him to the next town for a scan, just to be safe."

"Sounds good." Taz nodded.

Doc narrowed her eyes at Rue. "Now. Tell me about the date."

"What date?"

"Oh, come off it." The doc grinned. "You and Cole. Don't play coy, Ms. Maddox. I have a nose for these things."

"There wasn't a date," Rue said. "It got interrupted by a drunk miner and then...well, grumpy sheriff face."

Taz smothered a giggle.

"Oh, so nothing *happened* on the date?" Doc said innocently. "That still counts as a date."

Rue dropped her head into her hands. "Why is this town like this?"

"Because it's delightful. And because we live for gossip that doesn't involve hauntings or dead miners."

"She's right. The date was the most exciting thing to happen since the goat got into the mayor's office," Taz added, then frowned. "Well, until you started finding dead people."

Doc nodded. "Still don't know how Nacho picked the lock."

Rue changed the subject with a glare. "So...what's this I hear about night markets on tonight?"

"Oh, yes," Doc said brightly. "Tonight, town center. It's mostly crafts and candles and one guy who makes weird little sock puppets, but the food stalls are great, and the gossip is even better. You two can come with me. We'll nose around, maybe catch Sheriff Grumpy in a better mood."

Rue gave her a look. "You're enjoying this way too much."

"I live in a town where ghosts outnumber dentists. Let me have this."

"Also, Mayhew tried to throw us out of the hospital. That's why Cole was so cranky. He had to shut him down in public." Taz's eyes gleamed as she shared the gossip.

Doc rolled her eyes. "Of *course* he did. Mayhew's been gunning for Cole's job for months now. Figures if he catches Cole stepping out of line, he can take it to the mayor."

"Lovely," Rue muttered. "Now I'm not just a body magnet, I'm a professional liability."

Doc smirked. "All the best women are."

"We'll see you at the market?"

"Wouldn't miss it. And I want full date details. Even if you pretend it wasn't one."

Rue groaned again. "There was no date. It was just a meeting."

Doc just waved them off with a grin and a sip of her tea.

Outside, Taz linked arms with her, grinning. "Told you she'd be all over it."

"I'm changing my name," Rue muttered. "Maybe moving to a different cursed town."

"Too late. You're one of us now. You might as well just give in and join us."

"Are you sure the night markets will be such a good idea? With my track record, who knows how the night will end up?"

"Exactly. It's going to be great."

Famous last words...

FIFTEEN

By the time they wandered down to the town square, the sun had dipped behind the hills and left the town bathed in that golden glow that gave everything a warm ambiance.

The square was a couple of streets over from Main. Trees ringed the park, strung with fairy lights, and a vintage bandstand, one of those old gazebo-style ones that practically begged for a band, sat proudly in the center. Food stalls, trinket tables, and local trash and treasure stalls radiated outward in a cluttered, charming mess.

"Pure Ghost Vein. I see the town's commitment to its tourism hasn't diminished, even with a killer on the loose."

They found Doc Halliday lounging against a pillar at the rotunda, sipping something warm from a to-go cup.

"Ladies." She greeted them with a grin. "Perfect timing. I was just about to start asking complete strangers if they'd seen any signs of romance in Nevada."

"Please don't. No more talk about romance," Rue groaned.

"No promises." Doc raised her eyebrows. "Sooo..." She drew the word out. "Tell me everything. Did he wear cologne? Was there brooding? Did hands accidentally touch?"

Rue looked heavenward. "I am not giving you the slow-motion rom com rundown of a date that *wasn't* a date."

"Denial is the first stage of infatuation." Doc smugly sipped her drink.

"I might go eat some pickled onions until this conversation dies. The smell of my breath should keep nosy people away." Rue turned on her heel. But she didn't go far. The vibe around the square was too good. Lights twinkled through tree branches, a kid in a cactus costume sprinted past, and someone played a fiddle over near the fudge stall. Two witches in long flowing pink dresses juggled glowing pale blue orbs, occasionally throwing one at each other so they could catch and juggle it. Rue could see why Great Aunt Ruth had decided to settle here. Ghost Vein had a pulse, quirky and chaotic and stubbornly alive. Maybe it wasn't so bad to stick around. Taz and Doc followed Rue as she meandered around the square.

"Look." Taz nudged her. "Fight incoming."

They'd just passed a stall draped in black velvet and dried herbs, where Wynona sold *"dark curiosities"* alongside a discreet sign advertising *private consultations*. Standing in front of her was none other than Cole Dawson, face like thunder as he tried to keep his voice calm.

"This is standard procedure. We have to make sure all public magical consultations are documented with the town registry..."

"This is harassment," Wynona snapped. "You're just bitter because my sister told you I hexed the mayor's birthday punch."

Cole ran a hand down his face.

Nearby, Jesse leaned on a post. When he spotted Rue

and the others, he straightened and sauntered over, dimples on full blast. "Evening, ladies. You missed the opening act, but the encore's looking promising."

"We're just here for snacks and no stress. You can take your flirting and leave," Taz said.

"Hey. No flirting here." He held up his hands then turned to Rue. "How'd the date go?"

"It. Wasn't. A. Date," Rue blurted.

The entire cluster around Wynona's stall, including Cole, turned to look at her.

Jesse grinned wider. "I think she protests too much."

Rue flushed. "I hate this town."

"Sure you do, sweetheart." Taz patted her friend's arm.

Rue stormed over to Lynette's stall, fully prepared to bury herself in baked goods and ignore the fact that Cole stood in close proximity to her. Lynette's booth was a soothing balm to her chaotic mind. Jars of honey, stacks of shortbread, and bottles of herb-infused oil battled for space with colorful crystals.

"Don't let them get to you, dear." Lynette passed Rue a forkful of something crumbly and incredible. "They only tease because they care. Everyone sees how you and Cole mesh. They're just rooting for you two to make a match."

"I'd rather slow dance with a cactus right now," Rue muttered, chewing on the cake. "Although this is delicious. No weird herbs?"

Lynette chuckled. "No magic, I promise. Just butter, sugar, eggs, flour, vanilla, and my heart and soul."

"That tracks."

Lynette trilled a sweet laugh and offered Rue a cookie as a loud voice interrupted them.

"You called the cops on me again, didn't you?" Wynona

was back, black skirts flaring, face flushed with fury. "I *knew* it. You and your stupid calming tea and healing crystals."

"I did *not* call the police. The rule is if you offer private consultations in public, you must adhere to the council rules. You know that." Lynette calmly unwrapped a new loaf of something spiced. "You were performing unsanctioned divination in public. That's on *you*."

"Snitch."

"Chaos witch." Lynette sneered back.

Before Rue could back away, the wind picked up sharply. It tugged at her ponytail and sent paper flyers, scarves, and a very unfortunate taxidermy squirrel skittering across the square. She took a step back, cookie still in hand.

Something weird was brewing. And not the kind you could cure with a mug of Lynette's calming lemon balm tea.

A woman in a rhinestone-studded cowgirl outfit paused at Lynette's table and picked up a pale-pink crystal no bigger than a walnut. She turned it over, admiring it under the fairy lights, when a sudden red spark snapped across her hand with a crack. The woman shrieked and flung the crystal. "It burned me," she wailed, clutching her palm.

Instant chaos.

Rue didn't think. She moved forward, bent down, and scooped up the fallen crystal. It was warm, almost pulsing. And then...ow. *Ow.* A jolt surged through her hand, not pain exactly, but something...sharp. Buzzing. Hot. Like static and anger and everything she hadn't said today rising to the surface.

Something inside her twisted.

And then...nothing.

She opened her fingers.

The once-glowing pink crystal now lay dull and white

in her palm, no spark, no hum. Just...calm. Rue laid it gently on the table in front of her and blinked down at her hand.

Silence rippled through the crowd. Wynona and Lynette fell silent. Both stared at the crystal, then slowly turned their gazes on Rue.

Lynette's eyes widened with delight. "Curse-breaking."

Winona sneered automatically, but Rue caught the flicker in her expression. Pride? Surprise? Then the sisters glanced at each other, gave a mutual snort, and picked up their argument right where they'd left off.

Rue stared at her hand. What the heck had just happened? Before she could make sense of it, Doc and Cole rushed over, then half-dragged the wailing tourist toward the first-aid stall. The woman kept jabbering about curses, burning, and suing someone.

The arguing behind Rue spiked in volume, drawing her attention away from the injured woman.

"I *told* you those crystals needed to be cleaned before today. I asked you to make sure," Lynette barked.

"I *did* clear them last full moon," Wynona snapped back.

Groaning, Rue stepped in. Otherwise, someone would probably blame her. "Ladies, please."

Before she could utter another word, Deputy Mayhew barreled through the crowd.

"What in the blazes is going on here?" he barked. His gaze zeroed in on Rue. "Of *course* you're involved."

"I didn't do anything..."

"She broke a curse," Lynette interrupted proudly.

"She *interfered* with evidence," Wynona countered.

Mayhew scowled. "That's it. I'm sick of this circus. Maddox and both of you witches are disturbing the peace, inciting panic. I'm arresting the lot of you."

"Wait, what?" *How does it always end up my fault? Cole is going to love this. Speaking of the sheriff...*

Doc and Cole were still over by the first-aid tent, calming the tourist, completely unaware of what was happening to Rue and the sisters.

Jesse made a move to step in, but Mayhew waved him off with a sharp hiss. "Stand down, Walker."

Cole's friend looked helpless. "You're seriously arresting Wynona for being *Wynona*? Not to mention the other two. This is ridiculous."

"*Lock. Them. Up.*"

The next thing Rue knew, she was sitting in Ghost Vein's station holding cell with two arguing witches and a growing headache.

Deputy Mayhew slammed the cell door. "You three can cool off in here while I decide if this warrants charges." He strutted off to the station's reception.

Nacho, bless his tiny hooves, trotted in a moment later and curled up at the bars, guarding them.

Lynette and Wynona were still going at it. Rue sat on a bench and rubbed her head.

"You *hexed* the crystal."

"I didn't. I *had* hexed it. Past tense. That crystal was part of the lot that *disappeared*. That's not the same."

"Oh, right, and I'm supposed to believe your merchandise walks away on its own?"

Rue snapped. "*Enough*," she said, loud enough to make the goat flinch and both witches freeze mid-insult. "Can we *not* do this right now?"

Both sisters stared at her.

"Sorry, dear." Lynette coughed, delicately.

"Well, I'm not apologizing." Wynona flounced to the other side of the room and dropped onto the bench.

Rue exhaled slowly and leaned back against the bars. "Okay. What *just* happened with that crystal?"

Lynette sat beside her. "What did you feel?"

Rue ran a hand through her messy ponytail. "I...I don't know. It was hot. My hand burned. Everyone was yelling, and that tourist was hurt, and I just wanted it all to stop. And then...something snapped. In my chest. Like a twang. And the next thing I know, the crystal's cold, and I feel like I ran a marathon."

"That's normal." Lynette nodded. "Frustration's a great motivator for magic."

Wynona rolled her eyes. "Anything's a great motivator if you have magic. The trick is not frying bystanders."

"I didn't *fry* the tourist. I picked up the crystal after it burned her. That's different."

"We'll sort it out later." Lynette patted Rue's arm. "Right now, we need to figure out who really hexed that thing."

"That crystal wasn't supposed to still *be* hexed."

"Aha," Lynette crowed.

"But..." Wynona lifted a finger. "It went missing. Along with some other stock. Someone stole it. I haven't seen it in weeks. I didn't put it out tonight on your table, Lynette."

"Someone took the crystal?" Rue nibbled on the corner of her lip.

Wynona gave a reluctant nod. "But I doubt Mayhew's gonna listen to me."

"Has the mayor or Maribel been sniffing around your stuff lately?"

"Not them. But the dead tour guide, Tobias, had been. A couple weeks before he died. Asked a lot of questions. Seemed interested in old protective charms and some hexes."

Rue's thoughts spun. "Do you think he stole it? And maybe the killer took it afterward?"

"I know I didn't put that crystal on Lynnie's stall." Wynona pointed a finger at her sister. "Did you?"

Lynette shook her head. "No. I didn't even realize it was there. The markets were packed with locals and tourists. Anyone could have slipped it on the table. Especially if they didn't care who touched it."

"And since Tobias is dead, I guess we have to assume that whoever killed him snaffled up the crystal just to cause trouble down the track." Rue tapped her chin.

"Who took it?"

"I don't know. That's something I'm working on. Or I would be if I wasn't in here. That's probably the whole point. Distracting me and getting me away from snooping." Rue stood and kicked the bars close to Nacho, who bleated in protest. Rue knelt and patted him through the bars. "Sorry, Nacho. I'm just annoyed that someone played me."

"Played us all." Wynona glared around the cell. "This is not good for my reputation. Someone's going to pay for it."

"It isn't about us." Lynette rolled her eyes.

The squabbling began again and escalated toward *loud and annoying* when the door to the lockup banged open and Cole strode in, boots heavy, expression carved from granite.

"Enough."

The sisters froze mid-glare. Rue straightened, already bracing for another lecture.

"I'm letting you all out." Cole unlocked the cell. "On the condition that you agree to *leave each other alone* for the next forty-eight hours."

Wynona opened her mouth to protest her innocence but stopped after one look at the sheriff's face.

"I mean it," he warned. "You've got a market full of

scared tourists and one poor woman who thinks she's cursed. You want more bans from festivals? Keep going."

Lynette sighed. "For the record...she didn't hex the tourist. This time."

"Did you just..." Wynona blinked myopically at her sister.

"Don't make me regret it," Lynette muttered.

Cole's eyebrows lifted slightly. "Noted. For once, I'm surprised in a *good* way."

He stepped back as the three of them exited. "The tourist's fine," he added. "Doc treated the burns and a few of the healers had a go. The mayor was there within minutes handing out vouchers."

"Of *course* she was. The mayor. Always popping up like a bad smell that just won't go away." Rue gritted her teeth.

Cole's mouth twitched, but the glare he sent her was half-hearted. "Just watch yourself. All of you. I don't want to see any of you back in here tonight."

"This wasn't my fault. I was trying to help. I picked up a crystal, accidentally un-cursed it, and then got arrested for breathing." Rue stormed after the sisters.

Mayhew waited just outside the holding area, arms folded. He glared daggers at Rue as she passed. "One day, your protector won't be around. And when that happens? I'll be there. Because I *know* you're up to something."

Rue stopped. Her entire posture shifted. She was halfway into a hiss...an actual hiss, when Nacho trotted in, right on cue.

And promptly vomited on Mayhew's polished black boots.

The sound the deputy made was less law enforcement and more freaked-out child. He squealed, stumbled back, and nearly lost his own lunch from the smell alone.

Bending down, Rue scooped Nacho into her arms. "You're a good boy," she whispered.

Cole appeared in the hallway just in time to witness Mayhew retching and a smug-looking Rue cradling the goat. His expression remained unreadable except for the corner of his mouth, which tugged just slightly upward. The tiniest, guiltiest smile. "Go home, Rue. Get some sleep."

She straightened, lifting her chin. "That's the plan. Assuming nosy cops don't lock me up first." Rue marched past, Nacho in her arms. She didn't know who was stealing things. And she sure as heck didn't know why her magic had suddenly started waking up. But she was going to find out.

Because Rue Maddox is done playing nice.

SIXTEEN

The clink of crystals and Lynette's humming had become the background noise of Rue's life the next day.

Seated at a small wooden prep table in the kitchen of Lynette's diner, Rue glared at a line-up of crystals placed in front of her. Wynona stood nearby, arms crossed, her expression a blend of annoyance and superiority.

"Try it again," she ordered.

Rue reached for the cloudy green crystal in front of her. Nothing. She squinted, focused. *Still nothing.*

Wynona sighed like a teacher about to give up on a promising but thick-headed student. "You're thinking too hard. Magic doesn't like being analyzed."

"Great," Rue muttered. "It's judgmental, just like my mother."

"I keep telling her." Lynette sipped herbal tea as she leaned against the counter. "Her gifts are reactive right now. Emotional. Like a teenager."

"I heard that," Rue grumbled.

"Good. Maybe your magic did too." Wynona sneered.

Rue clenched her jaw. The frustration was a slow boil

in her gut. Everyone seemed to have expectations—the town, the sisters, *herself*. Curse-breaking wasn't just this foggy concept; it was a need. And she was nowhere close to controlling it.

The kitchen door creaked open, and Cole stepped in, hair slightly windblown, shirt sleeves rolled up in casual cop mode.

"Hey." He nodded at the room at large, but his gaze snagged on Rue. "Just stopping by."

Rue sat straighter. "Everything okay? Do you have any updates?"

Cole leaned against the doorframe. "That drunken miner from the other night? He insists he's being framed. And now he's suggesting that he wasn't drunk. He thinks someone set the incident up. He has spotty bits in his memory."

Her brow furrowed. "Same thing Arnold said. Sort of."

Cole nodded. "Arnold's memory still has fuzzy spots, but he remembers *someone* behind him before everything went black. Said it was more of a feeling than a memory."

Winona scoffed. "That's because you non-magicals don't listen to your gut enough."

"Well, now we have multiple victims and maybe-suspects. Still no proof."

"Welcome to Ghost Vein," Cole muttered.

Rue's fingers itched. Pressure built in her chest. Between the mystery, her own magic, the weird cool vibes from Cole at the hospital—it all churned together, a storm inside her. She reached for her mug of tea and...*the spoon hissed.*

Not hissed like steam. Hissed like it was *offended* by her touch.

Rue yelped, flinging the mug upward. Tea sprayed like

a geyser. The spoon somersaulted through the air, a tiny metallic projectile.

Lynette ducked as it whizzed past her ear.

Cole caught the mug before it smashed on the ground. Unfortunately, not before the lukewarm tea splashed across his chest.

Doc Halliday, who had just wandered in from the front, immediately doubled over with laughter so hard she had to brace herself on the doorframe.

Wynona stared at the ceiling. "This is what happens when you ignore a curse."

"You try to stir it, and it spits in your face. Like when you fry." Lynette nodded.

Rue, cheeks burning, looked down at the mug in Cole's hand, then up at the dark stain spreading across his shirt. "I am so sorry."

Blinking away tea droplets, he gave a short laugh. "It wasn't hot. I'm fine. Just need a new shirt."

"I'm blaming the spoon." Rue blew out a breath.

"Blame your untrained magical gift. You should have spotted the hex on that spoon and broke it," Wynona muttered.

"I *am* trying to learn," Rue snapped. "But this isn't easy. There's no manual. No YouTube tutorial. Just...chaos."

Wynona pointed a black nail at her. "You can't ignore magic. Especially not curse-breaking. If someone's aimed that at you, it's going to *demand* your attention. Whether you like it or not."

Lynette, for once, agreed. "There's always a learning curve. Sometimes it curves straight into a brick wall, and you go splat. But you'll get there. You're stubborn."

"That's not always a compliment," Rue muttered.

"It is in Ghost Vein." Lynette handed her a clean towel.

"For the record, I still hate how much I agree with her." Wynona curled her lip at her sister.

Cole smirked. "If your curse-breaking's half as accurate as your tea toss, you'll be just fine."

"Still sorry." Rue glanced at Cole, sheepishly.

"You're good," he said, his voice low and warm again. "Could've been worse. Could've been coffee."

Behind them, the sisters exchanged looks and giggles. And Doc fanned herself.

"You'd better get back to the Silver Tongue," Lynette said innocently. "It's getting dark. Why doesn't Cole walk Rue back? Make sure she's safe."

Rue rolled her eyes. "Subtle."

"Who's being subtle?" Wynona smirked. "We're witches. We live for drama."

Opening the door, Cole gestured for Rue to go first. Behind them, the diner erupted into laughter.

Rue sighed. "One day, I'd like to have a normal moment in this town."

Cole glanced sideways. "Define normal."

She laughed, surprising herself. "Fair point."

The streets of Ghost Vein were quiet, cool air settling over the town. Somewhere in the distance, a wind chime jangled. Tourists had begun to turn up, but the rush hadn't started yet.

Rue walked beside Cole, Nacho trailing behind like a bodyguard or a chaperone.

Cole kept his hands in his jacket pockets, steps unhurried. "I'm looking into the miner's statement. And Arnold's, as well as the tourist from yesterday. Although all she really remembers is picking up the crystal and it burning her."

"It's starting to feel connected."

"Yeah." He exhaled. "The tour guide. The missing artifacts. The crystal yesterday. Probably the same person behind it all."

"But you can't say for sure yet." Rue glanced at him.

His mouth twisted. "Not officially. I can't assume anything. I have to go by procedure. Evidence. Reports. Not gut feelings and magical hunches. Or Mayhew will jump on me."

"Well, that explains why you're such a joy at parties. By the book and noncommittal."

Cole gave her a sidelong look. "I've been told I'm a delight. Once. By my grandmother. After a lot of whiskey."

Rue snorted.

They reached the edge of Main and turned toward the Silver Tongue. The air was still, the kind of stillness that made everything feel heavy.

"There's a pattern. We just haven't seen it yet. But that's why you need to be careful."

Rue stopped walking. "Seriously?"

Cole stopped too, a step ahead. He turned back to face her, arms crossed now. "Things are moving around you, focusing on you."

She tilted her head. "You just walked me home, updated me on every moving piece of the puzzle, and now you want me to sit the investigation out?"

"I'm not saying that to be a jerk. I just...I don't want you in the middle of it. There's too much you can't see coming. And Mayhew is looking for an excuse to drag you in again."

Rue arched a brow. "So, you get to investigate. And I get to...what? Bake?"

"If that's how you stay away from crime scenes, I support it."

She rolled her eyes and kept walking. "You're impossible."

"Comes with the badge." He shot Rue a small grin.

They reached the steps of the Silver Tongue. Cole stopped, hand resting lightly on the porch railing like he was about to leave.

But Rue turned, stopping him with just a word. "Hey."

He paused. Looked back.

"Thanks. For being honest. And for updating me. I know you didn't have to."

His expression shifted, something behind his eyes flickering. She couldn't quite read it.

Rue sighed, brushing a hand over her ponytail. "I don't know how to talk to you half the time. You were cold at the hospital, and now you're back to...*this.*" She waved a hand at him.

Cole's jaw tensed. "I have a job, Rue. A job that gets a hell of a lot harder when Mayhew's snapping at my heels and the mayor's breathing down my neck. I can't afford to cut corners. Even for..." He stopped himself. "For anyone."

She frowned. "I wasn't asking you to cut corners. I just... It felt like you iced me out."

He looked away. "Maybe I did."

"Seriously?"

Cole exhaled and muttered. "I didn't plan on caring what you thought."

She stared at him.

He shifted his weight awkwardly. "But now I do. And I thought maybe it was better to keep it simple. Do my job. Keep you out of it. Safer for everyone."

His voice was low. Strained.

Awkward.

Rue felt something in her chest pull tight, then loosen.

"Well," she said after a long beat. "I didn't plan on

staying in a haunted town either. I guess we're both flying blind."

Cole looked up at her, eyes unreadable.

"I was supposed to sell this place," she said, her voice barely above a whisper. "That was the plan. Have a fun holiday then sell it. Never look back."

She gestured at the darkened windows of the Silver Tongue behind her.

"But here I am. Stuck. Spilling tea. Breaking crystals. Yelling at goats. And somehow...caring."

Cole didn't say anything for a moment. Then he stepped just a little closer. "You make Ghost Vein look good."

Rue's breath caught.

And just as quickly, he took a step back.

"Get some rest," he said, back to business. "And maybe stop touching cursed spoons."

She snorted. "No promises."

Cole nodded, the ghost of a smile tugging at his lips, and turned to go. He stopped halfway down the porch steps, turning back, his expression guarded.

"You said...you were going to sell." His voice was quiet. Careful. "Is that still the plan?"

Rue blinked, caught off guard by the question. "Honestly? Right now, my priority is figuring out what the heck's going on. Everything else can wait."

He nodded slowly, awkwardly, like the answer didn't quite settle the way he wanted it to.

Between them, silence stretched.

Until Nacho let out a loud, unholy *baaa-rrrup*, somewhere between a yawn and a judgmental goat laugh.

Rue glared down at him. "Et tu, goat?"

Cole's mouth twitched.

Cassie strolled by, carrying a tray of something sugary and looking far too smug. "You two gonna kiss and make up already? Or should I call the town gossips and sell tickets?"

Rue shot her a glare. "If I had a cupcake, I'd have thrown it at your head."

Cassie cackled and vanished into the café.

Rue groaned. "I hate this town."

Cole's grin was faint, but unmistakable. "You say that, but you keep not leaving."

"Maybe I enjoy being tortured."

His eyes softened again. "Be safe, Rue."

She nodded. "You too. And keep me posted. Even if I'm not officially involved."

"I will." He tipped his head and walked off into the dark.

Rue watched him go. She sighed and headed upstairs. The apartment sat quiet, but something felt...off. She unlocked the door, stepped inside, and froze.

A folded piece of paper had been shoved under the door. She looked down the hallway. Nothing but empty space, not even a nosy goat. The note was folded tightly. Plain. No markings. Rue picked it up, locked the door behind her, and threw every bolt she had. Inside, she unfolded the paper.

Leave before the curse makes you disappear.

Her stomach dropped. The handwriting was scrawled and rushed. The paper, thin and slightly glossy on one side, was torn at the top. Something about the paper felt familiar. Not from the café. Somewhere else she'd been recently. Her fingers curled around it instinctively.

It didn't feel ghostly.

It felt *intentional.*

Targeted.

And not magical. Just *human*. Which somehow made it worse.

Rue checked every lock, every window. Twice. Pulled the curtains closed. Turned on the TV, not because she wanted to watch anything, but because she needed the noise. Needed something to drown out the too-quiet apartment.

She sat on the couch, the note clenched in her hand. She'd tell Cole in the morning. After she slept. *If I can.* Because one thing was for sure. That note hadn't come from a ghost. And whoever sent it? They weren't afraid of curses.

They were using them...

SEVENTEEN

Monday morning smelled like slightly burned cinnamon muffins. Rue stumbled down the stairs from her apartment, armored in jeans and a bright, patterned T-shirt. Her hair was in a messy bun that had given up halfway through the night, and her eyes were only half-open. Last night had not been the most restful she'd ever had. She'd spent most of it awake on the couch watching b-grade disaster movies.

Cassie, already behind the café counter polishing cups, waved at her boss. Thomas swept the bookshop floor and nodded at Rue.

Grunting, Rue aimed for the kitchen, kettle, and a cup of tea.

Cassie took one look at her. "Rough night, boss?"

"She looks like she fought a poltergeist," Thomas muttered.

"I *wish* it was a poltergeist," Rue grumbled.

Taz popped her head out of the kitchen. She held a cup of tea out to Rue. "Let me guess. Spicy dreams of the sheriff keeping you up?"

Rue took the tea and looked over the rim of her mug.

"More like paranoia and handwritten death threats. Super sexy."

Taz's smile dropped. "Wait, what?"

Rue sighed and jerked her thumb toward the stairs. "Come up. I'll show you."

They made their way to Rue's apartment. Placing the teacup on a side table, Rue fetched the folded piece of paper and handed it over.

Taz unfolded it and read silently. She stilled. "This isn't a ghost." Her eyes scanned the paper again. "This is a *person*."

"Exactly. It's not magical, not ghostly. Just...creepy in the good ol' flesh-and-blood stalker kind of way."

"This is an escalation." Taz looked sharply at Rue. "You're getting close to something, and whoever it is isn't happy."

"Well, good. Maybe that means they're scared of me." Rue flopped onto her couch.

"Rue."

"I mean it." Rue rubbed her face. "What if this is a good sign? What if I'm finally rattling the right skeletons?"

"This paper...it looks familiar." Taz stared at the note again, frowning.

"Right? I've seen this exact kind of stationery before. I just can't remember where. That header was torn off for a reason."

"Cole might be able to trace it." Taz hesitated.

Rue winced. "Yeah, I know. But..."

"But?"

"But if I show him, he might try to shut the investigation down or worse, shut *me* down. Again."

"And lying to him is a better option?" Taz crossed her arms.

"I'm not lying. I'm...delaying the truth." Rue held up a hand. "I'll tell him. Just not yet. I need to be sure it leads somewhere first."

Taz looked heavenward. "Ruth? Seriously? You gonna let her be this reckless?"

They both waited for a beat.

Nothing.

Rue picked up her cup and sipped her tea. "See? No flickering lights. No spooky mirror messages. She agrees with me."

Taz narrowed her eyes. "Or she's ignoring your nonsense like the rest of us do."

Rue grinned. "Still, I need more. I don't have the full story yet. Not about the mine, not about Elias Grimshaw, not about the gold. It all feels...tangled. I'm missing something obvious."

"Speaking of missing, have you managed to pin Letty Navarro down yet?"

Rue groaned. "Ugh. No. I left her a note. Then went by the library twice. Nothing. It's like she's dodging me."

"The archive's her domain. If you want answers about Grimshaw, the gold, or the map, she's the one."

"I *know*. That's why I'm losing my mind."

"Saloon opens later today. Let's go now. I'll come with you. She might let you in if I'm with you."

They headed back downstairs. Cassie was halfway through slicing scones and humming to herself while Thomas glared at a large box of books.

"Cassie," Taz called, "we're heading out for a bit. If we're not back before opening, you and Thomas can handle it, yeah?"

Cassie looked up and gave Rue a casual thumbs-up. "Sure. Try not to die. Or find another body."

"No promises," Rue muttered.

As they stepped out onto the boardwalk, the early morning sun painted everything in soft gold. And the town looked deceptively peaceful.

Until Nacho popped out from behind a crate of discounted canned peaches in front of the general store and skipped along behind them.

"I swear that animal has teleportation powers," Taz said.

Rue smirked and patted her pocket to make sure the note was tucked safely inside. If Cole popped up on their stroll to the library, she promised herself she'd show him. She wasn't sure what she'd find at the archive. But she had a feeling it might change everything.

They pulled to a stop in front of the library, and Taz pushed the door open. The bell gave a cheerful ding that felt too optimistic for a Monday morning.

"The library's actually *open?*"

"Either that or we've accidentally crossed into another world where things go right for you."

"For once." Rue shrugged. "No poltergeists. No vomiting goats. No locked doors. Something's going to go wrong...trust me."

Inside, the library was quiet, except for the faint clatter of a rolling cart and the rustle of pages turning somewhere near the nonfiction section.

Taz led the way, veering around a display of monster-themed romances and flagging down a woman with silver hair pulled into a tight bun.

"Rue, this is Letty Navarro." Taz gave a mock bow.

Letty raised an eyebrow and gave Rue a once-over. "So, this is the Maddox girl."

Rue offered a tentative smile. "Rue Maddox. I come in peace. Promise."

"I've heard the stories. Thought it best to dodge a Maddox interrogation." Letty's lips twitched.

"I'm not here to interrogate you. I just want to learn. The mine. Grimshaw. The curse. Whatever's tied this town in knots. I need to understand it."

Letty gave her another long look, measuring her, but finally nodded. "You want answers? Go downstairs. That's where the good stuff lives." She gestured toward a narrow stairwell tucked behind a stack of biographies. "It's old school. Filing cabinets. Microfiche. You should find what you need there."

It looked like she wanted to say more, but the bell chimed again, and cheerful heels clicked across the hardwood.

"Fancy finding all my favorite people in one place." Isla Gray swept into the room. Her strawberry-blonde curls bounced as she approached, carrying a satchel stuffed with books.

"Isla." Taz greeted her with a friendly smile.

"Research day," Isla chirped. "The curator sent me on a project. Something about cultural rights, superstitions, and how the mine fits in."

Letty gave her a sharp nod. "You know where to go."

"Oh, perfect. I'll take Rue and Taz down with me." Isla winked at Rue. "Three heads are better than one, right?"

"Lead the way." Rue licked her lips, nervousness and anxiety all wrapped up in one hard ball in the pit of her stomach. She needed answers and hoped the archives could help.

The basement was every archive cliché in existence, and Rue kinda loved it. Tall filing cabinets lined the walls. A bank of microfiche readers stood to one side. There were old school display cases filled with faded photographs, brittle documents, and rusted mine equipment.

"It's like a museum down here," Rue murmured.

"Letty refuses to digitize." Isla grinned. "Says it disrupts the vibe of the archives."

"Charming."

"Before you start..." Isla headed to a book on a desk near the door and scrawled something in it. "You *have* to sign in. Letty's rule. She's obsessed with the archive log."

Rue opened the journal. Pretty standard, names, dates, reason for visit. Isla's name was already neatly printed on the day's entry. Rue scrawled her name and Taz's below it, then casually flipped back through earlier pages. Her breath caught. "Maribel Knox," she muttered. "And Mayor Agnes Flint. Why am I not surprised?"

Taz leaned in. "What were they researching?"

"No reasons listed. But Isla's the only one who's got a valid microfiche entry for today." Rue flipped back a few more pages. "Tobias Pike is in here too. And...Jackson Malone?"

"The bartender?" Taz frowned.

"Says he was here with Tobias. Guess they were closer than Jackson let on. Interesting." She shut the ledger and turned to Isla. "We're looking for anything about Elias Grimshaw, when the mine opened, the miners who disappeared, the first town documents. Anything weird."

Isla beamed. "You came to the right place." She bustled off and started digging through cabinets. Five minutes later, she had them set up with folders and a functioning microfiche reader.

As they worked, Rue began piecing together fragments of a story that was starting to feel more and more real.

Grimshaw opened the mine with fanfare. The first few

years were successful, with mainly silver found. Then came supply issues, accidents, people killed. Grimshaw tightened his hold on the mine and the town, forcing longer working hours, dangerous conditions.

They found articles detailing the original town charter, a black-and-white photograph of the first mayor shaking hands with Grimshaw, and vague incident reports about a death of a mine manager just before Elias Grimshaw took over the operating of the mine himself.

One article caught Rue's eye, a small piece about Grimshaw's wife and child vanishing from town a week after his disappearance. The article claimed they were later seen in Boston, photographed at a park ribbon-cutting event. "They just left? He vanished, and they ran?"

"Or someone made them leave," Taz murmured.

The articles kept coming, miners' names, haunting rumors, stories of cursed gold. Treasure hunters who never came back. Families who swore the mine whispered at night.

Rue printed the list of the miners who disappeared and folded it into her pocket.

"Is there a photo of Grimshaw anywhere?" she asked.

Isla frowned. "The only one I know of is the one in the museum. It's a formal portrait, a bit grainy. But I don't think there's anything better."

"I forgot about that. I'll have to go back and look again."

Rue was elbow-deep in newspaper clippings when Isla finally groaned, stretching her arms over her head.

"Okay, I officially can't read another word. I think I'm growing microfiche-induced wrinkles."

"We've been here *two hours*?"

Taz gasped at Rue. "Cassie's going to kill us."

Scooping up her notes, Rue gestured to Taz. "Come on.

Let's go before we find Nacho eating us out of stock." Rue cast one more glance over her shoulder, toward the shelves still packed with secrets.

Taz grabbed the handle to the archive door and jiggled it. Nothing. She frowned. "It's locked."

Rue stepped forward and tried it herself, rattling it harder. It didn't budge. "Is that normal?"

Isla stared at the door, confusion giving way to rising panic. "It's never locked. Letty doesn't even *like* the archives; she always says the ambience gives her the creeps. She won't even come down to check on us."

"Maybe she changed her mind about us touching her microfiche," Rue offered.

"I told my boss I was coming here," Isla added quickly. "If I don't show up, he might come looking. Maybe." She looked doubtful.

"Let's hope he doesn't wait until tomorrow to notice," Taz muttered.

A noise sounded on the other side of the door. Shuffling. Thuds. A dragging scrape.

Rue's heart seized. "Did you hear that?"

They froze as another scrape echoed beyond the door... followed by a faint, unmistakable *bleat*.

Rue bent double and let out a gasping laugh. "Oh my goodness. It's Nacho."

Taz giggled helplessly.

Isla sagged against the wall, eyes wide and slightly manic.

Rue dropped to one knee, leaning near the base of the door. "Nacho? Hey, buddy? Can you go get Letty? Bring her back, okay?"

They heard another snort and the tapping of hooves retreating.

They waited.

And waited.

Nothing.

Isla started pacing, arms hugging herself tightly. "He's not coming back. We're trapped. We're gonna die down here with microfiche and mold."

"Breathe," Taz told her. "It's fine. Rue can try her magic."

"Wait...*what?*" Rue's eyes widened in horror.

Isla looked up, desperate. "You're a Maddox. Everyone's saying you're probably a curse-breaker like Ruth was. Use your magic and unlock the door."

"I don't even know *how* it works yet. I don't want to blow the hinges off and flatten all of us. Or worse, nothing happens at all."

Taz placed a steadying hand on her shoulder. "Okay. Just breathe. Don't overthink it. Try what you did before. Focus on the lock, *want* it to open. Picture it breaking."

Rue stared at the door. Nothing. She took a deep breath. Focused harder. Still nothing. Frustration surged like hot water bubbling under her skin. She marched forward and slapped both hands against the door. "*Open, you cursed piece of junk.*" Something sparked in her chest. The air around her shimmered, then snapped.

Crack.

The lock exploded with a jolt of light. Rue, thrown backward, landed hard on the floor. Her vision wavered and her ears rang. She swore she heard a voice. Older. Female. *"You're learning. You're not alone. Be careful who you trust."*

"Rue." Taz scrambled over to her.

Footsteps pounded from the stairwell above. Nacho bleated triumphantly as the door swung open with a force that nearly smacked Rue in the head.

Cole and Jesse burst through, Cole's weapon holstered but eyes sharp. Dropping to one knee beside her, Cole ran his hands over Rue, checking for injuries. "Are you okay?"

"I've got a migraine, and I smell like burned toast," Rue responded.

Taz ran to Jesse, throwing her arms around him and talking a mile a minute. She let him go as Isla walked up to Jesse, repeated Taz's actions, and flung herself at him, holding him tightly. "You saved us."

Jesse patted Isla's back awkwardly. He gently pushed her to the side.

"*Rue* saved us." Taz's head whipped around. "She broke the lock using her *magic*."

Cole glanced down at Rue, still kneeling beside her. "You used curse-breaking?"

Rue rubbed her temple. "I didn't mean to. It just... flared. Something snapped. Then I was on the floor."

He touched the back of her head gently. "Small bump but no bleeding. You'll live."

"Lucky me." She winced. "Do you have six ibuprofen and a glazed donut?"

"Only one of those," Cole murmured, slipping an arm around her shoulders to help her stand.

They were halfway up the stairs when Letty appeared, arms crossed and eyes sharp.

"What on earth happened?"

"Someone locked us in." Rue groaned and rubbed the back of her head carefully.

Letty frowned. "I've been out front. I didn't lock anything."

"I'll need to investigate," Cole said. "For now, the archives are closed. Off-limits until we figure out who was down there."

"I'm glad you're all okay." Letty's eyes flickered to Rue. "Maybe next time, we can talk...properly."

Rue nodded, still leaning on Cole. "I'd like that."

Isla, pale and still trembling slightly, lifted a hand. "Thanks again, everyone, but I'm gonna go. Far, far away from the archives. Forever." She waved and vanished through the library doors.

"Everyone, out. We should get Rue checked out." Cole slid an arm around Rue's waist and helped her up the stairs.

"I'm fine. I just need to lie down. On a surface softer than a concrete floor." The ache behind Rue's eyes pulsed like a drumbeat, but her thoughts were sharp.

They hadn't found a smoking gun.

But they had found *proof*.

Grimshaw was real. The mine had been opened with fanfare and hope and closed with blood. His wife and child had made it out. There might be descendants out there. And the list of missing miners?

Rue reached into her pocket and pulled it out, the paper slightly crumpled but intact.

The legend was real.

And someone, *someone still alive*, was willing to kill for the gold...

EIGHTEEN

The next few days were quiet. *Suspiciously* quiet. The kind of quiet that made Rue glance out the café windows half-expecting a stampede of crazed killers or hangry goats to be promenading along Main Street.

Outside, the wind howled down the street. A few brave tourists trickled through town in oversized cowboy hats, mostly trying not to get slapped in the face by a gust. Inside the Silver Tongue, life had settled into something almost... routine.

Rue had finally stopped second guessing her bookshop skills and had catalogued books, stuck barcodes on spines, and slowly realized she *loved* rearranging displays. She'd built a whole new table dedicated to paranormal romances and was unreasonably proud of the way she'd managed to get a witchy-themed candle to match the cover of a vampire cowboy romance.

Her *To Be Read* list had grown into a *TBR shelf.*

Great Aunt Ruth's collection of books was wild. Heavy on Western history, mining, and cowboys, but peppered with cozy murder mysteries, supernatural encyclopedias, and ghost romances that ranged from sweet to *are-you-kidding-me* steamy. And Rue...kind of loved it.

Taz, Cassie, and Thomas helped in both the café and bookshop, floating back and forth, superpowered employees. Taz made it look effortless. Rue mostly tried not to spill soup on receipts. She was halfway through restocking the drinks fridge when Taz poked her head out of the kitchen.

"Hey, Sherlock," Taz called. "You've got a call on the café line. Lawyerly sounding guy."

Rue wiped her hands on her jeans and headed to the counter, picking up the old-fashioned rotary phone. "This is Rue Maddox."

"Miss Maddox," said a gravelly voice. "This is Carl Hewitt. Ruth's attorney."

"Oh...hi. Everything okay?"

"I've received an offer on the building. It's generous. Above market value. Full cash purchase and no conditions. They want to close within the week."

"Wait, what?" Someone wanted to buy the saloon and move in within a week? "Why the rush?"

"No clue. The offer was made through a real estate agent and a corporate trust. It's anonymous, at least on paper. But it's legitimate."

Rue's stomach did a little anxious flip. "Do you know who made it?"

"Not directly. I can't see through the corporate veil unless I subpoena documents, which I doubt you want me to do just to satisfy curiosity."

"Maybe..." Rue muttered.

"It'll cost you, and there's no guarantee I'll be able to do it."

Ruth's money would stretch only so far. "Don't worry. But if you hear anything, please let me know."

"No worries. They've given you a forty-eight-hour deadline," Hewitt added. "I'll need your decision by then."

"Okay." Rue forced her voice to stay calm. "Email me the paperwork. I'll...look at it."

"Do it soon. This kind of offer doesn't usually sit long." He hung up.

Rue stared at the phone for a beat.

Taz was already watching from behind the pastry counter, one brow raised. "Well?" she asked.

"There's been an offer on the building." Rue walked slowly back toward the café.

"Are you going to sell?" Taz stiffened.

"I don't *want* to." Rue shook her head. "But I should at least read it. Be fair. Ruth left this place to me; doesn't mean I'm stuck here. Or that I'm not. Does that make sense?"

Taz didn't say a word. She just nodded slowly and turned back toward the kitchen.

Before Rue could stew too long, a delivery from Lynette's diner of boxes of soup, cakes, sandwiches, and pastries arrived. She helped carry them inside, stacking things in the cooler and restocking the front display.

"I've learned more about food service in the last few days than I ever wanted to." Rue wedged a box of lemon bars into the pantry.

"You're doing fine. Honestly, the tourists barely notice what they're eating. They just want something warm in winter and cold in summer. It's more about the vibe."

"And avoiding being pinched by a handsy miner ghost," Rue added.

"Exactly." Taz nodded.

Midmorning, the peace shattered. Tourists came in, buzzing and gossiping. Someone told them the museum *and* the library had lost power the night before. Lights flickered, systems shut down, and displays had been...*moved*.

"Ghosts," someone whispered loudly.

"I heard they even shifted the mannequins."

"Opened locked cabinets."

"Moved the books."

Rue shared a glance with Taz.

"Ghosts are *not* vandals." Taz rolled her eyes. "They can't redecorate."

One of the tourists looked sheepish. "I mean...the mine ghosts are scary. But the museum ghosts? No one expected exhibits to move."

"They're harmless. They're more interested in reliving drunken shootouts and pinching butts. They don't care about display cases. Or books. They care about the good old days. Saloon girls, poker tables, and moonshine. You want to blame anyone? Blame the *living*."

Cassie came bursting through the door, face flushed, from her break. She slapped a flyer onto the counter. "You will *not* believe this. The mayor's called a town meeting. *Tonight*. Six p.m. Topic?" She pointed dramatically. "Ghost issues."

"Ghosts have *issues* now?"

Cassie grinned at her boss. "Apparently."

Taz let out a sigh. "If the mayor's going to be there, then Rue definitely is."

"Of course, I am." There went couch time and chill. She had a feeling the meeting would be the opposite of chill.

The old dance hall was packed. What used to be a space for polkas and line dances had been repurposed into the Ghost Vein community center and town hall. Folding chairs were lined up in tight rows. Lynette's catering table sagged slightly in the middle and offered nibbles at the back. The whole room buzzed with locals whispering about ghosts, curses, and *whatever the mayor was up to this time.*

Rue stood near the back, wedged between Taz, Cassie, and Thomas. Bonnie, Cassie's mom, hovered nearby with a pinched look and her arms crossed.

Up front, Cole, Jesse, and Deputy Mayhew were attempting to maintain order or at least not let the crowd descend into mob mode.

Cole looked about as cheerful as a man who'd just been asked to arrest his own mother. Jesse wore an unusually *nervous* expression. And Deputy Mayhew stood like a puffed-up rooster at a barnyard brawl, arms crossed, chest out, and three suspicious sauce stains blooming across his shirt.

"Classy," Rue muttered about her least favorite person.

The mayor banged her hand on the podium. "Ladies and gentlemen. If I could have your attention." The crowd grumbled but quieted as the mayor shuffled her stack of papers and squared her shoulders. "I've called this meeting because of a concerning rise in ghost-related activity over the past few days," she began, voice high and tight. "What started as minor disturbances has now escalated. There's been damage to the museum and the library. Books related to the mine have been moved or thrown and historical displays tampered with."

Taz shook her head beside Rue. "That's not the ghosts. They don't mess with that stuff."

"Feels like someone's *pretending* to be a ghost." With a

town full of bored old ghosts, it wouldn't be hard to frame them.

The mayor continued, flipping through pages. "Reports from mine employees include increased wailing, flickering lights, and moved equipment. No one has been harmed *yet,* but the potential for danger is escalating." She paused dramatically. "Therefore, I am ordering the *temporary closure of the Silver Vein Mine to all visitors,* effective immediately."

The room erupted. Chairs scraped. Voices shouted. Someone actually booed.

"You can't shut it down."

"We *depend* on that mine."

"Where's the proof?"

Taz muttered, "Oh, the ghosts are going to be *livid.*"

She wasn't wrong. Wind gusted through open windows. Curtains flailed. Chairs toppled over on their own. A stack of folding tables creaked, then collapsed in a dramatic clatter near the stage.

Someone screamed. Others yelled curses as they were bombarded with flying food. The smell of burned metal wafted through the air, and several spectral shadows flickered near the back of the hall. The ghosts were here and absolutely not thrilled at being blamed.

The mayor slammed her palm on the podium. "Enough. This is *my decision.* The closure is for public safety." She pointed sharply toward the front. "Sheriff Dawson and his team will be enforcing the shutdown. Deputy Mayhew, you have the stop-work notices. Signs will be posted. Tape barring entry will be erected over the front of the mine and the gift shop. Visitors will be barred until further notice."

Cole's jaw tightened, but he said nothing as he turned

and took a roll of crime scene tape from Mayhew. Jesse looked like he wanted to sink through the floor.

Rue caught Cole's eye as he approached.

He moved to her side and spoke low, voice laced with confusion. "None of this makes sense. Agnes was the one who *pushed* the mine as a tourism draw. Rebranded the whole town with the cursed gold angle."

"I know," Rue said. "I heard she practically printed bumper stickers."

"She never mentioned shutting it down. And we've only had a handful of ghost complaints reported, nothing like she's implying. Nothing violent." He gave her one last look, then moved to help Jesse calm the room.

She turned back to Taz, who looked as uneasy as Rue felt.

"She's hiding something." Taz folded her arms tight. "The mayor's acting *weird*. First Tobias, now this? Her name just keeps popping up."

"She wants that mine shut down, and it's not about ghosts," Rue agreed. "It's about *something else*. What if she's the one searching for the gold now that Tobias is out of the way?"

"Maybe I can get a key." Taz gripped Rue's arm.

"To what?"

Bonnie cleared her throat behind them. "I clean the mayor's office."

Everyone turned.

"She's never around when I'm cleaning. She hates noise and always leaves while I'm there. If you're careful, you should be able to get in and search her office."

Rue held up her hands. "I'm *always* careful."

Everyone burst out laughing. Even Thomas snorted.

Cassie leaned in. "I'll be the lookout. I help Mom clean sometimes. I know the routine."

Rue hesitated. "Cass..."

"I'm not missing out on a mayoral heist," Cassie said firmly.

From across the hall, Jesse appeared at their side, his badge slightly askew and his hair windblown. "Whatever this is, I want in," he whispered. "I can't sneak off now, but I'll come after. Cole and Mayhew will be at the mine putting up signs anyway."

"You're going to help us break into the mayor's office?" Rue raised both eyebrows.

"Technically, I'm going to *clean* the mayor's office. And if I accidentally overhear anything useful? Well, accidents happen." He winked.

"You're getting sneakier." Taz smirked at Jesse.

"I work with Mayhew. I've learned from the best...and the worst."

As the group began to shuffle toward the exit, Mayhew's eyes tracked them from across the hall. He narrowed his gaze on Rue.

Rue nudged Taz. "We might want to double up on the lookout."

The women were dressed as cleaners. Jesse's version leaned more toward a ninja than a cleaner. Heads down, cleaning supplies in hand, they made their way through the back entrance of City Hall. The place was silent, spooky even, all echoing footsteps and dusty windows.

Bonnie jittered, excited, bouncing slightly as she whispered, "I feel like a spy." She giggled, then smacked her own cheeks lightly. "Okay. Focus. I'll clean down here with Cassie. You two stick to the mayor's office."

"Bonnie, no heroics," Rue warned. "Same for Cassie. Plausible deniability, remember?"

Cassie nodded, clutching her phone. "If anyone heads your way, I'll call."

Rue and Taz crept up the stairs, vacuum and rags in hand. Jesse stationed himself outside the mayor's office as lookout. He leaned against the wall, imitating a bored security guard as the women entered the office.

They had the lights on, cleaning gear out. If anyone walked in, they'd just look like janitors. Totally legit.

Moving to the desk, Rue checked for cameras. *Nothing.* She rifled through drawers, then paused. An official council notepad with Silver Vein's town logo on the header caught her attention. She flipped through it until she found a page with a ragged edge. Rue compared it to the threatening note she'd received under her door. It matched. She turned to Taz and held the note and the notepad up.

"Is that...?"

Rue nodded. "The mayor sent the note. She wants me out of the way."

"Too much drama in this town." Taz shook her head and continued searching and half-heartedly cleaning.

Moving to the old filing cabinet, Rue couldn't believe the mayor hadn't gone digital yet. No computer. No digital system. Just metal drawers and creaky handles. "Who in this day and age uses filing cabinets?"

"It's Ghost Vein. My bet is she probably has a laptop that she takes home." Taz nudged a dead spider with her vacuum.

Inside the cabinet, Rue found a file labeled with Tobias's full name. It contained ghost tour expansion paperwork, with a council approval stamp, then *DENIED* slashed across the top in red. Beneath that were increasing incident reports, ghost sightings, missing supplies, and equipment failures. And a note scribbled weeks ago about missing mine artifacts from the museum.

The mayor had known about all of this *weeks ago*. Why shut down the mine *now*? Why hadn't she told Cole?

Another folder revealed ownership documents. The mine had legally reverted to the town after no Grimshaw descendants were found, meaning the town now made a tidy profit from its cursed gold attraction. And then Rue found it. *A private investigator's report.* She scanned the pages. Elias Grimshaw's wife and son had fled west to Boston in eighteen sixty, where they lived briefly lid style before the wife died young and the son vanished. The Grimshaw line was lost...

Rue's voice was low as she whispered to Taz, "There *could* be a descendant. If they showed up, the mine wouldn't belong to the town anymore. The council would lose a goldmine...literally."

Taz let out a low whistle. "And guess who just spent cash on a PI."

Shutting the drawer, Rue turned to the desk again. The mayor's diary lay on top. She opened it. Two entries stood out. *Meeting with guide, late evening. Follow-up re: pricing. Firm?* It was dated the night before Tobias died. Rue's gut twisted. "Was the mayor negotiating with Tobias? About the map?"

"It wouldn't surprise me." Taz bumped the corner of a shelf. A decorative box teetered, then tumbled to the floor with a *crack.*

Rue rushed over, heart in her throat. The lid had popped off. Inside sat a small gold nugget. And next to it, a torn piece of map. She sucked in a breath. "That's it. That's Tobias's nugget." She pocketed both items before her brain caught up.

Taz gawked. "Rue, does that mean...did she *kill* him? Or did she just find them?"

"I don't know. But either way, she was *there*."

They put the box back together just as footsteps approached. They dropped their heads and pretended to clean just as the door swung open.

Mayor Agnes Flint stood in the doorway, laptop clutched under one arm, eyes narrowing at the scene. "What in the blazes are *you* doing here?"

In perfect silent sync, they both pointed at the vacuum and the spray bottle.

Agnes was not impressed. "You think I'm stupid? Just like your annoying great aunt, always meddling. You two don't know the first thing about what really goes on in this town. You should've left well enough alone."

"Maybe if people weren't still obsessed with Grimshaw's cursed gold, we wouldn't have to meddle." Rue clenched her fists tight.

The mayor bristled. "I should have you both arrested."

Rue's heart plummeted. If Cole arrested her, he'd *never* let her live it down, and that weird almost-something they had going? Dead. D-E-A-D.

Taz jumped in smoothly. "Sure, you *could* arrest us. But that's not going to help your approval rating. The mine's already closed, the town's ticked off, and you're up for re-election."

Agnes hesitated. "Get out," she snapped. "Say *one* word about what you saw, and you'll be in the lockup so fast your heads will spin."

They grabbed their gear and bolted.

Jesse met them downstairs. "Sorry. I saw her coming in but couldn't warn you fast enough."

Cassie looked sheepish. "I had no signal. Look." She held up her phone. "I *never* lose signal here."

"It's okay. Taz had it handled." Rue gave her friend a quick hug.

Bonnie and Cassie shooed them out while they mopped the floor.

Outside, after they'd explained what happened in the mayor's office, Jesse grinned. "Taz, that was *epic*. Hidden skills much?"

The mayor had motive, means, and opportunity. She had Tobias's nugget and map piece. She'd sent the threatening note. And she'd *lied* about everything. But a bigger question gnawed at Rue. *Why the PI report?* Was Agnes trying to *find* a Grimshaw heir...or *hide* one? Too many questions and not nearly enough answers.

And I'm running out of time to figure it out...

NINETEEN

Rue stood at the counter, apron on backward, and tried not to lick the spoon again. Lynette had cracked open a worn recipe card she claimed she got from Ruth's files, *curse-warding muffins*. Apparently, they were good for stomach upsets and hex hangovers.

The diner, in all its fifties-style glory, buzzed with cozy energy. The red vinyl booths gleamed, the jukebox played something classic and twangy in the background, and even Wynona smiled. She'd snapped at Rue earlier, but still. *Progress.*

Rue wiped her hands on a dish towel and grinned. "So... these muffins actually *ward* against curses?"

Lynette shrugged, eyes twinkling. "Or maybe just ward off bad attitudes. Either way, they smell fantastic." She leaned on the counter, watching her sister frost a tray of cinnamon muffins with delicacy. "Wyn, are you...dare I say...enjoying yourself?"

Wynona gave her sister a dramatic sigh. "Don't make a thing of it. I'm allowed to be in a good mood. Arnold's doing better."

That tugged at Rue's heart. "Really?"

"He doesn't remember much." Wynona's voice softened. "He remembers hearing your voice. Says it made him feel safe."

Rue nodded. "Glad he's okay. He's tough."

Lynette glanced sideways, her tone casual. Too casual. "So, Rue...are you thinking of selling?"

"Wait, what?" How on earth did anyone find out about the offer already?

Lynette didn't meet her eyes. "Just...heard a rumor that someone made an offer on the saloon."

Taz suddenly became very busy wiping muffin tins.

Rue rolled her eyes so hard they almost fell out. "The gossip mill in this town needs a muzzle." But inside her, something...clicked. Not in a bad way. In a lightning-bolt-to-the-heart kind of way. She *loved* this town. Loved the chaos, the ghosts, the gold dust, the diner with its hissing spoons, even the mine. She loved her ridiculous saloon-bookshop-café and the strange cast of characters who kept barging into her life. She wanted to stay. The realization scared her. But there were things she needed to do first...

"I haven't officially decided anything," Rue said aloud. "I need to solve the murder first. Then maybe I'll decide if I'm staying."

The bell over the diner door jangled, and just like that, the temperature in the room dropped ten degrees.

Cole Dawson stood in the doorway, arms crossed, jaw tight. He didn't say anything. He just stared at Rue, then turned around and walked out.

Rue's stomach did a slow, dramatic flop to her toes.

Taz gently nudged a brown paper bag into Rue's hands. "Take these muffins back to the saloon. I'll package up the rest and bring them later."

Rue opened her mouth to argue. Shut it. Nodded. Outside, the boardwalk was quiet. She'd made it about three steps when...

"You're really going to sell?"

She turned and stomped toward the saloon, almost within sight of its door and relative quietness. Cole followed her, his grumpy storm cloud look back in full force.

"Seriously, Rue? I heard the rumor. And you didn't think to *mention* it?"

"I didn't know I needed to run my decisions by you," she snapped.

"You don't," he bit out. "But Ruth..."

"Ruth is *gone*. She left me the building. That means what I do with it is *my* business. Not hers. Not yours."

Cole stopped dead in his tracks. "She trusted you."

"I'm just trying to survive here, Cole. I haven't even made a real decision yet. But even if I had, you don't get to guilt me into staying."

He looked like she'd slapped him.

Before either of them could say something they'd regret, a syrupy voice floated in.

"Oh, wow. I *love* a good lovers' quarrel. This lighting is perfect."

Maribel Knox. With her phone out and recording. *Typical of my luck right now.* "Maribel," Rue growled. "What are you doing?"

Maribel just giggled and finally stopped recording. "Ghost Vein's going to love this. Or maybe my followers will." She slinked up beside Cole, hand fluttering onto his arm as she stared at Rue. "If you *are* selling, I'd love to buy. I adore the saloon. Such...*vibe*. Plus, I think I could really make the most of this town's potential. You know...ghost tours, influencer weekends, cursed gold retreats..." She trailed her fingers over Cole's sleeve.

He didn't move.

Didn't even glance at her.

But he didn't *shake her off* either.

Rue's stomach clenched, a weird, painful twist of jealousy and hurt. She turned away before her mouth could say something that would blow everything up.

Again.

Rue barely took two steps before Mayor Agnes Flint materialized at the far end of the boardwalk. She strode toward them, arms crossed, sensible shoes stomping, lips pursed.

"I heard something about an offer. If you're selling the Silver Tongue, I want first refusal."

Come on. What is with the gossip in this town? "What?"

"I have to protect the town's interests," the mayor continued. "And we can't have just *anyone* taking over such a central property."

"Oh, *wow*," Maribel drawled from beside Cole, already flipping her camera back on. "Is that shade I hear? Are you implying *I* don't have the town's best interests at heart, Mayor?"

The mayor didn't even blink. "If it looks like a goat, walks like a goat, and headbutts like a goat..."

Maribel gasped.

Rue snapped. "That's enough. Both of you." Her voice cracked. "If I decide to sell, *I'll* decide who I sell to. Not you. Not her. Not the town gossip train. Me."

"Fine." The mayor's eyes glittered. "Sell to me, and I'll *forget* about the breaking and entering."

Rue's blood ran cold.

Cole's head snapped toward Rue. "What?"

"I..." Rue opened her mouth, closed it, looked anywhere but at him.

The mayor smirked. "Oh, she didn't tell you, Sheriff? That's surprising."

Cole's jaw clenched so hard Rue was surprised his teeth didn't shatter.

"What did she mean by that, Rue?"

"I was trying to help," Rue muttered. "I didn't steal anything."

"You *broke into the mayor's office?*"

"Technically, I vacuumed," Rue shot back. The guilt twisted in her stomach. The nugget. The map piece. Both hiding upstairs in her apartment like a ticking time bomb. And she hadn't had a chance to even let Cole know yet. "I had a reason," she said weakly.

Cole's voice was low and deadly. "We'll talk later."

"Can't wait."

The mayor stepped closer, ignoring the firestorm she'd lit. "I'm offering you a clean solution. You owe me that much."

"I don't owe you *anything*. And neither does this town."

"*I* brought this town back from the brink. My tourism campaign *saved* Ghost Vein." The mayor's face turned a dangerous shade of tomato.

"And now you're closing the mine," Rue snapped. "Why is that? Something you don't want us to find?"

Taz appeared on the boardwalk, eyes wide. Jesse watched from the steps of the diner.

And Maribel? Filming everything, eyes shining with delight.

"You're completely out of line." The mayor's voice wobbled.

Rue took a step forward. "So are you. You're hiding

things. Tobias, Arnold. Things started going wrong after you started meddling. Or maybe it all started with you."

Cole hissed. "Rue, *stop...*"

"I'm not the one killing people," Rue shouted.

The street fell silent.

The mayor stared at her as if she'd sprouted horns. Then...she laughed. Loud, sharp, brittle. "Oh, Ms. Maddox. You'd better sell before someone declares you mentally unfit to run a business. Or before the health inspector finds something wrong with your little café." She turned to Cole. "Control her. Or I will." Then she stormed off.

Maribel clapped once. "Brilliant. Five stars. Incredible drama. Can I get that line again about the murdering?"

Rue spun toward her. "Get out of my face, Maribel."

"Yeesh," Maribel muttered, stepping back with a mocking bow.

"Rue, if you have *any* evidence, real or suspected, you come to *me*. Not accuse the mayor in public. Not tip her off. Not whatever this circus just was."

Her throat burned as she tried to swallow. "I was angry."

"Yeah. No kidding." He shook his head. "And now you've warned her. What were you doing? She knows. We'll talk about the break-in later."

He turned and stalked off without another word.

Her chest ached. Her eyes stung. That old familiar feeling settled into her bones like a weight. The *Maddox mad,* her mother used to call it. A family trait. A red-hot rage that lit up fast and left nothing but regret. She'd just proved the mayor's point. In public. On camera. And worst of all...she'd let Cole down. *Again.* Rue turned on her heel and fled inside the saloon. She barely made it inside the

Silver Tongue before she heard the telltale click of bedazzled boots behind her. Maribel. *Of course.*

For once, the influencer didn't have her phone out. She was shaking her head with mock disappointment. "You know, Rue, you catch more flies with honey than vinegar. Maybe it's something you should've learned by your age."

"I'm twenty-eight, not ninety."

Maribel tilted her head, all faux concern. "Still. Maybe leave the emotional outbursts to the teens." She took a step closer, voice dropping. "And a little warning, from one woman to another. Stop interfering in my life. Cole is out of your league. You don't understand him like I do."

Rue crossed her arms. "He's an adult. He can date whoever he wants."

Maribel smiled. All teeth and venom. "Exactly. And after that volcanic little meltdown out there? I think he'll be ready for a more *subtle flair*. Someone who actually *gets* him." She gave Rue a little finger wave. "Toodles."

Taz slipped in seconds later, eyes wide. "Okay. I missed something. What the heck just happened?"

"I lost it." Rue sagged against the counter, her brown bag of baked goods squished against her hip. "I said way too much. I basically gift-wrapped a murder accusation and blasted it at the mayor, with Maribel filming the whole thing. I blew it, Taz. I screwed everything up."

"No, you..."

"I did. Maybe I should just sell and leave before I make things worse."

"Rue..."

She held up a hand. "Please. I can't talk about it right now."

Taz exchanged a look with Cassie, who had just poked her head in from the kitchen.

Rue pretended not to see the concern in their eyes. She buried herself in busy work, shelving books, wiping down tables, and helping Thomas organize the book cartons, even though he clearly didn't need help. By mid-afternoon, she'd caught them whispering about her. She wasn't even mad. They were right. She was spiraling into an organizing fugue state. She didn't mention Cole. Didn't mention the mayor. Didn't mention the investigation. Just kept moving because if she paused, she might fall apart completely.

Early evening came and the saloon stood quiet. Thomas and Cassie offered to clean up.

Taz shoved a hoodie into Rue's hands. "You and I are going for a walk. No arguing."

Rue didn't argue, just followed her friend outside. The town was starting to wind down. Fairy lights twinkled along Main Street, and the wind carried the scent of baking and chimney smoke. They passed the general store just as Delilah was locking the front door. She spotted them and gave Rue a knowing look.

"I heard you had a bit of a set-to with the mayor."

Rue winced. "You could say that."

Delilah grinned. "You're not the only one. Everyone's wanted to take a swing at Agnes at some point, just not while being filmed for the entire supernatural internet. But still."

"I lost my temper," Rue muttered. "I shouldn't have."

Delilah threw her head back and laughed. "Honey, that's exactly how Ruth and I stopped being friends. Two stubborn women with short fuses and sharp tongues. We blew up and never fixed it. Wasted time." She stepped closer, eyes suddenly serious. "Be better than us, girl. Losing your temper's human. It's what you *do after* that shows your mettle. Make it right. Don't repeat the same mistake."

"Thanks," Rue said quietly.

Nacho bleated behind them, like he agreed.

The women kept walking, arms linked, the breeze cool on their faces. Tension started to lift from Rue's shoulders. They were almost past the library when Letty Navarro appeared.

She stood on the top step, library tote in hand, gaze flicking up and down the street. She looked...nervous. Shifty.

"Evening. Just closing up." Letty's voice was tight.

"Evening," Taz replied cheerfully, not noticing the tension in the other woman's voice.

Letty moved to turn back inside, then bumped into Rue, her papers spilling out of her bag everywhere. "Sorry, I'm clumsy sometimes."

Rue bent to help her. As she did, Letty's hand brushed hers, then pressed something into her palm.

A folded piece of paper.

Letty gave her a tight nod as she met Rue's gaze, then she scooped up the rest of her bundle and disappeared inside, locking the door.

Taz raised an eyebrow. "Well. That wasn't suspicious at all."

Rue switched sides so Taz was now between her and the street. "Pretend you're talking to me."

"I *am* talking to you."

"Talk more. Keep it normal."

Her friend immediately launched into a loud, animated explanation about the ethics of wearing socks with sandals.

Rue unfolded the hidden note in her hand. It was scrawled in tight, librarian-perfect script. *Meet me tomorrow night after the library closes. I have something you need to see. It's connected to your investigation. Come alone.* She refolded the paper and tucked it into her hoodie pocket.

What did Letty know? And why couldn't she just say it outright? Rue had a feeling the answer was simple. Whatever Letty had discovered...was dangerous.

And someone might already be watching...

TWENTY

Rue had been on tenterhooks all day, her mind a whirlwind of what-ifs and worst-case scenarios. She'd kept herself busy at the bookshop, but her nervous energy didn't diminish. She was dusting a bookshelf in the main room, with two books clutched to her chest, when someone cleared their throat behind her.

Cole. With Jesse right behind him. The sheriff scowled at Jesse, who gave him a nudge, then drifted off.

He cleared his throat. "I regret what I said yesterday. In the street. I shouldn't have snapped. And I'm not going to shut you up just because the mayor says so."

Okay, not what she expected.

He kept going, awkward but earnest. "Your opinions—they matter. You matter. But Rue...you *can't* keep sneaking around and breaking into people's offices. One of these days, I'll be the one who has to arrest you."

She bit her lip. "I'm sorry. I shouldn't have lost my temper. My mom calls it the 'Maddox mad.' It builds up, then explodes, and afterward, I always feel like a jerk."

Cole smiled. "Ruth had a version of that too. Though... she never really did it in public. On Main Street."

Rue gave a weak thumbs-up. "So, I've got one up on Ruth. Great." She sobered. "I *am* sorry. I shouldn't have yelled. I'm planning to apologize to the mayor. Even if it kills me."

Cole chuckled. "Maybe don't go that far. But...yeah. An apology probably wouldn't hurt." They stood in awkward silence for a second before he added, "I don't want you to sell, Rue. I hope you stay. Give Ghost Vein a real shot."

Rue nodded. "I'll think about it."

"That's all I can ask."

She debated telling him about Letty's note. The gold. The map. But she decided to wait and let him get his full mad out all at once later, after she met with Letty. She might text him just before, though. Just in case.

"See you later?" he asked.

"Yeah," she said softly.

He nodded, then headed back toward Jesse, who promptly grabbed him in a headlock and dragged him out.

Taz walked up, grinning. "Well, that wasn't so bad."

Rue grimaced. "I hate apologizing. But...yeah, I had to. That whole explosion was not okay. Now I've gotta suck it up and say sorry to the mayor too."

Taz smacked her gently on the back. "That's not the only thing you'll have to suck up."

"What's that supposed to..."

The bell above the door jingled. Maribel sashayed in, all smug expression and bounce.

Putting on her customer service smile, Rue placed her books on a shelf. "Good afternoon, Maribel. Can I help you find anything?"

Maribel smirked. "Oh, I just came to check in. After

your...*temper fit* in the street last night. I saw Cole leaving. Guess he wasn't impressed, hmm?"

She didn't take the bait. "Can I help you with any books?"

Maribel pouted. "No reaction? Hmph." She turned and flounced around the bookshop.

That's when Nacho trotted in from the café side. The goat zeroed in on Maribel and galloped toward her.

She squealed and tried to sidestep him, but he kept following. "Shoo. Go away," she snapped, trying to nudge him with her foot.

Nacho wasn't having it. He followed her faster, ears perked, tail flicking.

Maribel shrieked as he chased her out the door.

"Security's got teeth today." Rue giggled.

Taz popped up from behind the counter, snorting. "Goat patrol strikes again."

They high-fived as Nacho strutted back in.

Rue helped close up for the night, though she was more distracted than useful. She stacked three books on top of the coffee grinder and tried to put a cupcake in the till before Taz gently redirected her to a task that involved less...chaos.

As they wiped the last table, Taz nudged Rue with her hip. "Text me if you need backup at the library. Or better yet, want me to come with you?"

Rue shook her head. "It's not even dark yet. I'll be fine. I'll text Cole now, just so he doesn't freak out. I'll send it as I'm leaving so he can't stop me."

Taz winced. "Soooo...you might want to know I already texted Cole."

"Of course you did."

"He was being all weird and grumpy, and I figured he'd

want to know. I didn't tell him *everything*, just enough to make him twitchy."

Rue sighed. "Just try to delay him if he heads this way, okay?"

"I'll do my best," Taz said. "But you know how protective he gets when you get that 'I'm about to trespass' gleam in your eye."

Saluting, Rue grabbed her bag and headed outside, trying to beat Cole to the library. Her phone pinged. Text from Sheriff Grumpy.

Don't go in until I get there. I'm serious, Rue.

She read it, then closed the message and pretended she hadn't.

The sun had set, but Main Street still glowed under strings of fairy lights and old-timey lamp posts. People were out, enjoying the evening.

The breeze kicked up. A strange chill brushed past her. Rue stiffened.

A translucent shimmer drifted across the street. One of the miner ghosts. He winked at her and gave a raspy chuckle. Rue covered her butt automatically. "Rude," she muttered. "Spooky *and* handsy? Pick one and stick to it."

The ghost vanished.

She reached the library and stopped cold. The door was wide open.

From what she'd heard, Letty was meticulous. Not the type to leave a door unlocked, let alone *wide open*. Rue's stomach clenched, but she pushed forward. "Letty?" She stepped into the library.

No answer.

The lights were still on, the air still warm from the day. But the silence felt...wrong.

"Letty?"

Something gurgled.

Rue froze. "That's not a good sound." She moved toward the noise, pulling out her phone and clutching it like a weapon. The reading area was a mess. An overturned chair. A collapsed bookcase. Books scattered like confetti. A broken ladder lay nearby, one of those sturdy old wooden ones that belonged in a museum, not laying here with one leg snapped like a matchstick. Rue crouched beside it, her stomach twisting. The break was clean. *Too* clean.

"Sabotage," she whispered. "Someone did this on purpose."

A thud behind her made her whip around. Her heart did the can-can in her chest. She called out, "I'm over here." Only after the words left her mouth did she realize...what if it *wasn't* Cole?

Another gurgle answered her. It came from in front of her, buried under the books. Rue dropped to her knees and peered beneath the edge of the fallen shelf.

An arm.

"Letty." She scrambled forward, tossing books aside until she uncovered the librarian. "Help. Someone help."

Letty was barely conscious. Her face was bruised, her clothes rumpled, blood trickling down her temple. Her eyes fluttered open, and her hand reached out, grabbing Rue's wrist.

"Shhh. Don't talk," Rue whispered. "Help's coming."

"Under the front desk. A package," Letty's voice rasped. "Your name on it. It'll help you."

"You're the one bleeding and you're giving me homework?"

"If it's my time...no fussing's gonna stop it." Letty coughed. "Keep digging. There's more. Someone doesn't want you to find it."

The words sent ice down Rue's spine. Before she could reply, a scuff of boots echoed across the tile. Rue spun, phone raised.

"Easy, it's me." Cole crouched beside her.

"Thank goodness." Rue sagged with relief.

Cole didn't waste time calling the paramedics, the town doc, and Deputy Mayhew. "They're on their way. You okay?"

"Fine. I just...got here first."

He raised an eyebrow. "Didn't you get my text?"

Rue widened her eyes innocently. "Must've been delayed."

He grunted. "Sure it was."

Rue stayed beside Letty until medical help got there.

Doc Halliday arrived just behind the medics, took one look at Rue, and sighed. "Back up, sweetie. Let them work."

Cole gently steered Rue aside as the team moved in, working fast. Letty was alive but bruised, bloodied, and barely conscious. The sight of her motionless under the tangle of books and broken shelf churned Rue's stomach.

The doc turned to them. "We'll stabilize her here, but if she's strong enough, we're sending her to Reno. Better facilities. Better chance." Then she was gone, marching after the stretcher.

Rue stood frozen, arms wrapped tightly around herself. "She asked me to meet her. I was running on time, but if I'd been early, maybe I could've stopped it. Maybe—"

He cut her off. "Or maybe *you'd* be the one on that stretcher."

Rue bit her lip. "She wanted to talk. Whatever it was, it was important. Important enough for someone to *stop* her."

"Rue...you think this was on purpose?" Cole frowned.

"It looks like an accident or maybe a heart attack and she fell."

"She didn't just fall, Cole. Look at the ladder."

He hesitated, then walked over to where it lay. Rue followed, gesturing to one of the broken legs. "That's not a normal break. Too clean. Too straight. That wasn't age, weight, or bad luck. That was a *cut*."

Cole crouched, inspecting it closer. His brow furrowed.

Meanwhile, Rue moved to the front desk. She ducked behind the counter and there was the package Letty had told her about. A large manila envelope, her name printed across the front in Letty's tidy script.

"Rue?" Cole called.

She stood up, holding the envelope. "Letty left this for me."

He crossed to her, eyes narrowing as she flipped through the contents—handwritten notes, newspaper clippings, printed emails. The top page was marked in bold. *Elias Grimshaw Lineage. Missing Descendants.*

"Take it," Cole said quietly. "But don't let anyone else see it. Not yet."

He glanced over his shoulder. "Mayhew's outside. He'll be watching. Head back to the shop. We'll talk later."

Rue nodded. Her hands shook as she tucked the envelope beneath her sweater.

Cole turned to intercept Mayhew, buying her time. The deputy gave Rue a narrow look as she slipped past him, but he said nothing.

Outside, the air felt colder. Rue pulled out her phone with trembling fingers and called Taz. "It's me. Letty's been hurt. I'll explain everything when I get back but..." Her voice cracked. "We have to stop this. Before anyone else dies."

TWENTY-ONE

The next day, Rue and Taz sat at one of the saloon tables, Letty's package cracked open in front of them. The building hadn't opened to the public yet, but Cassie already bustled around, getting the café side prepped for the day.

Nacho contentedly munched on a berry muffin.

Inside the package were Letty's research notes, carefully written pages about the mine, the legend of Ghost Vein, Elias Grimshaw's rumored magical practices, and the cursed gold. Tucked inside her journal was a scribbled reminder about additional documents she'd left in her office.

One journal entry interested Rue. Letty had written about someone repeatedly breaking into the library and archives, moving her notes and rummaging through her research. She'd hidden things, but they always seemed to be...off. Shifted. Disturbed.

Rue pointed at the entry. "See this? She wasn't just being paranoid. Someone really wanted her research."

Taz nodded grimly. "Enough to maybe set up an accident. To stop her from talking to you."

"Exactly. So, at least one person is interested in more than just shiny treasure. They want the vault."

The notes dove deeper into Elias Grimshaw's obsession with power and control. Letty had a list of the miners who'd vanished, some names Rue had seen before, but Letty's version was more updated.

"Some of these families are still in town." Taz leaned closer to the list.

"Who?"

"Wynona and Lynette's last name is here. Their maiden name was Hennesey."

Cassie peeked over their shoulders. "Ramirez." She pointed at the paper. "That's my dad's side. There's always been weird stories in our family about Grimshaw." She pulled up a chair and settled in. "According to my grandma, who heard it from her mother, Grimshaw was paranoid. Paid people to snitch on their coworkers. He underpaid everyone and worked them to exhaustion. People were constantly sick. Some workers just vanished. But because shifts ran long and folks were always working overtime, no one noticed for a couple of days. When families did go to the police, the mine was investigated...briefly. But Grimshaw paid off the sheriff. Then Grimshaw disappeared. Gone."

"And no one ever found the miners?"

Cassie shook her head. "Nope. My grandma said before the miners disappeared, people spotted strange things near the mine late at night. Grimshaw, witches lurking. After he vanished, that's when the ghost stories really started."

"That matches what I've heard too." Taz nodded.

"I love a good creepy ghost story." Cassie beamed.

Taz rolled her eyes. "These ghosts aren't like the friendly, chatty types in town. The miner spirits barely show themselves. Mostly, it's just the wailing. The chanting. Occasionally, someone spots a ghost near the entrance or in one of the deep caverns. Tourists have caught glimpses before. But usually, it's just one ghost."

Rue shivered. The image of that miner ghost from her mine tour flashed into her brain, and she couldn't shake the icy feeling that followed. Rubbing her arms, she made her way upstairs to the apartment bathroom.

And froze.

Another message had been scrawled across her mirror. In lipstick.

Pay attention. They're getting close.

"Ruth, seriously? Lipstick?" Rue grabbed a hand towel and scrubbed the mirror. "Do you even know how much makeup costs now?"

No response, of course.

"How about actually showing up, huh? Face-to-face. Like a normal dead person." A soft clink behind Rue made her spin. The lipstick lifted on its own, hovered, then dragged itself across the mirror.

Soon.

It dropped to the vanity with a loud clang. "Fine. But hurry up. I'm going nuts here." Shaking off the unease, Rue headed downstairs. She found Doc Halliday already in the kitchen, sipping a cup of tea while Letty's packet of information sat tidied away on the counter.

Doc gave her a long look. "Letty survived the fall. She's stable...for now."

Relief hit Rue. "Thank goodness."

"She's in a medically induced coma. They're monitoring her for a possible brain bleed."

"Did she say anything before she passed out?"

"Funny you should ask." Doc studied Rue over the rim

of her mug. "She kept mumbling about her office. And you. Your name, over and over. Rue. Office."

A chill spread into Rue's bones. Letty had tried to tell her something.

"What exactly is going on?" Doc's expression turned sharp. "Am I about to get more patients? Is this town about to turn into a medical emergency zone?"

Rue glanced at Taz, who gave a subtle nod.

"Someone's hunting Elias Grimshaw's cursed gold and the map to the vault. Letty had some information. That's why she was targeted."

"Are you saying this wasn't a fall? That it wasn't natural?"

"Can you tell if her injuries were consistent with... anything besides a heart attack or accident?" Rue side-stepped Doc's question.

"She was in good health. No sign of a heart attack. The injuries match a fall, but I can't tell you if the ladder was sabotaged. That's Cole's job." Doc set down her cup. "Do you have any idea who's doing this?"

"I don't know *who* yet," Rue admitted. "But I'm narrowing it down. All signs point to someone hunting that map."

"There are always treasure hunters around." Doc rolled her eyes. "Why is this time different?"

"Because this isn't like before," Taz said. "This person is serious. Ruthless. People are getting hurt."

Rue hesitated, then spoke slowly. "Ruth said...the vault is a prison, not a prize. Trust no one."

Quiet for a beat, Doc nodded. "It's good to hear Ruth's hanging around. But I don't get it. *Prison?*"

Cassie piped up from behind the counter. "My family always believed the miners never left that mine. That they were sacrificed. The way we heard it, witches were involved. Blood wards. My gram said her mother told her that Grimshaw cursed the gold so no one else could have it. That if the gold is found, the town dies."

"There are angry spirits in there. Dangerous ones." Taz shuddered. "Cursed gold, cursed souls. I wouldn't want to be the one to open that vault."

Doc drained her tea and stood. "I don't know anything about gold or curses. I just know about my patients, and I don't want more of them." She strode to the door, then paused. "I'll prep the med bay and alert the next hospital over, just in case. But Rue?" She fixed Rue with a level stare. "Warnings from a ghost are all well and good. But Ruth's already dead. I'd rather you not join her." With that, Doc left.

Rue stood there, the silence ringing in her ears, the air in the room suddenly heavy. She crossed her arms, hugging herself. "How am I supposed to stop any of this? I don't know the first thing about curse-breaking. Or sleuthing, for that matter." A few lucky guesses. A few magical hiccups that somehow worked in her favor. That's all she had.

The floor trembled.

Bookshelves rattled.

Mugs in the sink clinked ominously.

"Pretty sure Ruth's saying *get over yourself and get moving.*"

Rue raised an eyebrow at her friend.

"Fresh air." Taz pointed toward the saloon doors just as they burst open with a dramatic squeak. "See? Ruth approves. Go stretch your legs."

Groaning, Rue grabbed her jacket. "Fine, I'll go inhale some Main Street dust and maybe track down a cupcake or three."

She slipped outside. Tourists had already begun to flood the street, posing in cowboy hats and hoop skirts, snapping photos like it was a Wild West Disneyland. She hadn't gotten far when Cole fell into step beside her.

"You okay?" he asked.

"Haven't yelled at anyone today, so that's a win." She gave him a sideways smile. "Just worried things are going to get worse before they get better."

"They might, but you're not in this alone. We'll handle it. *Together*. Just keep me looped in on what you're doing, and I'll run interference when needed."

Rue blinked, caught off guard by the offer. "Okay. That's fair. Taz already gave me a lecture. So did Doc."

He arched a brow. "What did Doc say? Any updates on Letty?"

"She's stable, in a medical coma up in Reno." Rue rubbed the back of her neck absently. Her skin itched like someone watched her. She glanced behind them but only saw tourists. "Doc said she kept mumbling about me. And her office. Over and over."

Cole nodded. "Doc mentioned she'd been talking but didn't have details yet."

They paused outside the library where yellow crime scene tape fluttered in the breeze, the *Closed Until Further Notice* sign still taped to the door.

"I've got to grab some photos. Want to come in? I promised transparency. I'm trying here. Unless Deputy Mayhew's lurking nearby, ready to tattle to the mayor."

Rue's heart gave a small, unexpected tug. He *was* trying. She nodded. "Yeah. I want to check Letty's office anyway."

Inside the library, they split up, Cole to photograph the

fall site, Rue to Letty's office. She hesitated, not wanting to violate Letty's space, but she *needed* answers.

Letty's files were immaculate. Nothing obvious about the mine or the gold stood out. Rue trailed her fingers across the bookcase, scanning the spines. So many genres. Letty had been a reader, and Rue respected that. Her hand snagged something, a small handful of loose newspaper clippings tucked between books. One headline caught her eye. *Maisie Grimshaw Donates Garden to Boston Historical Society*. Dated a year after Elias Grimshaw's death.

The photo was grainy, but the woman looked like the one from the museum display. Standing next to her was a small boy. A son? Rue's heartbeat faster. Another article, dated nineteen seventy-five, was an obituary. This time for a Miriam Grimshaw, age eighty-seven. No children, but she had a brother who had one son, age forty...in nineteen seventy-five. Rue frowned. That meant Elias Grimshaw's descendants could still be alive. One of them could even be in Ghost Vein right now. She tucked the articles back but found a torn scrap of paper stuck to one of the books. It was Letty's handwriting but messy, rushed. Not journal-neat. Rue read the passage out loud. *"Cursed with death's greed and power. Grimshaw's descendants walk hidden."*

It sounded...like a prophecy. What if Letty *had* discovered a Grimshaw descendant in town? Someone hiding their identity and willing to kill to keep it hidden.

Maribel? The mayor? Josiah Evans?

They all had a weird obsession with the gold. If one of them was a Grimshaw...it would explain a lot.

Cole poked his head into the office. "Find anything?"

"Bits and pieces. This note...and articles. I think Grimshaw's family didn't vanish. They scattered."

"You need to dig into it. I also just got word more museum artifacts have gone missing. We can't get a full list while Letty's out, but it's possible her archive was targeted too."

"And we need to solve it before anyone else gets hurt."

"By the way..." Cole hesitated before continuing. "Did you ever find out who made the offer on your building?"

Rue shook her head. "Just a real estate agent and a corporation. No names. I'm going to nudge the lawyer again. Honestly, it wouldn't shock me if the mayor was behind it."

"Funny you say that. One of Doc's nurses mentioned someone asking around about your saloon. Who owns it, its living conditions, whether it was zoned properly. Her brother works at one of the cafés. Heard it from a customer."

"Someone's trying to get dirt on me."

"Looks like it. Maybe they're trying to use local regulations to push you out."

Rue let out a breath. "Sounds *exactly* like the mayor. Especially after I accused her of murder. Maybe this is her revenge, to force me out of Ghost Vein."

"Not happening. I won't let anyone hurt you. Or run you out. You're a Maddox. You *belong* in Ghost Vein."

Rue met his gaze, tension crackling between them. Warmth bloomed in her chest, curling tight and hot. No one was forcing her out. Not before she found the killer.

And not before I uncover the truth about Grimshaw's cursed gold.

TWENTY-TWO

Early evening draped Ghost Vein in fading golden light. The town square was alive with chatter and clinking glasses. Tonight was the annual *Old-Fashioned Moonshine Tasting*.

Rue strolled between stalls with Taz and Jesse, eyeing the themed displays. "I thought moonshine was illegal?"

Jesse smirked. "Mayor got special permits. It's all above board. Cole and Deputy Mayhew are on patrol, making sure no one ends up trying to ride a goat or duel a lamppost. Happens every year. Tourists eat it up."

Taz snorted. "Tourists eat up the saloon girls in tight corsets and push-up bras."

Jesse clutched his chest. "How dare you? This is about the moonshine. The rich history. The craftsmanship. Not the corsets."

Taz rolled her eyes so hard Rue was surprised they didn't fall out.

Despite the sass, Rue was actually enjoying herself. The Western-themed chaos had its charm. Laughter echoed across the square, fiddles played in the background, and fairy lights twinkled overhead. They paused by a stall offering ghost-themed moonshine tasters.

Jesse handed her a tiny plastic shot glass. "Try this one, 'Miner-Begone.' It's mild."

Rue made a face. "You know I'm a lightweight. Alcohol doesn't like me. One sip and my face is a beetroot."

He grinned. "Exactly why this one's perfect. You've got to immerse yourself in Ghost Vein's...extracurricular activities."

She sniffed it, braced herself, and took a sip. It wasn't terrible. Slightly smoky with a sweet aniseed kick. Against her better judgment, she took a second sip before tossing the rest. "Okay, that's enough. I'm already feeling the flush."

"Lightweight." He handed a second shot to Taz.

Across the crowd, Rue spotted Cole, standing near the mayor and Deputy Mayhew. He gave her a small, private smile. The mayor didn't. She looked like she'd bitten into something sour. Mayhew's glare was frosty. Rue spotted Maribel lurking at the edge of the crowd with her phone out, filming. She sneered when she caught Rue's eye.

Rue turned away. "I need hydration and less judgement." She slipped away to a nearby stall selling bottled water. As she paid, she caught a raspy voice behind the stall next door.

"I'm tellin' you, it's part of a map," an old man said, slurring his words. "Old mine shaft, the layout, it's real. It's old paper. Torn but real."

The bartender, Jackson Malone, grunted. "You're drunk, Earl. Every month, someone claims to have a piece of the gold map."

"I'm not claimin' anything about gold. Just that the paper shows the mine tunnels. I'd be willin' to entertain offers."

"Tell you what. I'll cover your bar tab. Consider that your offer."

Earl sputtered in outrage. "I heard you were interested. Now you're mockin' me?"

Jackson spotted Rue standing nearby. His eyes narrowed, and he moved...fast. "Don't mind him." He strode over to Rue with forced cheer. "Moonshine makes old men talk nonsense."

Rue backed up a step. Jackson's body language wasn't threatening, just invading her personal space. He was *trying* to distract and herd her away. And she didn't like it.

Apparently, neither did Cole.

He crossed the square in a heartbeat, jaw tight. "Hands off, Malone. Back it up. Aggressive behavior's not what this town needs right now."

Jackson grinned. "Just sayin' hi."

"Try waving next time," Cole snapped.

A crowd was starting to gather, locals and tourists catching wind of tension. The man Jackson had been talking to, shot Rue a calculating glance, then sidled off, disappearing out of sight.

Jackson, never one to avoid drama, puffed his chest and stepped into Cole's space. "Don't like your tone, Sheriff."

"And I don't like you breathing on me," Cole growled back.

They were toe-to-toe, the kind of macho showdown that usually ended with someone getting punched.

Rue stepped between them, one hand on each chest, firm but calm. "Okay, easy. No one needs to end up face-first in the moonshine vat."

Jackson grinned at her. "Finally putting your hands on me, sweetheart?"

Rue didn't dignify that with a response. She looked at

Cole instead, giving him her best distraction smile. "Come on, Sheriff. Deep breaths. Think of all the paperwork."

Cole stared at her for a beat, jaw still tight, then exhaled and stepped back.

Jackson, of course, couldn't resist a final poke. "Didn't know the law was so sensitive."

Cole's voice iced over. "Watch yourself, Malone." He turned to Rue. "You know you can make your own choices. I respect that. But that guy? He's got a record for drunk and disorderly. And a reputation. He's not someone to trust."

Rue dropped her arms. "I don't like him. But one awkward half-date doesn't make *us* a couple, Cole."

Jackson winked from where he leaned against the nearby stall. "Still happy to buy you that drink later." He tipped an imaginary hat and sauntered off, enjoying every second of the attention.

Rue held up a hand to Cole. "I know you mean well. But you don't get to police who I talk to."

Before he could answer, the mayor stormed over. "This is *my* event. And once again, *you're* causing trouble. Just like your great aunt. Always stirring things up. Maybe it's time you sold that saloon and moved on. Ghost Vein's not for troublemakers." She didn't wait for a response, just flounced off in a cloud of righteous indignation.

"I guess now's probably not the best time to apologize for calling her a murderer, huh?"

Cole sighed. "You think?"

Maribel popped up, phone raised. "This is *gold.* If either of you wants to do an interview, I'd be *happy* to help you tell your side. I'll even make sure *you* get a flattering edit, Sheriff." She leaned into Cole's side, eyes sparkling as she practically purred at him.

"You're free to speak to whoever you want." Rue's face

turned to stone. "We're not dating, remember?" She pivoted and marched toward Jesse and Taz.

"That looked tense."

"I'm fine." Rue shook off Taz's concern. "Maribel's just…ugh. *Maribel*." She rubbed her temple. "And she made me forgot what I overheard, until just now." Rue glanced back toward the drink stalls. The old man was gone. So was Jackson. She relayed what she'd heard about the torn map and described the drunken old man.

Jesse frowned. "That sounds like Old Earl. I've fixed his truck a couple of times. Total boozehound, but harmless. Lives out past the mine road."

"Then you two should pay him a visit. I'll keep an eye on Cole. And the bartender."

Rue hesitated.

Taz smirked. "Don't worry. I'll behave."

Jesse gestured toward his truck. "Let's go before the trail goes cold."

They left the square and drove out toward the edge of town. Earl's place was a creaky cabin tucked near the base of the ridge, half-swallowed by brush and time.

"This place feels cursed." Rue made a face.

Shrugging, Jesse killed the engine. "Welcome to the neighborhood. Although I'm surprised we didn't pass the old guy on our way."

"More than likely, he's still in town trying to sell his part of the map." She frowned. "If that's what it was."

Rue knocked on the door of the lopsided cabin. No one answered. She tried again, this time banging with more force. Still nothing. She pushed, and the door swung open with a long, dramatic groan. Rue exchanged a glance with Jesse. "That's not creepy at all."

"Probably just a raccoon's den."

They stepped inside cautiously. The place was small, one room. A mix of stale alcohol and mildew permeated the air. Clothes were missing from wire hangers, drawers half-open, and personal items strewn across the floor.

Jesse gave a low whistle. "He probably had time to get back here before us if he left while Cole and Jackson were having words. He either left in a hurry...or someone else *helped* him pack. We must have just missed him."

"Or maybe someone came searching for something." Her gaze landed on a battered bookcase in the corner. A few books had been torn apart, spines split, pages scattered. She crouched and spotted a crumpled piece of paper near her boot. Smoothing it out, a strange tingle trickled along her spine as she stared at it. The paper, partially torn, looked familiar. The texture too. And at the top, a faded inscription. Her stomach flipped. "Jesse...I think this might be another piece of the map. It looks like what Tobias had when he died."

Jesse held it up toward the dusty light filtering through the grimy window...and sniffed it. "Yeah...except this paper is tea-stained. It smells like chamomile."

"Did you just *sniff* the paper?"

He ignored her, took another sniff, and recoiled. "And feet. Tea and feet. A not so good copy."

"You sure you're not part *fox* or something? You've got that whole sly, lets-make-trouble vibe."

"Fox, huh? That's new." He chuckled.

"It fits. You're quick, nosy, and you definitely steal things, like my snacks." She stared at the paper Jesse still held. "You think it's a fake?"

"Absolutely. Earl had a rep for scams. Probably made this to con someone, and it backfired. Whoever he tried to swindle didn't like it."

Rue frowned, holding the paper up to the weak cabin light. "It's similar enough to Tobias' that it might've fooled someone...at least long enough to cause trouble." She tucked the page into her jacket. "I wonder if he tried to sell it to someone other than Malone?"

Jessie crossed his arms, looking around the cabin again. "Malone definitely gives me shady energy."

She let out a tired sigh. "Great. Another name for my ever-growing suspect list. They all have means, motive, and access. It's like a murder mystery bingo sheet, and everyone's one suspicious glare away from a full card."

They both paused as something thumped in the corner of the cabin.

A possum waddled out from behind a pile of old boots, gave them a disapproving look, and hissed.

"Well, I guess that's our cue."

Rue backed toward the door. "Agreed. Leave the crime scene to the animals."

She couldn't help but wonder what other crime scenes were waiting in her future...

TWENTY-THREE

The night air was cool with desert chill, and the faint twang of a country guitar leaked out through the rickety door of *The Hole.*

Rue tugged her jacket tighter and eyed the bar with grim determination. "This is either going to be genius or the world's most embarrassing sting operation."

Beside her, Taz folded her arms. "Remind me again why we're back at The Hole?"

"Because, my skeptical sidekick, this is part of the plan." Rue grinned.

"Sidekick? I give out sidekick vibes?" Taz pouted. "We need a name."

"You're right. It's terrible branding. I need something with more pizzazz. Maybe...*The Sleuthers?*"

Taz's face twisted in horror. "Absolutely not."

A third voice chimed in cheerfully. "What about *The Clues Crew?* It has a nice ring to it." Isla strolled up, her smile full of mischief.

"You're both enjoying this way too much."

"Of course we are. Subterfuge. Deception. Late-night scheming. It's live-action theater."

Taz sighed. "How about we just...don't name ourselves anything? Ever."

Rue ignored her and refocused. "All right, here's the deal. We're setting a mini trap for the bartender."

"The same bartender who thinks you're hot for him?"

"Exactly. Best kind of bait. I'm positive he's tied up in something shady. The old guy, Earl, was talking to him about that map. The map's fake but there had to be a reason Earl approached Malone."

"Or one bad egg recognizes another," Taz muttered.

"Anyway, he's been acting twitchy ever since Cole started sniffing around. So, tonight, we're going to rattle him and see how he reacts."

Isla tilted her head. "How exactly are we rattling him? I'm still confused on the logistics here."

"Simple." Rue grinned. "I'm going to let it slip that some artifacts from the museum are missing, specifically items linked to the mine. Then I'll drop that the sheriff has promised to look the other way if the items are returned."

"You're just...lying to a possibly dangerous criminal?" Taz narrowed her eyes. "Does Cole know about this?"

"Strategic fibbing. And yes, Cole knows. He and Mayhew are staking out the museum."

"And then what?" Isla nibbled her lip. "I don't want the museum to be at risk."

"I tell Malone that if the missing artifacts magically return, the sheriff might back off. Then...bam." Rue clapped her hands. "He panics, tries to sneak the artifacts back, and the cops catch him red-handed. And your museum is safe."

"We set the bait, *he* takes it, and *Cole* gets the collar?" Taz grumbled.

Rue nodded. "Yep. It's the one part of the plan Cole insisted on. No civilian arrests. I'm on thin ice already."

Isla looked almost wistful. "I'd love to see those artifacts recovered. My boss has been losing sleep over it. He's obsessed, but the mayor keeps telling him to keep it quiet. She's terrified the news will tank tourism funding."

"Of course it's the mayor. It's *always* the mayor." Rue smoothed down her top and tugged the neckline just low enough to make her point. "All right, ladies. I'm ready for action."

They pushed through the door of *The Hole*, instantly assaulted by the wail of someone on stage murdering a Garth Brooks song.

"No," Rue groaned.

"It's karaoke night." Taz snickered.

"Really, *really* bad karaoke night," Isla added, hands over her ears as a cowboy in sequins hit a note that shouldn't be humanly possible.

"Perfect cover noise. Nobody notices small talk when their eardrums are bleeding." Rue winced.

The trio weaved through the crowd. Locals filled the booths, their laughter as loud as the discordant singing on stage.

"Grab that corner booth. I'll handle the bar."

"Try not to get us banned," Taz called as she and Isla slid into the booth.

"Or arrested," Isla added.

Shooting them a salute, Rue threaded through the crowd toward the bar.

The bartender, Jackson Malone, glanced up when Rue approached, and his expression tightened. "Well, look who it is. Bookstore lady. You here for a drink or another round of questions?"

Rue leaned casually against the counter. "Maybe both. You make a mean soda."

"You're easy to please."

"That's me," Rue said. "A soda and two beers, please."

He gave her a wary look but started pouring the soda. She took the moment to glance around the bar. Taz and Isla were pretending to study the menu, their heads pressed together. Totally subtle. Rue tried to keep her expression neutral. When the bartender slid the glass toward her, she smiled. "So...rough week?"

"You could say that. Town's going crazy, ghost stories, break-ins, cops poking around. Everyone's jumpy."

"Yeah." Rue lowered her voice. "Heard the sheriff's been busy. Something about missing artifacts?"

The bartender's hand froze on the cloth he was wiping the counter with. "Artifacts?"

"Mm-hmm." Rue took a sip and set the glass down. "Supposedly from the museum. Pretty valuable."

He frowned. "Who told you that?"

"Small town. Big mouths." Rue leaned closer. "Word is, if the stolen items quietly show back up, the sheriff might drop the case. No charges. Everyone walks away happy."

His expression didn't change, but a muscle in his jaw ticked. "Huh."

"Crazy, right? People do stupid things for shiny objects. Especially when they think nobody's watching."

He didn't answer, just grabbed two beers and shoved them at her.

Rue smiled, all innocence. "Anyway, just thought I'd mention it."

She turned, balanced her drink with the beers and sauntered away, heart pounding.

Back at the booth, Isla practically vibrated with excitement. "That was *brilliant*. He looked so guilty I thought he might blow."

Taz, less impressed, grabbed her beer from Rue. "Or he was just thinking about how weird you sounded."

Rue slid into the seat beside them, handed Isla her beer, and kept her eyes on the bar. The bartender had vanished into the back room.

"See?" Rue whispered. "Bait taken."

"And now?"

"Now we wait."

Taz raised her glass. "Here's to not getting caught doing something stupid for once."

Rue clinked hers. "Let's not jinx it." Hopefully, Cole and Mayhew had the museum handled. The plan was simple. If the bartender took the bait and tried to return the stolen artifacts, they'd catch him red-handed. When the next off-key rendition of *Sweet Caroline* started up, Rue declared the operation officially over. "Mission complete. I've laid the bait; it's up to Cole now." Rue slid out of the booth. "Let's go before I lose any more brain cells to bad singing."

Taz and Isla followed her into the cool night. The street was mostly empty, wind kicking dust across the cracked asphalt. For once, they were doing what they promised, heading straight back to the saloon instead of *accidentally* tripping over a clue. Rue felt almost proud. *Almost.*

Morning sunlight spilled through the front windows of *The Silver Tongue*. Rue hummed under her breath as she restocked a shelf, a rag tucked into her back pocket.

After a night of waiting for Cole's, *"We got him"* text,

which never came, she'd decided to channel her frustration into cleaning. Nothing soothed the nerves like alphabetizing fiction and threatening cobwebs with a feather duster.

The bell over the door jingled.

Rue smiled automatically. "Morning. Welcome to…" Her smile died the instant she saw the phone. And the smug woman behind it.

Maribel Knox, Ghost Vein's resident influencer and fulltime menace, sashayed inside, camera already rolling. "Oh, look at you." Maribel cooed, panning her lens across the counter. "Such dedication. Scrubbing shelves, restocking…the *cleaning-lady aesthetic* is so in right now. Very salt-of-the-earth."

"Thanks?" *Is this girl for real?*

Maribel beamed with syrupy sweetness. "I thought I'd drop by for an interview. My followers are dying to know how your little inheritance is going. You know, the down-on-her-luck-girl-inherits-haunted-bookstore angle really *resonates* online."

Rue set down her rag. "I'm not sure down-on-her-luck are the words I'd use."

"No, of course not." Maribel's eyes gleamed. "More like…inspirational. How you keep persevering despite your limited skills. So plucky. At least you're doing better than the woman before you. I heard she was useless with business things."

It took Rue three full seconds to realize she and her great aunt had been insulted. "Excuse me…"

"Don't worry." Maribel's smile widened. "I'm sure your customers will be forgiving. Although I heard you've been accusing townsfolk of stealing artifacts. That's quite the storyline."

Rue inhaled through her nose, forcing herself to stay

put. *Do not take the bait.*

Maribel circled the counter like a shark, her phone angled perfectly to catch Rue's expression. "Honestly, your cleaning technique is impressive. I've never seen someone polish away their reputation quite so diligently."

"You really are trying to get me to lose it on camera, aren't you?" Rue asked, voice calm but tight.

Maribel fluttered her lashes. "Who, me? I'm just documenting local color."

Rue smiled back sweetly. "Then make sure you get my good side."

Maribel's eyes narrowed. "You don't have one in this lighting."

Before Rue could decide whether homicide counted as bad PR, the bell over the door jingled again.

And just like that, the mayor walked in. *Seriously, how bad can my luck be?*

Mayor Agnes Flint swept inside in her usual cloud of disapproval. Her gaze locked on Rue immediately. "Ms. Maddox. I came for the books I ordered."

Maribel's smile faltered. "Mayor. I was in the middle of filming a..."

"Not anymore." The mayor brushed past her.

Rue tried not to grin. *Oh, this is going to be good.*

Maribel lowered her phone, jaw tightening. "You just ruined my shot."

"Then perhaps film somewhere else," the mayor replied without looking at her. "Preferably far away."

Muttering something that sounded suspiciously like a curse word, Maribel turned off the recording. "Fine. I'll edit around it."

The mayor ignored her, focusing instead on Rue. "Are my books in or not?"

Maribel crossed her arms and interrupted. "You could at least apologize for interrupting my segment."

Agnes Flint turned, her voice dripping with frost. "Apologize? For preventing more of your self-promotion? You're welcome."

Rue almost applauded.

"You have no idea how influential I am online."

"And yet? You're still here."

That was it. Rue nearly lost it. She bit her lip to keep from laughing outright.

"Enjoy your little bookstore, Rue. Try not to accuse anyone else before lunch," Maribel snapped.

"Thanks for the business advice."

Glaring daggers, Maribel muttered something about *"small-town nobodies"* and stormed out.

Rue watched her go, then turned to the mayor. "Thanks for that. Really. You saved me from going viral for throwing a book at someone."

Mayor Flint sniffed. "Don't flatter yourself, Ms. Maddox. I didn't do it for *you*. Bad publicity affects tourism, and tourism keeps this town alive. I'd rather not have Silver Vein trending online as *Murder Town, USA*."

"Fair. Though I think that ship sailed somewhere around the second or third attack."

The mayor's eyes narrowed. "And frankly, I can't stand her *or* you. You're both headaches in different packaging."

Rue gave a small, diplomatic smile. She wasn't here to fight, in public...*again*. "Noted."

Agnes crossed her arms, tapping one manicured nail against her sleeve. "Now. My books?"

Rue ducked beneath the counter, still biting her tongue, and came up with the neatly wrapped stack. "Right here."

"Put it on my tab."

Rue cleared her throat, smoothing her expression. "Before you go, I...uh...actually wanted to apologize."

The mayor blinked, clearly not expecting that.

"For accusing you in the middle of Main Street. It was wrong. I lost my temper, and that's on me, not you." Rue waited for the mayor to say something.

Finally, Agnes sniffed. "While I appreciate the sentiment, as a business owner, you should be more careful. Poor manners can affect your reputation and your profits."

"Understood." Rue nodded stiffly.

"Good." The mayor tucked the books under her arm and gave Rue one last measuring look. "Try not to cause any more drama this week." She spun on her heel and stomped out.

Rue let out a long, slow exhale. "And that concludes today's episode of *Everyone Hates Rue*." She waved Thomas over to man the counter, then slipped across to the café.

Taz was behind the counter, rearranging a pastry display while Cassie wiped down tables.

"Please tell me all the customers in this town don't hate me," Rue said.

"Nah. I'd say it's a fifty-fifty split right now." Taz slipped a pastry to Rue.

"So, one half waiting to throw confetti and the other waiting to throw rocks?"

"Pretty much. But hey, Cassie likes you."

Cassie beamed while Nacho bleated loudly, stamping a tiny hoof.

Rue smiled. "Three votes of confidence. I'll take it."

"Make that four."

"Who's the fourth?"

Taz tilted her head toward the doorway.

Cole Dawson stood there.

Her stomach did a slow, ridiculous flip. "Oh. That fourth."

"We need to talk," he said.

Rue followed Cole to the quieter book side of the store.

He waited until they were out of earshot before speaking. "The bartender, Malone, took the bait."

"He did? I knew he was shady."

"He returned some of the missing artifacts last night. We found them near the museum loading bay."

Rue grinned. "See? My plan worked. You doubted me, but it worked. Can I be in on the interrogation?"

Cole didn't look nearly as thrilled. "Don't get ahead of yourself."

"What do you mean? You caught him red-handed, right?"

His expression tightened. "Not exactly. Malone showed up, dropped the box, and took off before Mayhew could stop him."

"Wait. He *escaped*? How does someone like him escape from a trained deputy?"

"Apparently, by throwing a bag of flour at him and running."

She stared. "Flour. Like, *baking flour*?"

"Yep. A small bag. He carried it with him." Cole's jaw flexed. "Mayhew's fine, just...covered in what looked like ghost dust."

"Unbelievable. And why was he carrying flour?"

"I have no clue. Preparing for a distraction, I guess. Look, it's not ideal. But we've got his apartment under surveillance, and I've notified nearby towns. If he shows up anywhere, we'll know."

"Or maybe Mayhew just *let him go* so I'd look bad."

"Rue..."

"I'm serious. You saw how Mayhew acts around me. If there's even a chance, he..."

"Let's not accuse anyone again."

She huffed. "Fine. But admit it—my plan was solid."

He gave her a reluctant nod. "It was. The setup worked. We got proof that Malone had the artifacts, and that's something."

She brightened a little. "So...you're saying I was right?"

Cole's lips twitched. "I'm saying you were *not wrong*. Don't let it go to your head."

"Too late. I'm already planning my detective agency logo."

Cole's expression softened. "You did good, Rue."

Then he turned and walked out, leaving her standing there with a heart doing somersaults and a head full of new questions.

Rue leaned against a bookshelf, thinking. "Okay. Malone's a thief but maybe not the killer. Great. Another piece to a puzzle." Her gaze drifted toward the window. Somewhere out there, someone was still pulling strings, and she was running out of people to accuse without getting banned from every bar, museum, and diner in town.

"Just a small-town girl trying not to get murdered. Is that too much to ask?" Then she heard it. A whisper that hung in the air around her.

Have faith.

Rue froze. "Ruth?" No answer. Just the faint rustle of pages on the nearest shelf, though she hadn't touched a thing. She smiled faintly, the hair rising on her arms. "All right. I'll try."

Because maybe the dead knew something she didn't. *Have faith it is...*

TWENTY-FOUR

The saloon was quiet, the kind of hush that settled after a long day of customers, chatter, and the occasional goat-related mishap. It was late, the front doors locked, but none of them were quite ready to call it a night.

"Feels weird without the crowd," Taz murmured.

Rue nodded. "It's been one of those weeks. The kind that starts bad and keeps getting worse."

"That's one way to put it." Cassie reached for her bag. "I have to head over to the library. Mom's organizing a cleanup, just tidying after Letty's...accident."

Rue looked up. "Wait. They think she'll be back soon?"

"Not exactly. She's still in a medically induced coma. The doctors are waiting for the swelling in her brain to go down before they bring her out. Mom's staying in touch with the hospital. I'll let you know when she's allowed visits."

"Thanks. I hate sitting around while she's lying there. She knew something important, Cass. I could see it in her eyes when I found her."

Cassie nodded. "You'll figure it out. You always do." She waved and slipped out the back door.

Three seconds later, the door banged open again.

"Really?" Rue sighed as Nacho trotted in.

The tiny goat bleated imperiously and made a beeline for the counter.

Rue bent to scratch the goat's head. He leaned into her hand, then immediately headbutted her leg in protest when she stopped.

"Persistent little thing. Doesn't anyone ever complain about him wandering into their stores? Besides Josiah that is."

"Complain to *who*? Everyone knows he belongs to Delilah, and no one's brave or stupid enough to cross her. You try telling that woman her goat's trespassing and see how long you live."

Rue chuckled. "Fair. I wouldn't mess with her either." She looked up at the ceiling, her voice quiet. "Do you think Ruth's here? Really here?"

Taz glanced toward the doorway that led to the bookshop side. "Yeah. She's around. I can feel her sometimes. You probably can too."

"I do. She moves books, writes on mirrors. But if she's here, why can't we see her yet?"

"It takes time. Most spirits who hang around after death need to get the hang of it. Energy, willpower, whatever you want to call it. Some never figure it out. Ruth will eventually."

"We just have to be patient?" Rue laughed softly.

"Pretty much."

As if on cue, Nacho bleated again

Taz grinned and reached for a plastic container on the counter. "Savory mini muffins. Don't say I never spoil you."

But before Taz could open it, Nacho darted between her legs and clipped her ankle. The container went flying, and time slowed as a dozen golden savory muffins arced gracefully through the air. They hit the floor with soft, tragic plops. "Great," Taz muttered. "Five-second rule?"

Rue sighed, bending to help. But before she could reach for one, she froze.

The muffins...moved.

At first Rue thought it was a trick of the light or her tired eyes. But then the nearest one twitched. Another rolled an inch. Then another.

"Please tell me that didn't just happen."

"The muffins are...rearranging themselves."

And they were. Slowly, methodically, invisible fingers nudged them across the tiles. One by one, they wobbled across the floor, forming crooked lines that twisted, broke apart, and regrouped.

Taz's jaw dropped. "Okay. The baked goods are spelling things. I'm not caffeinated enough for this."

On the tiles, the muffins settled into a shaky line of words that read, *check the ledger.*

"Check *what* ledger? Like...the saloon's?" Taz said. "Because that'll just show who owes us for coffee and who tips in nickels."

Rue shook her head. "I have no idea. Ruth? Could you maybe clarify before we start harassing random ledgers around town?"

For a heartbeat, the muffins quivered like they might respond. Then...nothing.

The kitchen door slammed open again. "Why's everyone staring at the floor?" Jesse strolled in, smelling faintly of motor oil. He took in the scene, the scattered muffins, the startled women, the goat chewing in the corner, and raised a brow. "What did I miss?"

"Shh. You'll scare them." Rue pointed at the floor.

"The muffins?" Jesse asked.

"Yes, the muffins," Taz snapped.

He crouched beside them, expression half skeptical, half intrigued, until he got a look at the words. "Huh. You weren't kidding."

"Ruth's sending messages again, only this time through baked goods. Because apparently mirrors weren't enough."

Jesse's brows shot up. "Check the ledger..." He rubbed his chin. "I think I know what she means."

"You do?" Taz looked suspicious.

"I've helped out at the museum before, volunteer stuff, mostly fixing displays or lights. They've got an artifact register, kind of an old-school ledger that tracks every item in and out of storage. Maybe Ruth's talking about that."

Taz nodded. "That actually makes sense."

"Because I'm brilliant." Jesse flashed a smile.

Rue gave him a look. "Your ego's showing."

Before he could reply, one of the muffins gave a little hop. Then another. And another. Soon, all of them were dancing across the floor.

"Oh, come on. Was that a yes?" Rue crouched closer. "Ruth, if you mean the museum ledger, give us a sign."

The muffins shuddered again, then went perfectly still.

And right when the suspense was unbearable, Nacho trotted forward and started eating them.

"No," Taz yelped. "Nacho, stop."

The goat ignored her, chomping happily.

"Unbelievable. He's devouring evidence."

"Technically, he's recycling it," Jesse offered.

"Technically, you're next if you don't hush," Rue muttered.

Taz clapped her hands. "Okay, muffin séance over. I vote we trust Jesse's theory. He's probably right, and at least it's something we can actually *do.*"

Rue stared at the muffin massacre on the floor. "Ruth, if that's not what you meant, blink the lights or something."

Nothing.

"Good enough for me. Let's go raid the museum." Jesse dusted his hands.

"Raid?" Rue echoed. "We're not raiding anything."

He grinned. "Investigating, then. With style."

"You mean trespassing." Taz shook her head.

Jesse checked his watch. "Museum's open for another hour. If we get a wiggle on, we can get in, check the ledger, and get out before anyone notices."

"You say that like this isn't going to go horribly wrong."

He winked at Rue. "That's optimism, sweetheart."

"Fine. But the goat is definitely *not* coming."

Nacho bleated indignantly, crumbs still stuck to his chin.

Rue pointed at him. "You heard me. No heists for you."

The museum was quieter than usual. A small tour group lingered near the front door, most wearing cowboy hats or ruffled Western costumes.

Leading them was Isla. She spotted them the moment they slipped inside. Her expression flickered briefly, amusement and curiosity, but she recovered instantly and waved.

"Perfect timing," Isla chirped, then turned back to her group. "Now, if you'll follow me, we'll continue to the

Ghost Vein Mine tunnel exhibit, where you can see artifacts recovered from the original mining tunnels."

Rue waved back sheepishly as Isla herded the tourists down the hall.

Jesse nudged the women toward the opposite corridor. "Ledger's through the staff only doors."

"Won't the curator notice?" Rue whispered.

"He's front of house. He'll be hanging out somewhere round here," Jesse said. "I'll distract him."

"How?"

"Easy." Jesse straightened his jacket and smirked at Rue. "I'll tell him you want to make a donation. You know, cash, books, antiques, your eternal gratitude."

"This is going to cost me, isn't it?"

"Probably." He walked toward the information desk.

Taz grabbed Rue's sleeve, giggling as they ducked behind a display of vintage mining helmets. "He's totally enjoying this."

"Absolutely. He loves being the center of attention."

From the front desk, they heard Jesse's voice rise cheerfully. "Evening. I'm here on behalf of Rue Maddox. You know, the owner of The Silver Tongue. She's a little shy, so she sent me to discuss her donation plans."

"He actually said it." Taz giggled.

Rue shook her head. "I'm going to have to move when this is over."

The curator popped up from behind the desk and sounded intrigued and mercifully distracted. "Excellent. Why don't we discuss her generous donation?"

"He's terrifyingly good at lying."

"All charm, zero shame," Taz whispered back.

They made their way toward the group of tourists Isla was speaking to. Coincidentally, the group stood just in front of doors with a staff only sign on them. Rue and Taz slid in at the back of the group, pretending to listen. Isla caught Rue's gaze mid-sentence and raised one brow in silent question. Rue mouthed, *later*. They waved to Isla as she led her group toward the main hall.

Behind the heavy door marked *staff only*, the air was cooler, mustier. Faint light glowed from a desk lamp, illuminating stacks of old boxes and rolled maps. And on the desk, a large ledger.

Rue's pulse quickened. "All right, Ruth. Let's see what's in this ledger you want us to see." Rue flipped it open.

The listings were all written in tight, slanted handwriting. Names, descriptions, invoice numbers, and dates. Each entry tracked an artifact, where it came from, who logged it, and when. Except...some of the pages had been torn out. Rue frowned, brushing her thumb along a jagged edge. "Someone removed pages."

Taz leaned over her shoulder. "How far back does it go?"

"About six months. Here, look at this one." She pointed to a faded line near the top of a page. *Gold nugget and fragment of map.* Next to it a set of initials, *T.P.* Rue's stomach tightened. "Tobias Pike. The tour guide."

"He sold it to the curator? How did he have it in his hand when he died?"

"He had to have stolen it back. The curator should've reported those pieces missing. Why didn't he tell Cole?"

They turned the page. More listings, pickaxes, helmets, coins, bits of silver ore. And then...

Rue froze. "Here. A branding iron from the mine. A piece of metal from the mine hit Arnold in the back of the head. What's the likelihood it's *this* one?"

They stared at the entry in silence.

She kept reading. There were more "T" initials scattered across the pages, all with receipt numbers but no dollar amounts. "I wonder how much Tobias was paid?"

"That means a receipt or an invoice book." Taz's expression hardened. "Right. Let's go snooping."

Before Rue could protest, Taz tore out the ledger page with the gold nugget and map entry, folded it neatly, and handed it over. "For evidence."

Tucking it into her pocket, Rue hoped Cole wouldn't add grand theft stationery to her growing list of misdemeanors.

They crept back into the main museum, their footsteps muffled by the old carpet. Jesse's voice floated faintly from down the hall.

"...like I said, the donation's in the works. She's a little shy about attention. You know how creative types are."

He's really laying it on thick.

The curator's laugh followed, cheerful and unsuspecting. "Delightful. We're always thrilled to have contributions from local businesses."

"See? Told you," Taz whispered. "He's terrifyingly convincing."

They passed a side hall and spotted Cassie and her mother cleaning an exhibit case. Cassie waved, oblivious to their espionage. Rue gave a quick finger-to-lips gesture before they ducked around the corner.

The curator's office was just ahead. Closed door, but no lock.

Rue exhaled. "Okay. Fast and quiet. If this is all on computer, we're doomed."

"This is Ghost Vein. I bet the man still writes museum hours in chalk." Taz pointed to a black filing cabinet beside the desk. "There's your database."

Rue tugged on the top drawer. It squealed. She froze.

No footsteps approached.

Rue eased the drawer open slower this time. Inside were folders labeled by year, some so dusty they looked fossilized.

Taz rifled through the desk while Rue skimmed file tabs. "Bills, reports, catalogues...aha." Rue pulled out a thin folder jammed at the back marked *artifacts*. She laid it flat on the desk, flipping it open. "Bingo."

Inside sat a small receipt book with carbon paper copies, hand numbered. Rue flipped through and froze. Every second or third entry had the same name, *Tobias Pike*.

Each line listed an artifact and a payment. Five hundred here. Seven hundred there. And one that made her mouth dry.

Gold nugget and map fragment, One thousand dollars. Paid in cash.

Taz peered over her shoulder. "Whoa. That's not pocket change. He must've been stealing them straight out of the mine and reselling through the museum."

"Look, there's a note at the bottom of this one." In scrawled handwriting, someone had written. *Seems to be a lot of interest. Multiple inquiries to sell.* "The curator wrote that. He knew the items were valuable. Probably had a seller lined up."

"Tobias was a thief, and someone decided to shut him up permanently."

Before Rue could answer, Taz whispered, "Bingo."

Rue turned to see her smoothing out a crumpled paper she'd pulled from the wastebasket.

"It's a letter from the mayor," Taz said. "Denial of funding. Listen to this." She read aloud softly, "'Due to lack of tourist interest and budget constraints, the council has voted to cancel the mine expansion. Future focus should shift toward town history, not mining. Be aware the council is reconsidering all of the museum's funding.'"

Rue could practically hear the mayor's sharp tone. "Wow. That would've gutted the museum. The curator would've been furious."

"No wonder he balled it up and pitched it. His whole career depended on those mine displays."

"If the museum loses funding, he loses his job. And his nice little side hustle with stolen artifacts." Rue rubbed her temple.

"Motive, meet opportunity."

Turning to put the receipt book back, Rue rehearsed how she'd tell Cole she *found* the evidence, not *took* it.

But Taz wasn't looking at the file anymore. She was staring over Rue's shoulder, eyes wide.

She sighed. "Let me guess...he's right behind me, isn't he?"

"Uh-huh." Taz nodded.

A deep, familiar voice rumbled behind her. "Yes, I am. And I'm wondering why the two of you are ransacking the curator's office?"

Cole stood in the doorway, arms crossed, badge gleaming faintly under the overhead light.

"Oh, this?" Rue gestured vaguely at the office. "Just light tidying. With, uh...some side benefits." She waved the crumpled letter and the receipts. "Evidence. And motive."

He stepped forward, plucked the papers from her hands, and slid them into an evidence bag. "Good thing *I* organized a warrant this time. You know, so we don't get arrested for breaking and entering."

"You got a warrant? For here?"

He gave her a flat look. "Of course. I actually follow procedure."

Taz muttered, "Well, there's a first time for everything."

Cole ignored her. "As far as the official record goes, *I* found this evidence. You two were never here. Got it?"

They nodded in unison.

"Good." He gestured toward the hallway. "Out. Before the curator sees you." He escorted them toward the exit, expression unreadable, all professionalism. Not angry, just in cop mode this time.

When they reached the main hall, Jesse spotted them. His smile faltered at Cole's glare.

"Ah, there she is," Jesse said quickly, as if nothing was wrong. "Curator, meet Rue Maddox, the generous donor I mentioned."

The man's face lit up. "Ms. Maddox. A pleasure. We were just discussing your contribution."

"Right. Yes. My...contribution." Rue knew she'd end up paying somehow.

Cole turned to Rue, Taz, and Jesse. "Home. Now. I'll talk to you later." He shot a look at Jesse. "That means *you* too, Mr. Volunteer of the Year."

Jesse cleared his throat. "Right. Of course."

Cole turned back to the bewildered curator as Jesse linked arms with the girls and steered them toward the exit.

Once they were outside, Rue exhaled hard. "Well. That could've gone worse."

"Barely." Taz rubbed her forehead. "I thought we were seconds from matching orange jumpsuits."

Jesse grinned. "Admit it. You love the thrill."

Rue shot him a glare. "The only thrill I want right now is caffeine."

A bleat cut through the night air. Nacho trotted out from nowhere, looking smug.

Rue groaned. "Where were you five minutes ago when I

needed a distraction? What's the point of having a goat minion if the minion doesn't *minion?*"

Nacho headbutted her knee.

Taz laughed so hard she nearly doubled over. "He's the only reliable man in this town."

Rue couldn't even argue.

TWENTY-FIVE

Taz nudged a hot mug of tea and a muffin toward Rue.

Rue cracked one bleary eye, yawned, and reached for the mug. "You're a saint."

"Did you sleep at all last night?"

"Barely. My brain wouldn't shut up. Just kept...looping everything."

"Like the part where Cole caught you ransacking the curator's office? Maybe you were lying awake wondering how annoyed he'll be today?"

"Maybe. I don't want him upset at me. But at least I gave him the evidence. No guilt there." Rue frowned. "Except I forgot to tell him about the gold nugget and the map fragment."

Taz nearly choked on her muffin. "You what? Oh, Rue."

"I *know*. It's just, we've been arguing and people are getting hurt and I haven't exactly had a spare moment to say, 'hey by the way, I found a chunk of the missing cursed treasure.'"

"You need to *tell him*." Taz stabbed a finger at Rue.

Rue nodded. "I will. I just didn't mean to sleep in. Thankfully, I have amazing staff who roll with the chaos."

Out in the café, the morning bustle was well underway. The bookshop side was still quiet. Cassie had somehow roped Thomas into restocking display cases, and the girl looked downright *smitten*.

Taz covertly dropped a piece of muffin into her napkin. With a quick glance around to make sure no tourists were watching, she slipped it to Nacho under the table.

The goat bleated happily.

"We really need to stop feeding him in public. Last thing I need is the mayor slapping us with a health code violation because my goat minion likes blueberry muffins." Rue sipped her tea.

"Maybe we can bribe the inspector. You know, *after* the mayor stops putting a target on your back."

Before Rue could reply, the front door slammed open.

Deputy Mayhew stormed in, already scowling. "Your antics are gonna get you shut down, Maddox. Or worse."

"You threatening her now, Deputy?" Taz shot to her feet.

Mayhew looked taken aback for half a second. "No. I'm, warning her. All this poking around? Butting into investigations? It's going to get someone hurt. Civilians need to stay..." He paused, clearly hunting for a phrase.

"Civilians need to keep... *civiling*?" Taz offered, then turned to Rue with a deadpan expression. "Is that a word?"

"Pretty sure it's not."

Mayhew flushed. "You think this is funny?"

"No," Rue said. "I don't. But I also don't like being lectured in my own place."

Mayhew bristled and turned to stomp out but not before swinging a boot at Nacho.

Nacho let out a bleat of indignant outrage.

Rue surged to her feet. "You so much as *touch* him with that boot, and I will…"

Mayhew had already disappeared.

"Maybe he's right." Rue sagged back onto her stool. "Maybe I *should* butt out. I don't want anyone else getting hurt. And look at Nacho. He got kicked because I made Mayhew mad."

"Nacho's fine." Taz gave Rue a long look. "And Mayhew knows if he actually *connected*, Delilah would've strung him up by his badge. He wouldn't risk it."

Rue just looked down at her muffin. "I keep thinking… maybe Ruth trusted the wrong person with the Silver Tongue."

A loud *slam* echoed from the kitchen, followed by the soft *plunk-plunk* of muffins tipping over in the display case. Books rattled on their shelves.

Taz slapped the counter. "All right, both you Maddox women need to suck it up."

"Pretty sure one of us is dead." Rue looked confused.

"Ruth had faith in you. Maybe it's time *you* did too. And you…" Taz wagged her finger at the ceiling. "Control your temper. This is a place of business." She turned back to Rue, all business now. "Go downstairs. Read some journals. Soak up Ruth's witchy vibes. Then we'll regroup and figure out our next move."

Rue took a shaky breath and stood. "Okay." She headed downstairs to the basement and unlocked the hidden panel. This time, she jammed the door open with a heavy box. She was not in the mood to get locked in again. She collapsed into the overstuffed armchair in the corner and stared into the gloom.

"I don't even know if you're here, but I guess it helps to

talk to you anyway. I'm worried, Ruth. What if I don't figure it out in time? What if the killer strikes again, and this time...it's someone I care about?"

Her voice cracked. "It's all tied to the cursed gold. The mine. The map. I *know* it. But everything feels twisty, inside-out...and don't even get me started on my curse-breaking. I've had a few lucky flares, but it's mostly been a magical dud. I'm a failure."

A soft *thud* interrupted her self-pity spiral. A slim blue book tumbled off a small shelf and landed spine-first on the floor. "Of course." Ruth's books had a habit of falling whenever the ghost got dramatic. Still, Rue's heart gave a little flutter as she picked it up and flicked through it.

It wasn't just any book. It was a handwritten journal filled with Ruth's curse-breaking notes. Diagrams, recipes, magical procedures. It was practically a how-to manual. Rue clutched it tight to her chest, tears burning behind her eyes. "Thank you."

Behind her, the pins on the old corkboard rattled, shifting with a quiet, purposeful rhythm. Words formed in crooked cursive. *Find your own way.*

Rue let out a breath and gave a watery laugh. "Easier said than done, Aunt Ruth." Still holding the book to her chest, she nodded slowly. "I guess I do need to figure out how I do it."

It wasn't a full-on epiphany, but it was something. A beginning. A step forward. She stood up just as a soft knock sounded on the open door.

Taz poked her head in. "Message from Cole. Said to meet him at Wynona's ASAP."

"You think he's mad?"

Taz snorted. "Almost definitely."

Rue tucked the journal under one arm and squared her

shoulders. Whatever it was, she'd deal with it. Because she had to.

———

Rue zipped across town on Cassie's red scooter. Once there, she squared her shoulders and walked toward Wynona's porch, spotting Cole already waiting on the top step. Rue held herself tight, trying to keep her nerves from jangling too loudly.

Cole took one look at her and sighed. "Calm down. I said what I needed to say yesterday. I'm not here to yell. I just want you to stop taking risks and include me next time. That's all."

His voice was quiet. Steady. Rue's spine loosened an inch. "Thanks for saying that. And for the record, I *did* hand over the evidence. I'm not a *total* delinquent."

He quirked an eyebrow.

She snorted. "Besides, Mayhew already gave me a lecture this morning. Did his best fake lawman impression. *Keep your nose outta law enforcement business.*" She dropped her voice an octave and gave a grumpy scowl.

He laughed. "Yeah, well. Mayhew's got a...very narrow interpretation of what policing means. He's not wrong about the danger though."

She sighed. "No, he's not. But it doesn't mean I can stop caring."

"Just don't let me catch you snooping. It's not good for my blood pressure."

Rue giggled. "Noted." She stared at the Victorian house. "What's the deal with visiting Wynona?"

Cole pulled out a folded list. "These are artifacts Tobias sold to the museum curator. I'm hoping Wynona can tell us if any of them made the rounds on the underground market."

"Big if. She's not exactly a fan of badge-and-gun types."

A snort sounded from behind them.

"Wynona is standing *right here*," said a dry voice.

They both spun around.

Wynona stood in the open doorway, arms crossed, one eyebrow raised. Her black-gray hair was piled in a high twist on her head, and she was dressed in a black jogging suit. "If you're gonna ask me questions, you'd better get your butts inside. You're bad for business loitering on my porch."

Rue and Cole scuttled inside. Wynona slammed the door behind them and waved them toward the kitchen.

Rue smiled as she took in the calm serenity of Wynona's space, but Cole blinked a few times.

Wynona smirked as she stepped into her kitchen. "What? You expected a cauldron?"

"You've never seen her kitchen before?"

"You think I entertain law enforcement?" Wynona arched a brow at Rue. "I'm *very* careful. No cops for tea."

"I prefer coffee and cake," Cole muttered. "And no hexes."

The hex witch ignored him. "In all the years I've known him, I've let this one into my house *twice*. Neither time did he make it as far as the kitchen."

"You should feel honored," Rue whispered.

"Don't," Wynona said. "Now hurry up. Time is money."

Cole laid the list of artifacts on the counter. "These were sold to the museum by Tobias. Anything stand out?"

The witch squinted. "I don't work at the museum."

The sheriff narrowed his eyes. "I want your opinion."

Barking a laugh, Wynona slapped the counter. "So,

you're asking if any of this stuff has passed through the black-market witch circuit?"

He didn't answer. Just stared.

With an eye roll, Wynona pulled the list closer. Her lips pursed. "Some of these sound familiar."

Cole added a few receipts with Tobias's initials. "Anything ring a bell?"

"Please. Tobias's name is right here." Wynona sniffed. "Of course I recognize it. He liked money, a lot. Didn't care how he got it. I wouldn't touch anything he sold with a ten-foot wand."

Rue frowned. "Why not? If there's a market for dark artifacts, wouldn't that be good for business?"

Wynona's nose wrinkled. "Because karma exists. And that mine? It reeks. I'm not touching anything tied to it. Blood magic went down in there, no question. I'm not about to siphon death energy into my shop."

"But others might?" Rue asked.

"*Absolutely*. And Tobias knew it. He wasn't just selling; he was buying too. Probably for someone else. He didn't have the cash to collect the kinds of items I saw floating around."

"What kinds of items?"

"Little things. Talismans. Inscribed charms. Nothing valuable on the surface, but if they came from the mine, they'd carry a magical residue. Dark stuff. Some witches can siphon that kind of energy."

"Why didn't you tell me this before?" Cole frowned.

Wynona hissed. "Because I'm not a narc. I'm not your informant."

Cole bristled.

Rue gently touched his arm. "Wynona...anyone else try

to sell you mine artifacts? Something important to this case?"

The older woman looked at Rue for a long moment, then gave a reluctant nod. "Yeah. Once. Someone tried to sell me a piece of inscribed metal. Etched with old symbols. The aura on it was nasty. I sent them packing."

"Who?" Cole's eyes narrowed.

"Jackson Malone." Wynona's lips twisted.

"Figures. The bartender's as dodgy as they come."

Cole muttered something under his breath that sounded suspiciously like agreement.

With that, Wynona stood. "And now? Time for you both to leave. You're spooking my customers." She walked them to the door. Out on the porch, she hesitated. Her voice was low. "Be careful, both of you. There's more going on than you realize." Then she turned to Rue. "And keep practicing your curse-breaking, girl. It's going to matter more than you know."

Rue shivered. The wind had picked up, but that wasn't what gave her goosebumps.

She had a sinking feeling things were going to get worse before they got better.

TWENTY-SIX

Rue stood on the boardwalk outside the Silver Tongue. The streets of Ghost Vein were buzzing with costumed chaos. Tourists in cowboy hats and dollar-store corsets posed for selfies, and most of the locals had even turned up. Every café and bar was open, serving themed cocktails and over-priced root beer floats.

Nacho trotted between their legs, occasionally pausing to see who might drop a snack.

Taz leaned on the railing beside her. "This town is certi-fiable, but I love it."

"I know." Rue grinned. "It's exhausting. But also...kind of great?"

Even Delilah had emerged from the general store, standing stiff as a fence post with her arms crossed. She looked grumpy, but Rue had the distinct impression the old woman was secretly enjoying the mayhem.

Cole and Deputy Mayhew roamed the fringes of the crowd, keeping an eye on things. Cole looked mildly amused. Mayhew looked like he'd eaten something sour.

Jesse lounged casually on Rue's other side, arms folded and eyes scanning the crowd.

"He's under orders from Cole to keep an eye on you," Taz whispered.

Rue snorted. "Seriously?"

"Yup."

"I'm not going to cause a scene during a town shootout reenactment."

"Rue, you could trip over a rock and accidentally knock over a suspect. Chaos follows you."

"I resemble that remark." Rue snickered. Technically, her friend wasn't wrong. She had the worst luck lately. Things just seemed to go wrong around her. Even the reenactment had to be rescheduled after a drunken miner actor had tripped and knocked himself out. The town council, not wanting to miss the lucrative Saturday foot traffic, had insisted on a redo. Hopefully, nothing else went wrong.

Rue was kind of excited. For once, she wanted to forget about cursed gold and murder and just soak in the weirdness. "I vote we enjoy this. We've earned it."

Taz nodded. "Agreed. Sleuthing later. For now, corn dogs, ghost girls, and staged gunfire."

Jesse rubbed his stomach. "As long as there's red meat involved, I'm good."

Taz snickered. "Of course you are. You're a shifter."

"But what kind?" Rue giggled. She was enjoying the game of *guess what shifter Jesse is.* "If you're craving red meat, you're definitely not a vegetarian shifter. So, no bunny."

"No more bunny guesses," Jesse groaned.

Rue grinned wider. "Fine. Raccoon?"

He made a face. "No one wants to be a raccoon shifter, Rue. No one. Ever."

"Hey, raccoons are resourceful. You'd never lose a shiny object again."

He bared his teeth and gave a playful growl. "Keep guessing. But I'm not shifting on Main Street. Even if the tourists would lose their minds."

Rue held up her hands. "Spoilsport." She elbowed Taz. "Come on. You've known him longer. Spill."

Smiling, Taz shook her head. "Not getting involved. But I'll let you know when you guess right."

Rue groaned dramatically. She wasn't paying much attention to the crowd, focused instead on pestering Jesse with absurd animal theories until Delilah's bark cut through the chatter.

"You ghost girls have *no pride.*"

She turned to see Delilah pointing a stern finger at a trio of ghostly corseted saloon girls flirting shamelessly with a group of tourists.

Taz grinned. "Aw, Delilah. Don't be a prude."

"I'm not a prude," Delilah snapped. "I just don't see why the girls should get all the credit when it's clearly the ghostly push-up bra doing the heavy lifting. *That's* what should get paid."

Jesse choked. "You want the *corset* to be paid?"

"Darn right," Delilah muttered, stomping away.

The girls dissolved into helpless laughter.

As Rue wiped tears from her eyes, her attention snagged on two familiar figures loitering at the edge of the square.

The mayor stood by the old bank, arms crossed, eyes narrowed.

Across the road, Maribel held up her phone and angled it toward Rue's group, clearly filming.

"So much for forgetting about the murder."

Two of her four suspects. Watching her like a hawk, waiting to see what she'd do next.

The crowd shifted and surged around them as more tourists gathered for the reenactment.

Taking a step toward the edge of the boardwalk, Rue caught sight of Cole across the square.

He winked.

Her cheeks flushed before she could stop them. She gave a tiny wave, feeling like a teenager caught doodling her crush's name in a notebook.

Taz elbowed Rue in the ribs. "He doesn't *look* too mad at you," she teased. "Maybe he's finally getting used to you poking your nose into his investigation."

Delilah snorted from behind them. "Or maybe he's just given in to the inevitable. Maddox women are nosy and stubborn. Comes with the gene pool."

Rue responded with a vague shrug. *Delilah wasn't wrong, even if she wouldn't admit it to her out loud.*

Out on Main Street, the two reenactors were now center stage, one in a grubby miner getup, the other in a dapper cowboy fringed coat. Both had antique-style pistols strapped to their hips and were hollering insults across the dusty gap.

"Are those guns...real?" Rue squinted.

Jesse nodded. "Period correct replicas, mostly, but some are real weapons. A few are museum-owned, some council-owned. But they're all loaded with blanks. Supposedly totally safe."

"*Supposedly.*" Famous last words. Rue muttered to herself, just as a familiar weight pressed into the back of her knees. "Nacho." She reached down to rub his bony little back. "You scared me, buddy."

The tension dropped away for a moment as the actors

launched into their performance. The miner shouted something about gold theft. The cowboy accused him of cheating at poker.

It was all melodramatic and Rue loved it. And this time the miner actor wasn't slurring or swaying. He even winced convincingly when the cowboy "shot" him in the arm. Rue grinned as a few minor ghosts floated nearby, making snarky commentary. One loudly called the acting "amateurish," while another bemoaned the lack of historically accurate dirt.

Then someone shoved her.

Hard.

Rue stumbled, catching a flash of someone in a hoodie behind her before momentum took over. She fell just as the miner fired his gun again, and the *crack* of it was wrong. Too loud. Too real.

The first bullet hit near her boots, splintering the sidewalk.

"*Get down,*" Cole shouted. He dived toward her as a second shot hit the wood behind her. Screams erupted from the crowd.

Tourists scattered in every direction. Nacho let out an ear-splitting screech and launched himself at the stunned miner, head-butting and bleating.

Cole's weight pressed down on Rue, shielding her completely.

"You okay?" he asked.

Rue's heart hammered. "I...I think so. That wasn't a blank, was it?"

"No," Cole growled. "That was a real bullet."

Across the street, Maribel appeared, phone in hand, smirking and filming the chaos.

Rue's stomach churned.

The mayor burst forward, clapping her hands like a game show host. "What a show," she said with a forced laugh. "A brand-new direction for Ghost Vein."

Is this woman serious?

"Everyone head to your favorite bar or café. One free drink on the town. Courtesy of the Ghost Vein Tourism Board."

The crowd, dazed and hungry, let the mayor's explanation wash over them and began pouring into nearby buildings.

Cole hauled Rue to her feet. "You okay?"

"I'm fine." Rue brushed dust from her jeans. "A little dusty. But not full of bullet holes."

Taz and Jesse ran over, eyes wide.

"You good?" Taz asked breathlessly.

"I'm fine. Thanks to Cole."

Cole nodded, but his eyes were on the miner, still menaced by an enraged goat. Nacho had gone full berserker. The actor flailed, trying to ward off sharp hooves and relentless bleating.

"Nacho, down," Rue called. "I'm fine."

Jesse muttered, "That goat's got bloodlust."

Taz eyed the scene. "Rue, I love you, but you have the absolute worst luck with accidents at public events."

Rue let out a shaky laugh. "I mean, at this point, is it *luck?* Or bad karma?"

Nacho headbutted the man squarely in the shin before trotting back toward Rue.

Delilah rolled her eyes at Taz's words. "Are you *blind*, girl? That wasn't an accident. That was someone trying to kill her."

"I...yeah. I didn't trip. Someone pushed me. Just before the miner fired. Someone tried to *kill* me."

Cole marched over to the trembling miner, his jaw clenched. The ghosts that had been hovering for the performance drifted away. Only a disappointed looking ghostly undertaker lingered nearby, muttering about wasted paperwork.

The miner actor held up his hands up. "It was supposed to be blanks. It's *always* blanks. I swear, I don't know what happened."

"It's going in for testing. Every round, too." Cole confiscated the pistol.

Deputy Mayhew rushed up, out of breath. "This is exactly what happens when civilians stick their noses into active investigations."

"We *don't* victim-blame." Cole turned on his deputy, eyes flashing. "Go take witness statements. Then head back to the station."

Mayhew sputtered. "But..."

"Go."

Grumbling, Mayhew slunk off into the crowd.

Cole turned back to the miner. "Where'd the weapon come from?"

"Loan from the museum," the miner said, still pale. "I think it's an actual artifact, magically restored or something. I picked it up from the curator. Didn't load it. Didn't do anything."

The cowboy actor had crept over, white as a ghost. "Mine's the same. Same source. Same ammo." He offered the weapon to the sheriff.

"Where'd the ammunition come from?" Cole took the pistol.

Before either could answer, the mayor bustled up. "*I* organized the blank rounds. There was *nothing* live. I made sure of it."

Cole fixed her with a look. "Then you'll turn over whatever ammunition remains. We'll test everything."

The mayor looked offended. "Of course. I'll deliver it to Deputy Mayhew. And I'll be forming a *safety oversight panel* immediately. Perhaps it's time we introduce barricades. Or new reenactment protocols." She turned on Rue with a tight smile. "And maybe keep spectators where they belong."

Rue bristled. "I *was pushed*. That wasn't on me."

The mayor sniffed. "Regardless. I'll drop the blanks to the station."

"Mayhew's taking statements then he'll be back at the station. Give them to him, no one else."

The mayor flounced off, muttering about liability and legal teams.

Maribel slithered into view, phone still raised. She beamed. "Can you *believe* I missed the whole thing? I was in the bathroom. *Ugh.* Real bullets would've sent my views through the roof."

"Well, sorry to disappoint, but there was *no blood*. I'm fine."

"I *did* get some crowd footage, though. Might be something useful in there." She flashed Cole a flirty smile.

"Send me everything you've got."

She winked. "Only if you promise to owe me. I *do* collect." With that, she sauntered off in the same direction as the mayor.

Rue stared after her, a shiver skimming down her spine. She hated that woman with a passion, but Maribel did have flair. Maybe her footage would show the person who pushed her. Something was off in Ghost Vein. And it wasn't just the bullets or the push. It was the town itself. Something in Ghost Vein festered.

And she had a feeling her near-death experience was only the beginning.

TWENTY-SEVEN

Rue tugged at the hem of her shirt for the third time in thirty seconds.

She stood beside Cole in the foyer of the Ghost Vein Historical Museum, doing her best impression of someone who absolutely belonged. "You're *sure* you want me in the interview with the curator?"

He gave her a sideways smile. "If I don't include you, you'll just sneak in anyway."

She opened her mouth to protest...then closed it. "Okay. Fair."

"As long as Mayhew doesn't see you, we're golden."

"I just... Official stuff is different. If I say something wrong, it won't bounce back on me. It'll bounce back on *you*."

Cole met her gaze. "Don't worry. We'll get answers. And I trust you."

Her heart may have done a small somersault. She pretended not to notice.

The curator swept in from the back hall in a visible wave of nervous panic.

"Sheriff. Ms. Maddox. Come in, come in, what's this about?" Josiah Evans ushered them into his office and flopped into his seat behind a cluttered desk. "I haven't heard anything since you took that evidence the other day. Is this about the gold nugget? Or the map fragment?"

Cole shook his head. "No. This is about the reenactment incident that happened earlier this afternoon."

Josiah looked confused. "Reenactment?"

"There was a shooting on Main Street," Cole said flatly. "The actor playing the miner fired his weapon, and it wasn't a blank. It was a real bullet. Rue was nearly shot."

The color drained from the curator's face. "That can't be. That *shouldn't* be. Restored magical artifacts, yes, but only capable of firing blanks." He scrambled for a file and yanked it from a filing cabinet, shoving photos and paperwork across the desk. "Here. See? Photos of the weapons before they were loaned out. Receipts from the restoration. Everything was handled properly."

"Handled by *who*?" Cole asked.

"Wynona repaired them. She's our certified artifact technician. She and Isla Gray were both present when the restorations were finalized. The guns weren't supposed to be capable of firing *anything* lethal."

"Well, they did. A real bullet was fired. Which means we need to know if there is any live ammunition that fits that weapon stored or supplied by the museum."

Josiah's face twisted. "Not *intentionally*. But..." He hesitated, licking his lips. "There have been some...disturbances over the last few months. Some of the displays were tampered with. A few artifacts may have been damaged or even gone missing. I've been trying to do a full inventory."

Cole stiffened. "Period-specific ammunition might be missing. And you didn't report it?"

"Look, if I'd filed a report, our insurance premiums would've gone through the roof. The town's been chaotic lately. Vandalism is up. Ghost activity is spiking. If the council sees the museum as a liability, they'll cut our funding."

"You realize," Cole said coldly, "that if you'd reported the thefts, the shooting today might've been prevented."

He wilted. "I...didn't think..."

"No. You didn't."

Rue shifted uncomfortably. Honestly, Cole had it handled. He was in full cold cop mode, and the curator squirmed like a bug. She didn't really need to be here.

"The mayor used to support us, you know. Now she's denying expansion requests, cutting back marketing, questioning every artifact loan. She used to help me push museum growth, and now she barely returns my calls."

She nudged Cole with her elbow.

He glanced at her and gave her a tiny nod, stepping back half a pace to let her take the lead.

Rue stepped forward. "Rue Maddox. I'm consulting with Sheriff Dawson."

Joshia nodded, though his eyes flicked toward Cole for confirmation.

Cole gave a barely perceptible shrug. He wasn't stopping her.

Clasping her hands in front of her to hide the fact her fingers were fidgeting, Rue focused on the curator. "Can you tell me where the museum's artifacts come from?"

Josiah launched into a ramble about archaeological digs, partnerships with larger institutions, and loans from regional collections and private donations

Rue kept her tone pleasant. "Do you ever buy artifacts from locals?"

The curator stumbled again. "Well, some private collections in town have been generously donated over the years. Often these are heirlooms, passed down through generations. Very valuable from a heritage standpoint..."

"Do you *buy* from locals?" Rue asked again, this time sharper.

He hesitated, then reluctantly nodded. "Sometimes. Occasionally, a resident will bring something they found on their property or tucked away in a relative's attic. If we can authenticate it, we may offer a small payment as a thank-you for supporting the museum."

"Is that what you did with Tobias Pike?"

His mouth twitched. He clearly didn't want to answer, but finally, he gave a tight nod. "Yes. Mr. Pike sold several items to the museum. They were always high quality and... unquestionably authentic."

"Did he provide any kind of documentation? Provenance? Paper trail?"

The curator began to sweat. He wiped his forehead with the back of his hand. "In an ideal world, yes, provenance is preferable. Especially with more valuable pieces. But in small-town collections, sometimes it's difficult to..."

Rue cut him off. "Did Tobias give you *any* paperwork?"

He shrank back slightly in his chair. "No. But his pieces were always the real deal. Not forgeries. Never suspicious. He was just...very lucky."

She raised an eyebrow. *Lucky?* Or an *opportunistic criminal?* She stepped back from the desk. "Excuse me for a moment. I need to wash up."

Cole looked at her, concerned. "You okay?"

She nodded, forcing a smile. "Just need to splash some water on my face. I'm not used to doing the cop thing. Pretty sure I'm bright red."

He gave her a subtle nod, and she slipped out of the office.

The museum was mostly empty. Rue walked through the exhibit halls, taking the long way to the bathroom. She ducked inside, ran cool water over her wrists, and splashed her face. The red in her cheeks faded slowly as her breathing evened out. "Okay," she murmured, "you didn't yell. You didn't cry. You didn't accidentally accuse someone of murder. You're doing fine."

She dried her hands and made her way back through the main exhibit hall. Her feet slowed instinctively as she approached the large photograph she'd noticed last time.

Elias Grimshaw and family.

It was an old black-and-white photograph. Elias stood front and center, tall, lean, and scowling. His eyebrows were heavy, his nose aquiline. There was something cold in his stare. Rue doubted the man had smiled once in his life. She could definitely see him committing murder.

The woman sat stiffly beside him, though not *close* to him. There was space between them. Distance. Even in a formal portrait, she hadn't wanted to pretend things were fine. Rue stared at the photo for a long moment. It all came back to Grimshaw.

The cursed goldmine.

The missing miners.

The obsession.

Absolute power corrupts absolutely, Rue thought. She still stared at the photograph of Elias Grimshaw when Isla appeared at her side.

"Pretty impressive, huh?" Isla nodded toward the photo. "I helped put this exhibit together. Just imagine how amazing it would be if we found a *living* Grimshaw descendant. Now *that* would make a killer exhibit."

Rue tilted her head. "Do we know if any descendants are still around?"

"Just rumors. All we really know is that Maisie Grimshaw and her son skipped town one night and showed up in Boston. After that, they vanished. No records, no trail."

Rue's mind flashed back to Letty's clippings, those articles she'd found. There *were* Grimshaws out there. At least as of nineteen seventy-five. But where had they gone? She shifted gears. "Where do the museum's artifacts come from, exactly?"

"I'd *like* to say they're all aboveboard, but...I honestly don't know. The curator gives me things to catalog, and they're always authentic, but I have no idea where he gets some of them. After Tobias visited, there were always new pieces. I didn't ask questions. I had a gut feeling he was either digging them up himself or getting them from the black market. I didn't want to be involved. I wanted to keep my job. And sometimes that means looking the other way."

"Did you see the shootout earlier?"

"Most of the town did. Are you okay?"

"Thanks to Cole. But those guns were loaded with *real* ammo, specific to the gun and the era. Not blanks."

Isla paled. "That's impossible. Wynona and I restored those guns. We watched the mayor load them with blanks. No one used live rounds. That would've required specific period ammo. And we didn't have any."

Rue hesitated. "The curator mentioned something about old ammunition going missing. Could that have been what was used?"

Isla's face darkened. "Actually...yes. Things have been going missing. Then reappearing in the wrong spots. It's been driving me insane. And that ammo, yeah, it was one of the items that vanished." She led Rue through the museum to a display of antique weapons. A handwritten sign was taped to the glass. *Closed for Maintenance.*

"Weapons and ammunition disappeared from this case. The curator refuses to report it because he's afraid the council will pull our funding. And to cover it up? He's been trying to *buy the stolen stuff back*, with museum funds. He thought he'd get the grant. But now the mayor's blocked it, and he's panicking." She lowered her voice. "That's between us, okay?"

Rue nodded. Isla slipped an arm through hers and gently steered her back toward the Grimshaw exhibit.

"Is there anything else suspicious going on here we should know about?"

As if summoned by the question, the overhead lights flickered, faint sizzles crackling through the fixtures.

"Those lights were *just* repaired six months ago. But the ones over the mine exhibits? They always glitch. Things move around. And I *know* it's not us or the cleaning crew."

She led Rue through a staff-only door and down to the familiar desk where she and Taz had found the ledger.

"This thing always gets moved." Isla pointed to the ledger. "Open one day, closed the next. Pages marked or missing. Someone else is accessing it. I just don't know who."

Rue kept her expression neutral. "What's the ledger?"

"It logs every artifact that's come in and out of the museum," Isla explained. "Who brought it, what it is, if they got paid. That sort of thing."

Nodding, Rue feigned ignorance.

The power flickered again, this time more violently. Then a loud *bang* echoed from deeper inside the museum.

They both rushed out into the main hall.

Glass rattled. A few artifacts tipped and fell inside their cases. Shadowy ghosts flitted through the room like smoke. A transparent face pushed out of an old miner's pickaxe, eyes hollow, then flipped into the air above their heads and disappeared into the ceiling.

Isla grabbed Rue's arm. "This has been happening *all day*. The ghosts are seriously rattled. I don't know why, but something's wrong. *Really* wrong."

"That's not something I ever want to see again." Rue turned toward the Grimshaw exhibit, her stomach knotting. "This can't keep happening. The accidents, the increased ghost activity. Someone's *stirring it up*."

"If you need help, anything, you've got me. I trust you, Rue. You're the best person to solve this."

"You've got more faith in me than I do most days."

Isla gave her a playful nudge. "Have a little more faith in yourself. At least more than Deputy Mayhew."

Rue cracked a smile despite herself.

She looked around the dim museum, at the portrait, the rattled displays, the shadows that hadn't quite gone. Then she looked back at Isla.

"I might just have a job for you."

TWENTY-EIGHT

Rue was having a perfectly nice dream. Something about chocolate, handcuffs, and a certain grouchy sheriff.

Then Nacho started bleating.

Loudly.

The dream twisted, grew darker. Her cozy saloon bedroom disappeared, replaced by the overgrown entrance to the mine. Not the cleaned-up, tourist-friendly version, but something older. Abandoned. Wind howled through the scrub, carrying voices that sounded far too much like crying. A figure stepped into view, curly red hair, jeans, flannel shirt, and boots caked with mud.

There was something familiar about the woman. *Is that a younger Ruth?*

The wind wailed louder. Rue twitched in her sleep. In the dream, Nacho's cries faded, replaced by the mournful chorus of the mine.

Ruth stepped forward, and Rue followed, her dream-self shivering from the cold. Her fingers brushed the tunnel wall; rough stone sliced her skin. She flinched, sucking at the cut.

They twisted deeper through narrow passages until they reached an open chamber. A landslide had half-collapsed on one side, revealing a small hollow behind it.

Ruth turned to her and pointed.

Rue had a bad feeling, but she stepped up and peered inside.

Mold. Dust. Rot.

And bones.

A tangle of *human* bones, jumbled and broken, trapped behind the rubble.

She stumbled back, horrified. *Had they been alive when they were walled in?* She looked to Ruth, but her great aunt had vanished. Panic swallowed her whole. Rue spun in circles. *How did she get out?*

Then, faintly, Nacho's bleats echoed through the mine.

Rue ran toward the sound, until she reached a sliver of daylight and the entrance again. She gasped for breath, and there, just beyond the threshold, Ruth stood again. Silent. Sad. She opened her mouth to speak...but the words didn't come. Instead, she shook her head slowly and whispered...

"Wake up, Rue."

She bolted upright in bed and promptly rolled off the edge, landing with a thud that nearly flattened a crying goat. "Nacho? How the heck did you...?"

He bleated in protest.

"Okay, thank you." Rue rubbed his head. "You're a very loud dream interrupter. But you did good."

She stumbled out to the living room and stopped cold. The front door was wide open. She *knew* she'd locked it. She exhaled slowly. "Thanks, Ruth. But next time, maybe use the phone?" She shooed Nacho back into the hallway. "Go home or get some snacks from Taz. I need to get ready." Rue locked the door behind him.

Today, she had a plan. A risky one. But if it worked, they'd finally have the proof they needed to nail whoever killed Tobias. She shuffled to the bathroom, still half-dream dazed. She washed her hands and hissed in pain.

Blood dribbled from a clean cut on her finger.

She froze. Her eyes flicked to the mirror. Then to the tiny wound. The same one she'd gotten *in her dream.* "It was real. The mine...the bones..." The truth cut through the daze. Ruth had shown her where the miners were buried. She wasn't dreaming. *The miners are real. And they've been buried alive. Waiting.*

A sharp knock shattered the moment. Rue jumped, then realized she was still wearing fuzzy pink rabbit pajamas. She padded to the door and yanked it open. Whoever it was would have to deal with sleep fashion choices.

The mayor stood on the other side, gray hair lacquered into place, black skinny boots gleaming, and shoulder pads that could take someone out.

"Clearly not an early riser." The mayor looked her up and down.

Rue didn't rise to the bait. "Why are you here?"

She held out a thick, padded envelope. "A generous offer for the entire building. Saloon, bookstore, apartment. All of it."

"What's in it?"

"Money. Enough for you to live comfortably in Florida. Build a new life. One more suited to your talents. Ruth had a feel for this town. *You* do not."

"You want me gone."

"Let's call it...encouraging relocation. No torches. No pitchforks. Just a very large check."

"Silver Vein is my home. No amount of money will make me leave."

The mayor's smile never reached her eyes. "There's no time limit on the offer. Just something to think about, for your own safety."

"Was that a threat?"

"Just a word to the wise." She tossed the envelope over Rue's shoulder. It landed on the floor with a soft *thud*.

Nacho trotted up, grabbed it with his teeth, and chewed through it with a vengeance.

Rue crossed her arms. "Feel free to have breakfast, Nacho. But chew slowly. It's a high-fiber bribe, and I'm pretty sure corruption causes indigestion."

The mayor turned on her heel and stalked away.

Rue slammed the door shut behind her and got ready for the day. She headed downstairs and into the saloon café. The place was already bustling.

Cassie and Taz juggled orders behind the counter, and Thomas restocked shelves.

"Thanks for letting me sleep in." Rue offered Taz a sheepish smile.

Taz raised an eyebrow. "Let you? We pounded on your door for ten minutes. Thought you were dead until I let myself in and found you snoring like a chainsaw. You're lucky Nacho didn't get creative with breakfast." She winked. "Hope you had good dreams."

Rue stared down at her bandaged finger. "Not exactly."

Taz frowned and stepped out from behind the counter, pulling Rue aside. "Okay. Spill."

She hesitated, then told her everything. The dream. The younger Ruth. The mine and the bones. The cut on her finger that still bled when she woke up. And how Nacho had cried until she snapped out of it.

Nacho trotted in when he heard his name. He still had shredded paper clinging to his chin.

Taz stared at him. Then at Rue's bandaged hand.

"Ruth showed me the miners. They're still in there. Walled up. Buried. She wants me to find them."

"That's...a lot."

"And that's not even the worst part. The mayor showed up ten minutes ago. Tried to buy me out."

"How much?"

She pointed at Nacho. "Ask him. He ate the offer."

Taz looked at the goat, aghast. "You didn't *read* it?"

"Didn't want to." Rue straightened. "I'm not selling. I'm not going anywhere. This is my town now. And I'm finishing what my aunt started."

Behind her, someone grunted. Rue turned as Delilah leaned against a bookshelf.

"You keep poking around like Ruth did, you'll end up just like her."

Rue bristled.

Delilah folded her arms. "I told Ruth the same thing right before she died. Had the same fight with her. The mayor tried to buy the saloon back then too. You think all this is new? The curse of the Ghost Vein mine isn't something one person can take on. Keep stirring the ashes and your fingers are gonna get burned."

As if on cue, the bookshelves shuddered. Cups and saucers rattled. The chandelier creaked and swayed overhead.

Nacho darted in from the café, pressing against Rue's side.

Delilah yelped and waved her hand wildly in the air. "Don't you start with me again, Ruth. I'm just telling her the truth. You always hated it when I didn't sugarcoat things. Truth's supposed to be blunt and nasty. You want her to survive in this cursed town? She needs her eyes open, not coddled shut."

The coffee machine let out a banshee shriek.

A familiar voice piped up behind Rue.

"This is *content gold.*"

Maribel. Phone out. Smirking. Filming. *I am so sick of this woman.*

Delilah spun around and stormed across the room like a tiny tornado in orthopedic sandals. "You little parasite." She got right up in Maribel's face. "You leech off everyone's misery and call it a hobby. Get my good side, did ya?" She leaned even closer. "Hope your followers prefer prune-face close-ups."

"Ugh." Maribel reared back. "Old people are *so* rude. No wonder this place has no classy clientele."

A nearby plate tipped off the table, spilling food straight onto Maribel's designer boots.

She shrieked.

Nacho took that as his cue to lick the cream off her shoes.

Rue couldn't help it. She laughed. "Ruth isn't happy with either of you. Maybe it's time for you both to take a little break from the bookshop."

Delilah muttered something that sounded suspiciously like *hussy,* shot Rue one last look, and stomped out.

"This is a health code violation. I'm reporting you. I'll have this whole dump shut down." As Maribel spun to leave, she nearly collided with a man standing silently in the doorway, a figure in a ratty gray hoodie. Maribel shoved past him with an angry huff.

Rue caught a brief glimpse of the man's face as he ducked away.

The bartender. Jackson Malone.

He slipped off in the opposite direction without a word.

She stared after him, breath held, heart thudding.

Maribel still ranted as she flounced out. "You'll be hearing from my lawyer. You owe me for the boots. You'll be paying the cleaning bill or I'll sue…"

Rue turned to find Taz staring at her like she'd grown horns. "Is now a good time to tell you the plan I have to catch a killer?"

TWENTY-NINE

Cole stood beside Rue, sharp in a navy-blue suit that hugged his broad shoulders and made his already handsome looks almost criminal. Rue, in contrast, had gone practical. Her sleek black jumpsuit looked fashionable, but she'd picked it for one very important reason. She could run, duck, climb, or throw in this thing if the plan went sideways. *Which it absolutely would...*

Rue chewed on a nail and clutched a wine glass like it might be her last lifeline. It held soda—she wasn't stupid. She needed her head clear and her bladder ready for combat.

"It'll be fine. Your plan will work."

"I hope so. I mean...we're dangling the juiciest bait we've got and hoping the killer bites. What could possibly go wrong?"

He raised a brow.

"Right." Rue sighed. "Everything could go wrong." She'd filled Cole in about finding the stolen gold and map fragment in the mayor's office. He hadn't been thrilled she'd kept that detail to herself, but he was here. In a suit. Participating. Which counted as forgiveness in Rue's book.

"I still can't believe you got Josiah to agree."

Cole shrugged. "He wanted off the hook for not reporting the missing artifacts. Hosting a fancy gala was a small price to pay...plus he's charging an entry fee. Man's making bank off this sting operation."

Isla had leaned into the trap idea with full enthusiasm. She'd gone full glamour in a long-sleeved copper dress with matching gloves that made her look like an old Hollywood actress.

The exhibit was real, technically. Rue had handed the map fragment and gold she'd taken from the mayor to Isla and the curator. They'd built a whole historical display around it, complete with dramatic lighting and velvet ropes. What the public didn't know was that it was all one big shiny lure.

The curator had gleefully told the mayor about the new exhibit while very *pointedly* refusing to say where the artifacts came from. The mayor had nearly popped a shoulder pad in rage but wasn't about to miss a PR opportunity. She stood near the temporary podium now, arguing with Josiah.

The rest of the museum was packed with a weird but familiar mix. Jesse and Taz wandered toward the appetizer table arm-in-arm. Jesse looked like a rogue playboy in a slate-gray suit, while Taz rocked an emerald-green jumpsuit that nearly matched Rue's.

Wynona and her sister Lynette already bickered in the corner near the drinks.

Doc Halliday stood by the snack table shoveling hors d'oeuvres into her mouth.

Arnold, the old tour guide, hovered behind Wynona in a baby-blue suit about two sizes too small.

Maribel floated near the wall in a pastel-pink gown, phone up, livestreaming to whoever subscribed to her channel.

Delilah stood near the entrance with her husband and Nacho, who had somehow acquired a tiny glittery purple bowtie.

Ghosts floated among the guests, mostly miners in various states of translucent grumpiness. Tourists and locals mingled, oohing over the new exhibit while the overhead lights flickered ominously.

Rue swallowed hard. She placed her glass down and locked her fingers together, trying to will away the tremble.

Cole rubbed her back gently. "It's okay. You've got this. You worked the puzzle out. Now we just wait for them to make a move."

She didn't feel like she had this. Not even a little. But there were no more backup plans tucked in her boots. Rue took a breath and looked toward the curator. She nodded once she had his attention.

It's showtime.

The curator stepped up to the temporary podium, pointedly ignoring the mayor's scowling presence at his elbow. He tapped the microphone, unleashing a high-pitched screech that had half the crowd cringing and the ghosts blinking in confusion.

"Apologies. Delighted to see such an enthusiastic turnout for tonight's unveiling." He threw a smug smirk at the mayor. "Running a museum takes passion, dedication, and often a touch of theatrics. But not every exhibit sparks *this* much drama. Thankfully, this one is not only legitimate, but significant."

He launched into a practiced spiel about Ghost Vein's history, Elias Grimshaw's legacy, and how the fragment found with the "late lamented Tobias Pike" had been authenticated as a genuine piece of Grimshaw's original mine map. The gold nugget had tested true as well, its composition matching other samples from the mine's oldest tunnels.

Josiah flung out a dramatic arm. "All of this information, we owe to the talented Isla Gray, who graciously authenticated the donation. We are now thrilled to present it to the public, thanks to the generosity of an anonymous benefactor and my assistant's efforts."

Isla gave a sunny wave.

Rue had to admit they sold it. No one watching would've guessed they'd been frantically cobbling the display together just hours ago. The set-up was flawless.

Then the lights flickered.

The chandeliers flickered off completely, plunging the room into an eerie hush. For a breath, it was darkness and silence.

Music screeched to a grinding halt as the lights flared back on.

A figure stepped from the shadows, cloaked in a long, hooded jacket that obscured their face. They hurled something small and round into the center of the room.

A burst of smoke erupted, thick and choking.

Panic rippled through the crowd as the smoke alarms shrieked.

Rue's heart kicked into high gear. Through the flashing emergency lights, she caught a glimpse of movement, a blur as the cloaked figure lunged forward and *tackled the curator*, sending him sprawling to the ground.

The attacker pivoted, sprinting for the display case behind the podium.

"The gold. They're going for the gold and the map..."

Before she could finish her sentence, the mayor launched herself at the thief.

"You'll regret this," the mayor shrieked, flailing her purse like a weapon.

Wrong move.

The figure grabbed her by the wrist and yanked. A flash of silver glinted in the chaos, *a knife*. The blade was pressed to her throat in the blink of an eye.

The thief backed toward the exit, dragging the mayor as a human shield. The crowd screamed and scattered.

"Stay back. Nobody follows," the attacker roared.

Cole was already on his radio, barking instructions. "Deputy Mayhew, target's heading out the west door. Possibly toward the parking lot." He turned to Rue. "Mayhew's tailing them now."

She gritted her teeth and shook her head. Her pulse thundered in her ears. "He doesn't have to. I know exactly where they're going."

"Where?"

Rue's voice dropped to a growl. "The mine."

She walked toward the mine's main entrance, the gravel crunching beneath her boots. Ghosts shimmered along the edges of the path. Their faces flickered in and out of focus as they passed. Their presence weighed heavily on Rue's chest. A sudden chill slipped over her hand, but it was cool and comforting. Just for a moment.

Rue didn't need proof. That had been Aunt Ruth. They both had unfinished business here. She sensed Cole and Jesse right behind her. Taz had taken a lot of convincing to stay behind at the museum, but Rue refused to drag her friend into the mine. *Not now.* She'd nearly pieced it all together. A few details still nagged at her, but she knew who the killer was. She just needed the why.

A voice rang out from the shadows. "I think that's close enough, don't you?"

Jackson Malone stepped out from the darkness, a smirk stretched across his face. He had the mayor in a tight grip, dragging her closer to his knife. She twisted, trying to break free, until he gave her a sharp shake.

"You surprised?" he said, his tone cocky.

Rue rolled her eyes. "Please. You're dramatic, not clever. Took me all of five minutes to connect the dots."

"But didn't you accuse *her* of murder?" Jackson pouted. He jerked the mayor's arm.

"She earned a spot on the list. She's a politician. Probably up to her ears in secrets. But she's not the killer." Rue let that hang in the air.

The wind howled low and eerie through the mine's mouth. Cold and hungry.

Then...

Slow clapping. A figure stepped out from the shadows, pulling back their hood. "Bravo." Maribel said, her voice singsong. "Honestly, you nailed it. Ten outta ten deduction, Rue. I'm almost impressed."

Rue gave her a dry smile. "That's a lot of praise from someone about to be arrested."

Maribel grinned. "Not yet. But that trap with the gold and the map? That was your idea, wasn't it?"

"Guilty. Like you're about to be, Maribel. If that's even your name." Rue chuckled.

"Technically, I go by Susanna Maribel DeLong. Maribel's just my middle name. But yes, I'm *also* a podcaster. I'm currently on holiday. Using my camera was a way of getting information. It worked."

"You should watch out." Rue turned to Jackson. "Someone that good at acting could turn on anyone."

Maribel snapped. "This is *for my family*. We've been cut off, ruined, forgotten. This was our chance. Our only one."

Rue stepped forward, her tone sharp. "And killing people is what? Your version of a startup business?"

"You don't understand," Maribel shrieked. "The cursed gold...there's *power* in it. Power from blood. The miners didn't disappear. They were sacrificed. That magic is tied to this place."

Jackson, looking increasingly pale, stammered, "What about me, babe? You still need me, right? We're forever."

"You were convenient. That's all."

Jackson's face crumpled. "I killed for you. That old guide, Arnold. I hit him just like you said."

"Please." Maribel sneered. "The old man wasn't supposed to live. You were useful. Now? Not so much."

Using their conversation as a distraction, the mayor stomped hard on Jackson's foot.

He yelped and let her go.

She scrambled away, hurling curses that would've made a cowboy proud.

"Good help really is hard to find." Rue shook her head.

Jackson lunged for Maribel's arm, but she was ready. A rock, hidden at her side, swung up and connected with a *thunk*. He crumpled at her feet.

Maribel dropped the rock on top of him. Her eyes blazed as she pointed a trembling finger at Rue. "This is all your fault. I *won't* fail. I won't let you win." She hurled a glass vial toward Rue, green liquid glowing in the moonlight.

Bubbles exploded and fizzed on Rue's chest, and her magic surged. Heat pulsed from her chest, racing to her fingertips. Her hands flared with light, and the vial *exploded mid-air*, shattering in a burst of flame.

Maribel screamed and tossed another. Then another.

Rue blocked them, barely, but one got through. A purple haze exploded around her. She gasped, bent over, hands clawing at her throat. Her vision blurred, and her knees wobbled. Thoughts spun wildly in her head. Cole, Jesse, Taz. She didn't want to leave them. She didn't want to die. Then, through the haze, *light*.

A silvery figure formed and solidified. Ruth.

Rue stared, stunned. Her hands still scrabbled around her throat as she fought for breath.

Ruth lunged for Maribel, who shrieked and stumbled backward, arms flailing. She didn't see the shape rising behind her.

Baaaah. Nacho, glorious, meddling goat minion, head-butted Maribel square in the knees.

She toppled, flailed, and hit the ground *hard*, smacking her head on the ground next to Jackson.

The purple haze began to fade. Rue dragged in a ragged breath. Air never tasted so good.

Ruth winked. Her voice echoed faintly. *"Told you. Just have a little faith. You know what to do now."*

And then, she was gone.

Jesse, Cole, and Taz rushed in, weapons and curses at the ready. Taz had, predictably, ignored Rue's instructions and followed the boys.

Deputy Mayhew ambled up last, grumbling as he

cuffed both Maribel and Jackson and muttered into his radio for paramedics.

Cole knelt, pulling Rue into his arms. "You have *got* to stop almost dying," he growled. "You're gonna give me gray hair. And high blood pressure."

Rue sagged against him, weak but grinning. She reached up and touched the silver strands at his temple. "Newsflash, Sheriff. You already have them."

"They showed up the day *you* did," he said dryly.

Taz squeezed in and hugged Rue tightly. "You okay?"

She nodded. "Thanks to Aunt Ruth. And Nacho." She glanced toward the mine. The wind whistled again. Cold and sharp. "The gold's safe. The mine's safe...for now." Her friends gathered around her. Laughing. Crying. But Rue's smile didn't quite reach her eyes.

I have a feeling the mine isn't done with me yet.

THIRTY

The next day, Rue stood once more at the shadowed entrance of the Silver Vein Mine.

A thin, silvery figure shimmered just ahead of her. Great Aunt Ruth, looking more solid than ever and just as bossy. She didn't speak. Just turned and started gliding into the darkness. Rue swallowed the lump in her throat and followed. Maribel might be gone, but there was still a threat that loomed.

This was like her dream. Only now she had backup. Arnold the tour guide was beside her, flashlight in one hand, pickaxe in the other. Jesse followed, annoyingly chipper despite the fact they were walking into a haunted mine. Cole brought up the rear, quiet but alert, eyes flicking at every shadow.

Ruth paused deep in the tunnel. Rue's steps slowed, a shiver running through her as she reached out to touch the wall, the same one where she'd cut her finger before. The skin throbbed sharply, and when she looked down, a bead of blood welled up.

"She's pointing," Cole said softly.

They all turned to look. Ruth's translucent arm stretched toward a crumbling section of wall, old wood supports bowing under the weight of rock and time.

Rue cleared her throat. "I think she wants you to bring it down."

Cole, Jesse, and Arnold exchanged glances. Without a word, they stepped forward, pickaxes in hand.

The first strike rang out, harsh and echoing, bouncing down the tunnels. Rock cracked. Dust fell. The air grew tighter with each hit.

After what felt like forever, the wall gave way with a dull crunch.

Bones spilled out like the mine was exhaling. Expelling the dead.

The men stepped back fast, faces pale under their headlamps. The skeletons were jumbled, collapsed together like they'd died sitting side by side.

"The missing miners," Rue whispered. "They're not missing anymore."

A sudden gust of wind tore through the tunnel, blasting past them as if it had somewhere to be. It howled out into the outside world, carrying something with it. Justice? Freedom? Rue hoped the miners were finally at peace.

Ruth smiled and faded like mist on the breeze.

Rue's breath hitched. "Wait, Ruth. Don't go." Panic flared. "What if we can't get out without her?"

Cole reached for her hands. "We've got this. Arnold knows the tunnels."

Arnold nodded confidently. "I do. Left at the old shaft, then up past the storage nook. We'll be out in fifteen."

Rue let out a shaky laugh. "You've got tracking talents, huh?"

Cole grinned. "That's not even the half of it. Stick around. You'll learn all my secrets."

"I plan on it."

He peered into the exposed chamber. "Bones. But no gold."

"I'm not surprised. I get the feeling Elias Grimshaw wasn't exactly the 'bury it with the victims' type. That guy had tricks up his cursed sleeves."

***

The café buzzed with noise, laughter, and the smell of three kinds of cake.

Wynona, Lynette, and Delilah had gone full baking competition. Nacho was clearly the winner. He had his own plate and frosting on his nose.

Rue leaned against the counter, tea in hand, watching her strange little found family fill the space. Taz, Jesse, Arnold. Even Delilah argued animatedly with Ruth's ghost in the corner.

It was weird. And it was perfect.

"Any word on the vault?" someone asked.

"No vault. No gold." Rue shook her head. "We found the miners, but that's all. If Grimshaw left behind treasure, it wasn't at that spot in the mine."

Disappointment rolled through the room. It quickly dissipated when Cole stepped in with an update.

"Maribel's been moved to the Reno jail. She's singing like a canary but still denies hurting Letty. And she swears she didn't swap the blank bullets."

"Maybe Jackson Malone did?" Taz suggested.

Cole shook his head. "He's awake too. Turned on

Maribel as soon as he could speak. He admits to Tobias and the attack on Arnold. But that's it."

A chill curled down Rue's spine. "Someone else is still out there...with a grudge and an obsession with maps and cursed gold."

Ruth floated closer, calm and faintly glowing. "You did well. It doesn't matter what else is out there. You're right where you're supposed to be, sweetheart."

"Home?" Rue's heart squeezed.

Her great aunt nodded. "Exactly."

Rue blinked away tears and turned to the window. Main Street bustled, tourists waving, kids with balloons, someone dressed as a ghost cowboy handing out flyers.

Jesse cracked a joke about surviving the next festival season without being hexed or hospitalized.

Cole joined her, brushing a kiss over her forehead. "I won't let anyone else hurt you. No matter what's coming."

She leaned into her grumpy sheriff, a small smile curving her lips. Until she saw it. Across the street, half-hidden in the shadow of the old apothecary, stood a hooded figure. Watching. Rue straightened. A shiver skated up her spine. The cursed gold. The broken bullets. Letty. All unsolved pieces whispered *this isn't over*. Rue hoped like heck Jesse was right.

She just had to survive.

The end.

Want More?

You can sign up for my mailing list. It's for new releases and no spam. Be the first to grab specials, new releases, and freebies.

Sign up now
https://www.kellyethan.com/newsletter

LEAVE A REVIEW

Did you like this book?

Please leave a review for it on Amazon!
Ghosts and Gold Dust

ABOUT THE AUTHOR

I want to thank everyone who spent the time to read my novel.

My world is small town magic, mystery and mayhem, with plenty of snarky laughs along the way.

With an overactive imagination and a love of all things that go bump in the night, it was natural to write cozy paranormal mysteries, but I also love paranormal romance. No matter the genre, I love sarcastic heroines who like to save the day and solve the puzzle.

With a busy and chaotic household, writing is my outlet for madness. I live in Australia and when not writing, I can be found plotting my next fictional murder or chasing after the family's ferocious hellhound.

Visit me today at my website or say hello on social media.

Website:
https://www.kellyethan.com

facebook.com/KellyEthanWriter

instagram.com/kellyethanauthor

tiktok.com/@authorkellyethan

COZY PARANORMAL MYSTERY:

Point Muse Cozy Paranormal Mystery Series

The Wicked Witch and the Christmas Chaos
The Wicked Witch and the Stolen Snow Globe
The Conniving Carver and the Jeering Jack-O-Lantern
The Wicked Witch and the Ultimate Smackdown
The Wicked Witch and the Abominable Snowman
The Wicked Witch and the Killer Grinch

#0 The Pernicious Pixie and the Choked Word
#1 The Killer Knight and the Murderous Chairleg
#2 The Dastardly Dragon Killer and the Poisoned Breath
#3 The Murderous Monster and the Stony Gaze
#4 The Cursed Crow and the Deadly Hex
#5 The Slanderous Siren and the Grievous Gift
#6 The Vengeful Villain and the Cursed Treasure
#7 The Fiendish Foe and the Deadly Jewels
#8 The Nefarious Nemesis and the Wedding Jinx